THE BUTCHER OF GLASTONBURY

David Bowker was born in Hazel Grove in Cheshire. He is the author of *The Death Prayer*, the first novel to feature Chief Superintendent Vernon Laverne, and *The Secret Sexist*. He lives in the Bedfordshire countryside with his best friend and their young son.

Also by David Bowker

THE DEATH PRAYER
THE SECRET SEXIST

DAVID BOWKER

THE BUTCHER OF GLASTONBURY

VISTA

First published in Great Britain 1997
by Victor Gollancz

This Vista edition published 1998
Vista is an imprint of the Cassell Group
Wellington House, 125 Strand, London WC2R 0BB

© David Bowker 1997

The right of David Bowker to be identified as author
of this work has been asserted by him in accordance with
the Copyright, Designs and Patents Act, 1988.

A catalogue record for this book is
available from the British Library.

ISBN 0 575 60203 1

Printed and bound in Great Britain by
Cox & Wyman Ltd, Reading, Berks

98 99   10 9 8 7 6 5 4 3 2 1

FOR DAD

There is a bridge in Glastonbury; an old timbered bridge that spans a quiet brook. On the northern side of the bridge, a rough dirt track curves away into a dense pocket of woodland. Above the trees, above everything in this listening landscape, rises the dark mass of Glastonbury Tor. But it is night, and the tower that pierces the hill like a Calvary thorn has merged with the blue-black sky.

In the opposite direction lies a house where a tragedy is about to occur. The bridge leads only to this house, where lights shine in the windows. The sound of a piano, played badly, drifts out of the house, up into the still night, a humble offering for the cold spring stars.

Lights sweep through the trees, followed by the crackle of tyres on loose gravel. A car appears, a red family saloon. The car stops before the bridge, the front passenger door opens. A young girl gets out, leans back into the car. Laughter and mingled childish voices. When she re-emerges, the girl is clutching a plastic carrier bag. She thanks the driver, waves to her friend in the back seat, slams the door and walks across the bridge, pausing half-way to turn and wave again. The car headlights flash in farewell.

The driver waits, watching until she is safely out of sight, then skilfully and speedily reverses back down the rough track, the engine singing into the distance. Then the girl reappears and walks back on to the bridge. She knows that her friend's father would not have driven away if she had remained standing there. But she often walks out here alone, late at night, listening to the water running over the rocks and studying the movement of the planets. She is not afraid of the dark. Besides, she is almost thirteen-and-a-half years old.

Looking up, she sees the Great Bear, and her eyes trace a slanting line from its tip until she finds Arcturus, the brightest star in the sky.

In the woods to her right, something catches her eye. She turns and sees a faint light moving through the trees. She stares and the light disappears. She waits. It reappears, hovers along for a short distance and then disappears again, as if someone is carrying a lantern through the wood. The light seems to draw nearer, without growing brighter. This makes her apprehensive, but pride, curiosity and her proximity to home compel her to wait on the bridge for a few moments longer.

Suddenly, the strange glow vanishes. The woods are in deep shadow again. The trees seem to heave a sigh of relief; their breath wafts over her, rich and damp and sweet. She watches intently, unwilling to ignore the testimony of her own eyes. Yet there is nothing there.

She turns, walks over the bridge and crosses the lawn. Before reaching the house, she glances back sharply, hoping to catch the prowler by surprise. But all around her, the countryside lies dark and still.

She enters the house through the side door, which is open, as usual, and slings down the carrier bag. The piano music has ceased. The door leads into a large empty kitchen, with a separate pantry.

She opens the pantry door and enters. It is deep, dark and cool. On one shelf lies a plump half-moon of apple pie, covered in foil. Lifting the foil, she finds a wedge of pie waiting for her, ready-cut. She drops it casually on to a clean plate, closes the pantry door behind her.

Licking her fingers, she moves down a short hallway and into the front room. The room is bright, its plain walls white-washed. Her father is sitting beside her brother on the wide piano stool, searching seriously through a song-book propped on the music stand.

As the girl enters, her father's face brightens. With his thin hair, thick sideburns, and the badly-broken nose that is a vestige of his rugby-playing days, he has always reminded her of a rough-and-ready farmer. In fact, he is an unemployed nuclear physicist who ekes out a living by reviewing software for computer magazines.

Tess wants to tell him about the light in the woods, but before she can speak, he says, 'Tess, Tess: tell Andrew what I mean by *feeling*.'

With her mouth full, frowning, she asks, 'What kind of feeling, Rich?'

'Musical feeling. I'm trying to explain to him that it's not enough just to hit the notes in the right order. If he ever wants to play properly, he has to put a bit of emotion into it, doesn't he? Tell him.'

Tess looks at her father. His name is Dr Richard Martin, but to everyone, including his own children, he is known simply as 'Rich'. Rich is not a stereotypical scientist. He has always been receptive to dreams and imagination. If a Disney cartoon is showing at the cinema in Wells, and no one else is interested, he will usually drive there to watch the film alone; a forty-six-year-old child, marvelling at the screen, tangle-haired forearm buried in a tub of popcorn. His hero is Albert Einstein, who also had the wonder of a boy in his eyes.

Unhurriedly, still eating, Tess looks at her father, then inspects her ten-year-old brother, Andrew. He is glowering at her, warning her not to make his life any more difficult. It is bad enough that he is expected to practise piano every night. He feels that it is outrageous of Rich to ask any more of him.

Tess considers the problem for a few seconds longer than her father wishes to wait. This is so like her. She will not be rushed, particularly when she is thinking.

At last, she says, 'If you ask me . . .'

'Not with your mouth full, Tess,' Rich admonishes mildly. 'I can't tell what you're saying.'

She nods, swallows, tries again. 'What I'd say is that feeling probably comes after skill. Andrew hasn't got any skill yet.' Her brother howls in protest. 'When he can play something all the way through without mistakes, then he can think about feeling. But it's too early to talk about feeling when he's still rubbish.'

Turning red in the face, Andrew addresses his sister. 'I'm not rubbish. *You're* the one who's rubbish.'

'All right, son,' smooths his father. 'She's only trying to wind you up. It's nothing to get worked up about.' He turns to Tess. 'Don't just insult him. That's too easy. Show him how it's done.'

She gapes. 'How what's done?'

'You can play with feeling. Give us a demonstration.'

'I can't play with feeling,' she retorts flatly.

'Yes, you can. I've heard you. What about the way you play "Annie's Song"?'

She shrugs, impervious to his flattery.

Rich thumbs through the song-book, searching for the piece in question. 'Now, where the sodding hell is it?'

She says, 'It's not in that book. It's in the blue one. But I don't want to play it. I don't feel like it.'

Her father sighs heartily, as if he is surrounded by ingrates. The sound of a crying baby approaches, coming down the stairs, increasing in volume. The noise is so familiar that none of them react to it.

'So you won't play it, then?' he repeats slowly, as if he wishes to be absolutely certain of her intractability before taking offence.

'I don't feel like it, Rich. Besides, I don't play it with feeling. I don't play it with skill, either. I just play it.'

'Perhaps you can't play with skill,' he concedes. 'But you *can* play with feeling. Which just goes to prove my point.'

She pauses, knowing that it would be churlish to answer him back. But she cannot help herself. She is thirteen-and-a-half years old. 'How do you know? You don't know anything about music.'

He shakes his head firmly. 'No. That's not true.'

'Yes it is, Rich.' She raises her voice. 'You know even less than Andrew.'

He knows that she is missing the subtlety of his reasoning, but can't be bothered to argue. So he merely shakes his head and says, 'No.'

(Afterwards, this scene will return to haunt her. Why could she not have agreed with her father? Or pretended to agree? Or simply have played the piano for him, as requested? Instead, she will be forever left with an image of him staring down at the piano keys, thwarted and undermined.)

She takes her empty plate out into the kitchen, where her mother is cradling her baby sister. Mrs Martin is a small, fair-haired woman in a gingham dress. Her smile is warm and expansive. She smiles now, as her eldest child lightly touches the back of the baby's head.

'Licky Lickul Helen. Why are you always crying?' pouts Tess playfully.

Tess's mother is too shrewd to be distracted by this show of affection. She has a bone to pick with her daughter. 'Hey, young lady. I thought we agreed on ten o'clock.'

For a second, Tess looks caught out. But she has an excuse prepared. 'Yeah. I know,' she sighs, as if staying out late is a difficult burden to bear. 'But Gudrun's dad took ages getting his car out. And then he went and stopped for petrol.'

Mrs Martin walks over to the door, rubbing the baby's back,

11

then turns to stare, awaiting acknowledgement of her grievance, some small gesture of atonement. 'What did we agree? Eh?'

At first, Tess resists. She forces herself to look her mother in the eyes.

'What's the matter? Do you think your dad and me are making impossible demands or something?'

'Sorry,' says Tess, unable to justify her own defiance.

'If you're really sorry, you can make us all a cup of tea,' replies her mother, leaving the room without looking back.

'Bum, shit, fuck. You old bag,' grumbles Tess as she fills the kettle with water. While she waits for the water to boil, the family cat, a ginger tom, walks into the kitchen and brushes against her legs, angling to be fed.

'You've got no chance, Harry. No chance at all,' she declares. The cat is immensely fat, with a small handsome head and a flared middle. He looks as if he has swallowed a goldfish bowl.

She crosses the kitchen and the cat follows her, purring loudly. A cold, bright light flashes past the kitchen window and she freezes, momentarily startled. Then she leaps to the door and rushes out, in time to see an image that she will remember for the rest of her life.

For a few moments, Tess remains rooted to the lawn, trembling with awe, almost forgetting to breathe, waiting to see if anything else happens. Then, when it is apparent that the excitement is over, she storms back into the house to tell her parents what she has witnessed.

She bursts into the front room and the horror of what she finds there sends her crashing violently backwards into the door frame. For the room's white walls are awash with blood. There is blood all over the ceiling, the floor and the sparse, simple furniture. Her family have gone, to be replaced by glistening scarlet mannequins, missing arms and legs. In contrast, the small figure lying atop the piano appears to be intact. The body is thickly caked in gore and wears her brother's trainers on its twitching feet. Its chest jets blood

12

into the air at regular intervals, reminding her, absurdly, of a whale expelling sea water through its blow-hole.

The room is now spinning so much that Tess is forced to close her eyes. She cannot move. She is appalled beyond endurance. But, in an odd way, she is not really surprised. The scene before her holds a dull, aching familiarity, as if she has already lived through it, many times. And she knows that smell – that hot metallic smell. Is it the odour of her own fear?

Or the stench of fresh blood?

Something round and heavy rolls across the floor, coming to rest by her feet. But she dare not look down. Jesus, she dare not look. She keeps her eyes screwed tightly shut and releases one strange, faltering wail of grief. After this, she makes no sound.

It will take a long time of standing and waiting and shaking before Tess can accept that the people lying in this room once belonged to her, and that she once belonged to them. While she waits, she remembers.

She remembers that her father's last word to her was 'No'. That her mother walked away without looking back.

That her brother sulked, her sister cried.

1

THE KILLER OF ALL TIME

It was the kind of day when even tourists seem lovable. York was bathed in brilliant sunshine and to celebrate this singular event, Chief Superintendent Vernon Laverne had daringly loosened his tie and folded his black Abercrombie coat over one brawny arm.

He ambled through Duncombe Place and entered Low Petergate. His way was blocked by a large-bottomed Italian woman in vast khaki shorts. She was attempting to photograph two clowning children who refused to stand still. Laverne politely waited for the camera to click before passing by, lest his likeable but undeniably plain face should inadvertently appear in the family album back in Milano.

In England, such weather would have been exceptional at any time of year. For early March, it was remarkable. Since daybreak a gentle winter sun had reigned over the city. A fresh, un-English breeze spirited through the ancient cobbled streets, sweetening the air and making Laverne think of childhood and seaside holidays, and people he had loved or wished he had loved.

Yet his mood was far from maudlin. He was almost happy to be alive. His last case had been ridiculously easy to solve. A husband had brained his wife with a brass door-stop and then left her lying on the kitchen floor for a week, until a window cleaner had noticed the corpse and alerted the police. An obvious and unintelligent crime with an easy solution, and to Laverne, a welcome relief from the pressure and anxiety of hunting down seasoned serial killers. Yes, he was bored, but it was a pleasant kind of boredom. Let all the criminals in York be as obvious and unintelligent as they pleased. He'd had enough excitement for one lifetime.

During the previous year, he had ended the reign of a sadistic murderer called the Animal and this event, added to his past successes, appeared to have conferred privileged status upon him. Not only had he been promoted, but he now noticed that he could walk out of his office any time he wanted, without being paged or pursued. Last month, he had taken a whole day off without authorization, just to see what would happen. And nothing happened. It was almost uncanny.

After years of arousing suspicion with his rather negligent approach to detection, Laverne suddenly found himself in the position of an elite senior pupil at a public school. His good intentions were taken for granted. Laverne's partner, DI Lyn Savage, had been nagging him about his lack of professionalism for years, but lately she had shown a worrying tendency to trust in his judgement. Even his arch-foe, Chief Constable Neville Wood, appeared to have finally accepted that, despite his faults, Vernon Laverne was a credit to the CID. He could go anywhere, do anything, and no one asked questions.

Apart from Angela Roth.

She was pleasant enough, but she was an American, and, like many of her compatriots, nurtured a questing and deep-rooted desire to get to the truth, however unpalatable that truth might be. In Laverne's case, the truth was so preposterous and far-fetched that he preferred to keep it quiet, which was why Angela and her endless questions were proving a major source of irritation to him.

Angela Roth was an FBI Officer on a two-month placement from the National Center for the Analysis of Violent Crime at Quantico, Virginia. In return, Farrell, the only member of Laverne's team with a university education, had gone to Quantico to familiarize himself with the latest FBI thinking on the apprehension of violent criminals.

In short, Angela was only in England to shadow Laverne and make his life a misery. His reputation had travelled across the Atlantic, and the Americans were eager to know how the Chief Superintendent's working methods compared with their own. With this in mind, the Bureau had approached Neville Wood and Neville, aware of the kudos involved, had instantly agreed. Without consulting Laverne. Laverne knew that he only had himself to blame for this situation. It served him right for catching so many murderers.

But Ms Roth's questions were getting more and more awkward, and, to make matters worse, DI Savage had befriended her. They talked to each other, actually talked, in his office, when he was trying to think. Sometimes, they talked when he was trying *not* to think. They never stopped talking. He was consequently being forced to take longer and longer lunch breaks, just to get some peace. Not that it really mattered. Work was slack, and the sun was shining. Despite Angela, despite everything, Laverne was almost happy to be alive.

The smell of fried onions drifted out of a café's open doorway, suddenly making him hungry. There was a small blackboard by the café's entrance, on which someone had chalked TODAY'S SPECIAL: BURGER, BEANZ AND CHIPS = £3.95. Always alert to a bargain, even at the risk of food-poisoning, Laverne entered and approached the counter. He was served by a tall girl with a glazed expression. He ordered a 'Special' but asked if he could possibly have his beans without a 'z'. The girl didn't smile, merely handed him a ticket with the number fourteen stamped on it.

He found a table in a quiet room at the back of the café. A light breeze blew through a door which opened on to a paved yard. After a while, someone shouted 'Fourteen!' and Laverne, foolishly, thrust his arm in the air like a schoolboy. Then, realizing what he had done, he hastily retracted the guilty limb and shouted 'Here!' in a suitably masterful voice.

A diminutive waitress arrived with his meal. He began to eat, then looked up and saw Angela Roth standing over by the counter. He scanned the room, looking for a possible escape route, but it was no use. There was nowhere to hide. Before he had time to collect himself, Angela had turned, noticed him, and was smiling in his direction.

Laverne managed a strained grimace as she walked over to join him. He couldn't escape the dark suspicion that she'd deliberately followed him here. She pulled out a chair and sat opposite him.

'Mind if I join you?'

'You're supposed to ask that *before* you sit down, not after,' commented Laverne bluntly.

She acted as if he hadn't spoken. Although she had only known him for a matter of weeks, she was already immune to his unique brand of old-English rudeness. She opened her shoulder bag and took out a small black notebook and a pen. This accursed notebook was rapidly becoming all too familiar to Laverne, and he subjected it to one of his coldest stares.

Sensing his resistance, Roth said, 'What's the matter? Can't I ask a few questions?'

'Angela, I'm trying to eat.'

'So you can't eat and talk? What's the matter with you?'

'Have you been following me?'

'No. No way. I've been trying to *catch up* with you, Vernon.'

Since her arrival, she'd insisted on calling him by his Christian name. Perhaps this was the custom amongst FBI officers. If so, it was a custom that Laverne found impertinent. He didn't particularly like the name 'Vernon' and as far as he was concerned, only his wife, Lyn Savage and the Deputy Chief Constable had earned the right to use it.

Roth was still talking. 'I've been trying to catch up with you

17

since I got here. In case you'd forgotten, I'm expected to file a full report on you when I get home and so far, I've found out nothing I couldn't get from old press cuttings. How about it? Don't you think we need to touch base?'

The expression in his eyes was not encouraging, but she persisted. 'I took your report on the Animal back to the hotel last night. I read it in bed. I've never seen a report like that before. Know what? It didn't tell me diddly.'

For a second, Laverne thought she was speaking in a foreign tongue. 'I beg your pardon?'

'Diddly squat. Meaning nothing. It's a report that doesn't report *anything*, Vernon.'

He looked down at his plate, forked chips into his mouth and chewed them belligerently.

She studied him calmly, noting his defensiveness. 'All I got from that report was that you and the Deputy Chief Constable went out to the Yorkshire Moors . . .'

With his mouth full, Laverne said, 'Dales.'

'What?'

'Yorkshire Dales. You said Moors.'

'Dales . . . Moors. Whatever. You go there in a snowstorm acting on . . . what was the phrase?' She opened the black notebook and quoted Laverne's own nonsense back at him. 'Here we are: "Acting on certain information from an anonymous informant . . ." OK. What informant?'

'If I knew that, they wouldn't be anonymous, would they?'

'So someone phoned you, right?'

He said nothing and stared moodily over her shoulder at the weeds springing up between the flagstones out in the sunlit yard. Go away, woman. Please. Just go away.

'OK. They didn't phone. So what *did* they do?' No reply. 'Did they mail you a letter? Did they put a billboard up outside your house? What?'

18

'Not now. Another time,' said Laverne. 'Let's just eat.'

She pursed her lips and stared at him, her head tilted at a meditative angle. She was in her late thirties, above average height, with brutally cropped dark-brown hair and an aggressively square jaw. Her eyes were blue-grey, and when she was displeased, as now, they grew cold and watchful.

'What's that on your neck?' she asked suddenly.

She was pointing to an area of discoloured skin on Laverne's throat which had appeared twelve months ago after a fight to the death with a lunatic called Thomas North. The bruise should have faded by now, but Laverne suspected that it was his for life, one more battle scar to add to the collection.

'It's a birth mark,' he lied. 'And don't be so bloody personal.'

Her food arrived. Like Laverne, she had gambled on the 'Special' and lost. As she ate, she began to complain about the way the British cooked chips, which she referred to as 'fries'.

'I mean, what are these things, for Christ's sake? They look as if they've been scraped off somebody's shoe. Taste like it, too.'

Laverne said nothing. He sipped his tea and did his best to ignore her.

That afternoon, at the police station on Fulford Road, Laverne and Savage interviewed a murder suspect. It was standard police work, a case of routine everyday nastiness. An inadequate man in his forties with a history of psychiatric disorders had kicked his elderly mother to death. The son couldn't hold down a job or form relationships. Until the incident, he had been living at home with his mother and had attacked her on several previous occasions. This time, he had gone too far.

In a case like this, no detection skills were needed. Hercule Poirot wasn't about to walk in, gather everyone together, and reveal the murderer's identity. The murderer's identity was crushingly obvious. It was simply a matter of getting him to talk.

19

Angela Roth, watching the proceedings on a video monitor, had seen it all before. First the 'interviewee' would sit in sulky silence. Then the constant questioning would make him aggressive, with all the usual oaths and threats that such a state entailed. After a while, the abuse would be peppered with small confidences. Sooner or later, the tears would come. Finally, almost asking his accusers for understanding, he would weep and rant and swear and confess all.

In the event, the dialogue didn't progress beyond the swearing stage before the interview was concluded for the day. Whenever the suspect was asked a question, any question, he gave the same answer: 'Up Jack's arse'. Roth had never heard the expression before, and its constant repetition lent a surreal flavour to the proceedings.

Savage: 'Do you realize that you're in a very serious situation?'

'Up Jack's arse.'

Laverne: 'Where were you at the time of your mother's death?'

'Up Jack's arse.'

Afterwards, Roth met DI Savage for coffee in the police canteen. Savage paid for the coffee. The two women sat at a corner table, under the window. Lyn Savage, dark rings under her lucid blue eyes, was apologetic about the tedium of the afternoon.

'I'm sorry. We seem to be going through a rather dull patch at the moment.'

'Forget it. Not your fault. Life in the Bureau gets pretty dull too, you know. Don't believe everything you see in the movies . . .'

Savage aped surprise. 'Gosh. You mean Jody Foster isn't really in the FBI?' Roth smiled, glanced around the busy canteen. 'Where's Vernon?'

Savage shrugged.

Roth smiled again, but not with her eyes. 'That guy's like the Road Runner. Every time I look round, he's gone.' She illustrated this point by swiftly turning her head from side to side and making cartoon sound effects.

Savage said, 'He's not an easy man to get to know.'

'No shit.'

'But believe me,' added Savage, 'getting to know him is well worth the effort.'

Roth wondered whether this was the right moment to discuss the clumsiness of Laverne's report on the Animal, his general evasiveness, the fact that none of his most famous arrests had ever been satisfactorily explained. She looked into Savage's startlingly blue eyes. Seeing nothing there but bland friendliness, she decided to keep her doubts to herself.

'This is just a thought . . .' began Savage.

'Yes?'

'I was wondering . . .'

'Yeah?' Roth noticed that DI Savage, normally so composed, was blushing slightly. What on earth was she about to suggest?

'I mean, you may have other plans . . .'

Roth said, 'Hey, Lyn. What is this? A marriage proposal?'

'No. I just wondered whether you were free on Saturday night.'

Roth's face brightened. 'Yeah. Sure. Why?'

'I wondered if you fancied coming round to my house for a meal. You could meet Ian and the children . . .'

'That'd be really great. I'd love to.'

'Just supper. It won't be anything exciting . . .'

Roth grinned. 'Lyn, after what I just sat through this afternoon, *anything'd* seem exciting.'

Early that evening, Laverne's wife Dawn turned her latch key in the front door of their Huntington cottage. The smell of cooking enveloped her as she entered the hall. She'd been shopping in York, and placed her carrier bags down in the hall before walking through to the kitchen. Laverne was standing over the stove, humming tunelessly while he stirred a large pan of vegetable soup. At the sight of her, he stopped humming and beamed boyishly.

'Thought I'd start the tea, ready for when you came in,' he announced proudly, unaware that such a mundane feat merited no congratulation. Vegetable soup was the only meal he could make, and Dawn was getting weary of it. All summer, whenever he'd arrived home early, he had taken it upon himself to drop a mound of diced vegetables into a pan, boil them and call the result 'soup'. He'd been arriving home early rather too often.

But she snaked her arms around his aproned waist and feigned gratitude. 'Nothing doing at work?' she asked him.

'No. No.' He shook his head, but Dawn thought she saw a guilty shadow dart across his face.

'What? So York's become a crime-free zone, has it?'

Evading the question, he said, 'That bloody woman's been following me around again.'

'Who? "Special Agent" Roth?'

He nodded, pulled a sour face. 'Giving me the damn third degree. It's getting embarrassing.'

'Be fair, now. She's interested in you. I can see why. You're an interesting case.'

Dawn pinched his bottom. He winced, grabbed her hand and turned to face her, drawing her body close to his and smiling down into her eyes. He said, 'Right! That does it. I'm charging you with common assault, contrary to section 39 of the Criminal Justice Act of 1988 . . .'

After dinner, the Lavernes went out for a walk. Birdsong pealed in the trees around them as they ambled lazily through the country lanes, relishing the sweet evening air. Dawn held Laverne's hand, then released it when they reached the village, knowing that he was old-fashioned and would deem it unmanly to be seen looking romantic in public. They passed the village pub and turned right, heading towards Huntington Parish Church.

They walked by a row of simple houses. The church spire appeared, almost unbearably beautiful in the violet dusk. On the bridge that led to the church, they paused, looking over the slow-running stream to fields in which plump white sheep were grazing. It was like gazing at a dream of Old England, although both of them knew that beyond the green horizon cars thundered round a busy ring road.

Laverne had been chatting all the way there, but he now fell silent. Dawn understood that it was not because he was stricken dumb by the pastoral splendour of the scene, but because their son was buried in the nearby churchyard. She knew that he didn't want to visit the grave, or wallow in melancholy, but would nonetheless do whatever she wished. Knowing this, loving him, she steered him back towards the village. 'Come on, Big Boy. Let's get back. My programme's on in half-an-hour . . .'

Immediately, she felt him relax, sensed the tension lift from his shoulders. Ten minutes later, they turned into the narrow lane where their cottage was situated. There was no one in sight, so Laverne was holding her hand again. She decided to voice the worry that had been eating away at her.

'Vernon: all this coming-home-early, this taking-it-easy-at-work. It's not for me, is it?'

He gave her a quizzical frown. 'What d'you mean?'

'You're not doing it just for my benefit? I mean, I know I've sometimes moaned about our lives revolving round your job . . .'

'"Sometimes"?' he mocked gently. 'Try "all the time".'

They were silent for a moment. After pondering, he went on to say, 'No. No, it's been for me, really. For years I've been running round, losing sleep, actually risking my life, while all around me, ninety-five per cent of my fellow police officers are just biding their time, putting in the hours, waiting for retirement and a nice fat pension.'

'Lyn Savage isn't like that.'

'No. But a lot of 'em are. The way I see it, the police have had more than their money's worth from me. Maybe it's time for *me* to take it easy for a change. I think it's about time I took more care of myself.' He winked at her. 'And you.'

'So this *is* about me?'

He jeered, shoved her playfully. 'About you? What makes you think that everything's about you?'

They arrived at the cottage. Someone had left a message on the telephone answering machine. While Dawn brewed a pot of tea, Laverne played back the tape. The caller had a deep voice with a strong Mancunian accent. It was Geraint John, the Deputy Chief Constable. 'Vernon, old flower. It's your darling friend Geraint here. Where were you at five o'clock, you skiving bastard? Came all the way over from Northallerton and you'd fucked off home. Oops. Sorry Dawn. Anyway, ring me at home, would you? It's a bit important.'

Laverne wondered what 'a bit important' meant. But he had no intention of ringing Geraint to find out. He went into the living room, turned on the TV and flopped on to the sofa. Dawn brought in the tea tray and they settled down to watch an insipid police drama series. Laverne made sarcastic remarks every time the main character, a world-weary detective with a tragic past, uttered phrases like 'prime suspect' and 'key witness'.

'Rubbish,' mocked Laverne. 'Nobody talks like that.'

'I don't care,' said Dawn, crossly. 'Shut up. You're ruining it.'

Suitably chastened, Laverne left the room, moved into the kitchen and helped himself to a chocolate digestive biscuit that he didn't really want, or need. It was getting dark outside. He was half-contemplating an aimless stroll through the garden when the front door bell rang.

Mildly curious, he walked up the hall, scattering biscuit crumbs over the carpet on his way. He opened the door and saw Geraint John standing on the step.

'Hello, my little chucky egg,' beamed John.

Laverne laughed and clasped the Deputy Chief Constable's arm in a friendly way, while inwardly cursing him. It wasn't that he didn't like Geraint; he was deeply attached to the man. But Laverne valued his privacy, and loathed surprise visits, whether he loved the visitor or not.

Geraint's walking stick entered the hall before him, followed by the towering frame of its owner. Laverne and Geraint were exactly the same height: six feet four inches; but since the Animal had blasted a hole through his belly with a shotgun, Geraint appeared to have shrunk slightly.

'I've been trying to ring you,' he pointed out.

'I know ... I got your message. Actually, I was just about to phone you back,' said Laverne.

'You are *such* a fucking liar!' retorted Geraint, rocking with ribald laughter.

They walked through to the kitchen. Laverne offered Geraint a cold beer and a glass, and poured one for himself. They sat down at the kitchen table. Laverne noticed that Geraint, ominously, had brought a slim leather portfolio with him. He now placed this squarely on the table between them.

Biding their time, the two men touched glasses, drank to each other. Laverne took in Geraint John's pale blue polo shirt, his grey corduroy trousers, the white teeth and bright eyes flashing in the tanned, handsome face.

'You're looking better, Geraint,' commented Laverne. 'No one'd believe you were at death's door a year ago.'

'I'm still not right, Vernon. I get very tired . . . no energy. I'd be fucked without my walking stick. Let's face it: I'll never dance the cancan again.'

'You couldn't dance it before.' Laverne took a mouthful of beer. 'Anyway, what can I do for you?'

Geraint's face darkened, becoming serious, almost soulful. 'It's not me who wants you, chuck.' He patted the portfolio. 'We've had a letter from Avon and Somerset Police. Not so much a letter . . . more of a request. A case of "Avon calling". They need your help.'

'The answer's "no".'

Geraint held up his hand like the traffic policeman he used to be. 'No . . . listen . . . hear me out. It's about that murder in Glastonbury. You know . . . where the whole family was wiped out, apart from that little girl . . .'

Laverne nodded warily. The case had received intensive media coverage.

Geraint said, 'Well, the lads down there are having problems and they fear that whoever did it is going to strike again. The inquiry's being led by a fella called Holebrook. Seems like a good bloke. But he's got bugger all to go on.

'There's some photos in the folder. And a report. Have a look, later on. You've never seen anything like it. No prints. No sign of a forced entry. Whoever did it went in and out like the invisible fucking man, and wiped out four people in seconds. If it was done by a gang, that's bad enough. But if it's the work of one man, we could be talking about the killer of all time.'

Laverne, who disliked hyperbole, sniffed at this. 'Sounds like a headline from the *News of the World*.'

The Deputy Chief Constable frowned, struggling to justify himself. 'What I mean is, the worst killer we've seen in this country. And if he does the same thing again . . . Jesus. Imagine the panic. Which is why Somerset have asked us . . . just asked . . . if there's any chance that you could go down there to offer any, er, well, you know . . .'

'What?'

'Advice.'

Laverne grimaced sarcastically. 'I'll bet . . .'

Wide-eyed, Geraint said, 'No. Just advice . . . I'm not lying. The letter's in the case if you don't believe me.'

Laverne sighed. 'I don't care. The answer's still "no".'

'Why? You haven't exactly been worked off your feet lately, have you?'

'Neither have you,' retorted Laverne.

Geraint grinned. 'Go on. It'll be a nice little holiday for you. Ever been to Glastonbury?'

'No.'

'Me neither. Too westerly for my liking. Too full of stupid bloody yokels. It's pretty, though. You could go and see the sights . . . visit the castle of King Arthur.'

Laverne couldn't help smiling. 'There isn't a castle at Glastonbury.'

Geraint looked mildly affronted by this information. 'Isn't there? Really?' Laverne shook his head. 'Well, where am I thinking of, then?'

'Tintagel. In Cornwall.'

'Oh, well. Whatever. It's meant to be pretty. Nice scenery. If you like watching New Age Travellers shitting out of caravan windows.'

Geraint laughed riotously, showing the fillings in his teeth. Laverne half-smiled, resisting his friend's indisputable charm. But Geraint refused to be beaten. 'Oh, go on. You can take Lyn Savage with you. They'll put you up in a nice hotel. All expenses paid . . .'

Laverne scowled. 'Did you hear me say "yes"? I said N-O.'

Geraint half-drained his glass, shook his head. 'Ooh, you can be a miserable fucker sometimes.'

Nodding in agreement, Laverne stared at the kitchen table. The two men were quiet for a moment. Through the open window came the sound of a tender breeze rustling the branches of the trees in the garden. Geraint patted the leather portfolio with something akin to affection. His eyes narrowed shrewdly as he watched Laverne's face. 'I can't say I blame you, Vernon. None of us are getting any younger.'

'What's that got to do with anything?' demanded Laverne sharply.

The Deputy Chief Constable shrugged, examined his fingernails. 'Oh, I'm not saying you're old. But you're not exactly young, are you? Neither of us are. Let's face it. You're probably sick of running around. Perhaps you should apply for that promotion ... settle yourself behind a nice desk and grow a few piles on your arse. More money for less work. Why not? You've earned it.'

Laverne's cheeks coloured and Geraint John knew his words had travelled straight to their target. 'All right, Geraint. I'm not ready for a Bath chair yet. And I'm not turning you down because I'm decrepit. I just feel . . .'

'Yes?'

Laverne squirmed. He disliked making personal admissions almost as much as he disliked hearing them. But his self-respect compelled him to tell Geraint what he had told his wife earlier: that he owed it to Dawn, and to himself, to retire in one piece.

Geraint John listened sceptically. 'It doesn't matter how you justify it to yourself, Vernon. Any fella who starts living his life to please his missis is past his prime. It happened to me years ago, as soon as I landed this twat-of-a-job. Overnight, I turned from a busy bobby into a glorified fucking office boy.' He stared at Laverne gravely, sighed and shook his head. 'I just never thought it'd happen to you.'

When the Deputy Chief Constable had departed, a rather deflated Laverne made his way upstairs. He undressed, brushed his teeth and donned a pair of overly flamboyant purple silk pyjamas

28

that Dawn had bought him for his last birthday, in an attempt to 'jolly him up'. He wore them because they were comfortable, and because he didn't want to hurt his wife's feelings. But he wasn't jolly, and never had been. He was steady and serious and preferred to dress in brown, grey and tweedy olive green; colours that his daughter Jennifer had once memorably described as 'seven shades of shit'.

Nevertheless, he buttoned up his inappropriate pyjamas, climbed into bed and began to flick through a glossy periodical called *British Cars*. But he couldn't concentrate on the magazine. Geraint's remarks about his age had left him feeling jaded. Dawn entered the room. As she undressed, she asked what their visitor had wanted.

Laverne answered without raising his gaze from the magazine. 'Oh, it's about that murder in Glastonbury. Could I go down and offer some "advice"?' He turned a page with exaggerated care. 'Don't worry . . . I didn't commit myself.'

She said nothing, eased into her nightdress, went out to the bathroom. Twenty minutes passed. She did not return. Laverne started to feel irritable. Geraint John's visit had left him with a headache. It had been a troublesome day and he needed to sleep. What was keeping her?

Eventually, he threw down the magazine and went out to the bathroom. She wasn't there. He descended the stairs and found her in the kitchen. She was sitting at the table and on its surface she had laid six ten-by-eight black-and-white photographs. Laverne walked up to her, saw that Geraint's leather portfolio was open. His stomach churned in dismay. He had meant to stash the folder in the spare room, out of Dawn's way, but had forgotten to take it upstairs with him. Now it was too late.

Silently, almost serenely, Dawn contemplated the images before her. The photographs recorded a scene of absolute carnage. In one picture, a baby that had been sliced in two lay across its prone mother. Her hands clasped each half of its sundered body, as if trying to put the infant together again. Her right leg was severed at the thigh, and her head was missing from her shoulders.

Elsewhere, the man of the house roared in death at his attacker, his gore-blackened face frozen between agony and defiance. The top of his head had been sliced off at a jaunty angle, as if guillotined by a flippant executioner. His intestines were trailing from a ravine-like wound in his midriff. His left hand was only attached to its wrist by a hanging tendon. The right arm had been hacked off at the elbow.

'Dawn, no . . .' Laverne reached forward to gather up the prints.

Gently, firmly, she stayed his hand. 'No. Leave them.' There was a resigned calm in her voice.

Laverne blushed. He was ashamed. It was as if she'd found a pornographic magazine in his bottom drawer; he wished that he could snatch the prints away, ease her mind with some innocent-sounding explanation. In the past, he had always managed to keep sights like this from her.

The police photographer had documented the massacre well: frankly, unblinkingly, with no concessions to sensitivity or good taste. Consequently, the pictures were hideous to behold, impossible to disregard.

He noticed that Dawn was holding something in her right hand: another photograph, not one of the official police exhibits, but a small colour portrait. Gently, he eased it out of her fingers and held it up to his face. It showed a young girl in school uniform, grinning exuberantly at the camera. She looked about eleven years old.

'That's her, isn't it?' said Dawn, not looking up. 'The little girl who survived.'

Laverne hummed in accord. 'Suppose it must be.'

Dawn passed her hand over the photographs on the table. 'And this is what she saw. Can you believe that? Can you even begin to imagine what that child is going through?'

Laverne felt that he could imagine this only too well. He placed the snapshot over the murdered infant, in a belated bid to censor the horror.

Laverne said, 'That's enough, now. Put them away.'

She looked up at him, anguish in her eyes. 'I hope you're going to help them find whoever did this . . .'

He opened his mouth to protest, then paused.

Dawn squeezed his hand emphatically. 'Vernon, you *must*.'

He nodded, and smiled at her, almost hearing the rush of air as his new-found life of ease flew out of the window.

Ian Savage smiled unctuously as he refilled Angela Roth's glass with the cheap and mildly offensive Bulgarian claret he'd picked up from the supermarket. 'I bet you'd like to know how Laverne does it, eh? So would I. Been trying to find out for years.' He nodded rudely at his wife. 'No point asking her. *She* won't tell you a bloody thing.'

A few drops of wine missed the proffered glass, spattering the white linen tablecloth with fake blood-spots. Savage winced, embarrassed by her husband's blustering bonhomie. Technically, the evening had been a success. The fillet steak with mushroom stuffing had arrived on their plates at the same time (and at approximately the same temperature) as the vegetables. Ian had taken an instant liking to their guest, and Officer Roth had returned the compliment by laughing dutifully at all but his most leaden attempts at wit.

But Savage was moderate in her habits, and wary of all mood-changes induced by drink. Her father had been an alcoholic. An angelic man while sober; bitter and abusive on his return from the pub. Growing up with him had left her with a deep distrust of all drunks, including the gregarious kind.

'There's no secret about it,' retorted Savage as she gathered their plates together. 'I don't know any more about Laverne's methods than anyone else. And I've given up worrying about it.'

'Yeah, but come on,' prompted Roth, her dark eyes glittering in the candlelight. 'How long's it been? Seven years? You must have your suspicions.'

Savage smiled enigmatically. 'Yes, I do. And someday, if you're really good, I might just share them with you . . .'

'Why not now?' challenged Ian. 'Why not share them now?'

Savage shot him a warning glance, which he either missed or ignored. As she walked into the kitchen, she heard him embarking on a familiar monologue. 'Know how he caught the Bolton Strangler? No? Surprise, surprise. Neither does anyone else. He was driving past a graveyard . . . I'm dead serious. What are you laughing for? He was driving past this graveyard. Lyn was sitting right next to him . . .'

Savage returned with the dessert: a large home-made cheesecake, crowned with blueberries and fresh cream. Roth whistled at the sight of it. 'Made to an American recipe,' explained Savage. 'So you ought to like it.'

Ian sniggered for Roth's benefit. 'Hear that? She's more or less saying that it's your own fault if you *don't* like it.'

Roth had no idea what he was talking about, so acted as if she hadn't heard. Savage crossed the dining room to slot another bland CD into the bland hi-fi, while Ian made a ham-fisted attempt to lever three slices of cheesecake on to awaiting plates.

They devoured their dessert. Apart from a few obligatory murmurs of dietary delight, all three were silent for over a minute. Then Roth said, 'I don't know what to say about this Laverne business, Lyn. I really don't.'

Savage feigned innocence. 'Sorry?'

'If he doesn't know how he catches these guys, and you're not sure, and I can't even begin to guess, then come on, let's be honest, this report of mine is destined to read like the biggest dumb-ass joke since Madonna called herself a singer.'

'Oh? I think she's rather good,' Ian interjected.

Roth responded to this with a look of disbelief that was only a fraction away from outright derision. Ian noticed the look, and boyish hurt flickered in his eyes. Seeing this, Savage felt an involuntary gush of affection for the father of her children, despite his penchant for embarrassing her in company.

'Madonna,' Ian stumbled on. 'She's all right, isn't she? I thought she was very talented. Sexy, too.'

Roth was unwilling to debate the point. Turning to Savage, she said, 'You gonna help me, Lyn?'

Savage found herself nodding automatically before she'd had a chance to consider the request.

'Yeah? Right. That's good. 'Cause Glastonbury's my one chance to salvage something from this situation. You watch me. I'm gonna hang on to Laverne's tail 'til he squeals for mercy.'

'I should imagine that'd make anyone squeal for mercy,' remarked Ian. Roth, who had never watched a *Carry On* film in her life, mistook the vulgar jest for a compliment.

'That's right,' she reaffirmed. 'That is *exactly* right. One thing you should know about me, I don't give up without a fight. Or several fights. OK, I've let him kid me around up 'til now. It's been easy for him. Since I've been in England, all he's had to do is push around a few drunks and no-hopers.'

'That's no way to talk about the North Yorkshire Police,' quipped Ian. This time, both women laughed. To mark this small victory, Ian refilled their glasses.

'But the crime in Glastonbury,' continued Roth. 'This is major league homicide. It's my territory, believe me. I've seen whole families wiped out before, by which I mean I've seen what's left of those families after the event. I've played hunt-the-entrail in homes from New York to Nebraska. Family murder is my specialty, you could even call it my forte, and if Laverne thinks he's going to push my nose out of this one, Christ, is *he* in for a big surprise . . .'

Hearing the stridency in her own voice, Roth paused, emitted a dry laugh, smiled apologetically. She took a mouthful of wine and shook her head. 'And I'm sorry. You don't need a lecture, I know that. Way I see it, your only crime tonight is feeding me one of the greatest meals I've eaten in my entire life . . .'

Savage attempted to deflect the compliment.

'No, truly,' pressed Roth. 'It's sublime.' She intoned this adjective as if she thought it was a word that only English people used, and would therefore appreciate hearing. Then she forked a diamond of cheesecake into her mouth and chewed. 'Truly sublime.'

A devilish grin played across Ian's mouth. 'Angela, Laverne does *know* you're going to Glastonbury with him on Monday, doesn't he?'

Roth shrugged. 'Who the hell cares?'

Savage shook her head emphatically. 'Nothing's been said. As far as he knows, it's just going to be him, me, and two hundred officers from Avon and Somerset. But as far as I see it, and as far as the Chief Constable sees it, Angela has every right to be there. The terms of her placement require that she observe Chief Superintendent Laverne for a period of two whole months. She's with us for another five weeks.'

Ian Savage had always been slightly envious of the high regard which his wife held for Laverne. He threw back his head to emit a mirthless cackle. 'Oh God, that's priceless . . . I'd give anything to see his face when he finds out . . .'

2

WE WILL NOT ALL SLEEP

For most of Monday, Laverne remained in blissful ignorance of the
horror to come. Should he ask about Angela, Savage had made up
her mind to confess all. But not once during the four hour drive to
Glastonbury did Chief Superintendent Laverne refer to Roth or the
organization she represented: the FBI, which he suspected to be an
acronym for the Female Bureau of Interference.

Displaying an uncharacteristic optimism, and reasoning powers
worthy of an ostrich, Laverne equated Roth's absence from the
back seat of his car with her permanent and prayed-for return to
somewhere-unpronounceable-in-Virginia.

As Laverne and Savage approached Glastonbury from the north-
east, their first glimpse of the Tor, imperiously reigning over the
Somerset plain, forced them to postpone the argument they'd been
having about police accountability while they observed a respectful
two-minute silence.

Laverne was seldom given to lyrical utterances, and did not make
one now. But the appearance of Tor Hill unsettled him. Over the
years, he had seen this famous landmark hundreds of times, often
in books, mainly in the kind of television documentary that made
him switch channels after the first ten seconds, usually after hearing
the words, 'The Ancient Isle of Avalon'.

But nothing had prepared him for the sight of the Tor itself.
The Matterhorn, viewed during a family coach tour of Switzerland,

had cast a similar chill through his heart. Yet the Matterhorn, being a jagged, shimmering Alp, had a right to be awesome. Glastonbury Tor was nothing more than an unremarkable hill with a ruined church on its summit.

'Seems to be saying something, don't you think?' ventured Savage.

Laverne grunted, hoping that Savage would mistake this for some kind of intelligent response.

'Seems so familiar, somehow,' she ventured.

Laverne grunted again, knowing that Savage was thinking exactly what he was thinking, and that here was a chance for them to discuss something more demanding than the pros and cons of clipping juvenile offenders around the ear. But Laverne, without knowing why, let the conversation die. With mingled apathy and regret, he reflected that his life was full of similarly missed opportunities.

An hour before, Laverne and Savage had stopped at the neighbouring town of Street, where the Avon and Somerset Police, anxious to create a good impression, had booked them into the three star Abbot Whiting Hotel. They were checked in by a charmless receptionist who confirmed that Savage and Laverne had been allocated a twin room and a single. 'Twin room, eh?' commented Laverne as they entered the lift. 'You'll be able to spend half the night in one bed, and the next half in the other.'

Savage smiled thinly, but said nothing.

On entering Glastonbury, Laverne left his Rover in a small car park while he and Savage took a stroll around the town. They turned into High Street, passing the fifteenth century George and Pilgrims Inn on their left and walking uphill towards the parish church of St John the Baptist. A clock opposite the church gave the time as two thirty-five. They were not due to dine with Detective Chief Inspector Holebrook until seven.

Glastonbury was smaller than Laverne had imagined: a pleasant but unspectacular town that happened to be steeped in history. There were hippies everywhere. The Love Generation may have failed to conquer the world, but it had certainly conquered Glastonbury. Every other shop seemed to be devoted to the quest for inner truth and spiritual meaning.

Laverne put this point to Savage over tea and cakes in the Guinivere Tea Rooms. 'Lowers the tone, don't you think?' he complained. 'Attracts the wrong kind of visitor. You can't move without bumping into people with green hair and rings through their noses.'

Savage was scraping butter over a scone. She paused to look into his eyes. 'That's unworthy of you.'

He was surprised by her evident disappointment in him. He then surprised himself further by blushing like a schoolboy.

Savage went on to explain herself. 'I expect that kind of reactionary rubbish from men like Geraint John and Neville Wood.'

'Ah. You mean senior police officers.'

'Exactly. But not you. Never you. You're better than that.'

'Am I really?'

'Of course.' She smiled. 'Why do you think I keep working with you?'

Pleased, Laverne stirred his tea. 'Dunno. I thought it was my calm and noble demeanour ... my battered but undeniably virile good looks.'

She laughed and shook her head. 'Sorry.'

He glanced up at a terrible frieze of knights and dragons that besmirched the walls and was reminded of his theme.

'It *is* cheap, though, isn't it? This must have been a nice little town, once. It used to be a place of pilgrimage, but they've turned it into a mystical version of Blackpool.'

'True. But it was the monks who brought the King Arthur trade here in the first place, remember, by claiming they'd found the bones of Arthur and Guinivere in the Abbey.'

'I know that,' countered Laverne, who actually knew nothing of the kind. 'All I'm saying is that Glastonbury represents England. A dream of England, if you like. And the dream'd be potent enough without all this nonsense about knights and dragons and signs of the zodiac.'

Laverne gasped sharply and doubled up as if he'd been punched in the solar plexus. Savage wondered if he was in pain. 'Are you all right?'

With his head lowered, he hissed, 'Don't look round. For God's sake, whatever you do, don't look round.'

But in common with Lot and Orpheus, Lyn Savage suffered from a fatal weakness for the backward glance. She peered over her shoulder and saw what she'd been expecting to see: Angela Roth, buying coffee and cake at the counter, handing over money with all the disconcerting confidence of the American abroad.

'Is she still there?' said Laverne, his voice muffled by the hand that half-covered his face.

'Afraid so.'

He lowered his guard to glance furtively at the counter, saw Roth cheerfully nodding back to him as she pocketed her change.

'Aw, it's no good,' he groaned. 'She's seen us.'

'Yes,' said Savage simply.

The casual nature of her response instantly aroused his suspicions. 'You don't seem very surprised.'

Savage shrugged. Further pretence was useless. The game was up. 'Vernon, why would I be surprised? It was me who arranged to meet her here.'

There is a cosy eighteenth century restaurant on the first floor of the Abbot Whiting Hotel, where, in or out of season, a disproportionately high number of genteel old ladies can usually be found, sitting in pairs, sipping the soup of the day with consummate slowness and holding polite disagreements in loud, indiscreet voices.

Two such old dears were present now, adjacent to the table occupied by Laverne, Roth and Savage. The police officers were awaiting DCI Holebrook, who, by way of welcome, was supposed to be meeting them for dinner. Holebrook had been due to arrive at seven. He was now twelve minutes late.

Laverne wasn't speaking to either of his female companions, so he had the freedom to eavesdrop on the more strident of the elderly diners, a gaunt septuagenarian whose stoop owed something to age and a great deal to the weight of the sizeable pearl necklace around her neck. She resembled Alastair Sim as the headmistress of St Trinians. Her squat companion reminded him of Margaret Rutherford. As a policeman, accustomed to dividing people into easily identifiable social groups, Laverne found it rather reassuring that such stereotypes actually existed.

'Who would have believed it?' Alastair Sim was saying. 'To think that we could ever have been reduced to such *penury* . . .'

This declaration puzzled Laverne. Observing the two diners, he could discern no outward evidence of their straitened circumstances. They were both elegantly dressed, and dinner at the Abbot Whiting was not particularly cheap. He guessed that their idea of a reduced income amounted to considerably more than a policeman's pay.

Laverne sipped his beer and waited for Margaret Rutherford to respond. But Margaret merely nodded, her spoon inadvertently chinking against the rim of her bowl. Pleased with the effect she'd created, Sim repeated herself. 'Such *penury*.'

At his own table, Savage and Roth were chattering away with relaxed familiarity. Savage was seated to his right, with Roth facing her. To his chagrin, neither appeared to have noticed that he'd ostracized them. That was the trouble with being habitually surly, brooded Laverne. When you wanted to be surly to make a point, rather than just surly for the sake of it, no one could ever tell the difference.

Officer Roth was telling Savage about ley lines. 'That's another

39

thing. Glastonbury is the meeting place for a record number of leys.'

Savage's incomprehension was all too apparent.

'Don't you know about this stuff? "Ley" is an Old English word, meaning 'old straight track'. Ley lines link places of spiritual power, and when you get a crossing of the leys, well, that usually means fireworks.'

'What kind of fireworks?'

'Well, you know. Hauntings. Miracles. Visions. Or maybe even mass murder.'

'You really believe that, do you?' asked Savage, in a tone that implied mild disapproval.

'It's not a question of what *I* believe, but what the killer believes. Think it over. This place is a Mecca for freaks and occultists. Four members of a family murdered. A fifth member is spared. Why? Does the number four have some significance here?'

Laverne's face prickled with indignation. The audacity of the woman! She'd only been here five minutes, and she was already trying to take over. Feeling the coolness of his stare, Roth languidly turned her head to look directly into his eyes. Laverne detected a hint of sweet mockery in the curve of her mouth. She raised her gin and tonic to him and smiled. 'Not that it's any of my business.'

'No,' agreed Laverne tightly.

Goaded by his manner, she added, 'Not yet, anyway.'

'As far as I know, I'm the only person who was actually invited here,' snapped Laverne. 'Unless I'm very much mistaken, you weren't invited at all.'

The ill grace of this remark made Savage lower her eyes in embarrassment. But Roth refused to be cowed. 'No. Way I remember, your Chief Constable invited me. Unlike you, he seems to think the FBI counts for something.'

'Oh. I *see*. I'm supposed to feel honoured, am I?'

'Vernon, drop it,' warned Savage.

40

Roth touched Savage on the shoulder lightly. 'No. Let him talk. I want to hear what he's got to say.'

'I doubt that very much,' sneered Laverne.

'Try me.'

Laverne swallowed the remnants of his beer and slammed his glass down petulantly. He noticed that the two old ladies had laid down their soup spoons and were watching with great interest. Let them gape. He could no longer contain himself. 'I've caught four serial killers in my career, and I did it without the benefit of psychological claptrap. I don't accept that every murder holds the key to a killer's personality, or that murderers themselves can be neatly divided into psychopaths or sociopaths or paranoid schizophrenics. I consider these terms to be misleading and primitive, because I believe that the human capacity for evil is far more complex and elusive than psychologists and, for that matter, behavioural scientists would have us believe. In short, Ms Roth, I consider you and the organization you represent to be laughably self-important.'

Savage attempted to leap to Roth's defence. Once again, Roth expressed a desire to fight her own battles. With icy self-control, never once shifting her gaze from Laverne's face, she said, 'Know what I think, Laverne? I think you see me as a threat.'

'No,' returned Laverne. 'I see you as a bloody nuisance.'

Roth's face coloured. 'Well, now ... maybe I don't give a blind shit for your opinion of me or behavioural fucking science or practically anything you could fucking mention. Now, how about that?'

One of the eaves-dropping old ladies groaned with dismay. Laverne knew how she felt. 'Now that's enough!' he blustered. 'I don't want to hear that kind of language, and neither does my Inspector.'

'Oh, Vernon, do shut up,' sighed Savage.

Roth took a deep breath. She immediately regretted her outburst and knew that a great deal depended on the wording of her next utterance. 'Listen: I don't want to fight and I'm not here to convert you to my point of view. Quite the opposite, in fact. I came to find out how you see things. You got quite a reputation for yourself. I don't think you take kindly to fame. Tough. You're in the record books, whether you like it or not.

'Now, whatever you may think to the contrary, the people I work with aren't idiots. They realize that you've achieved a great deal without our help. Without any help. Jesus, the police in England operate with *no money*. Frankly, your budget for a murder hunt wouldn't buy me a new pair of shoes. And yet without funds, without technology or criminology, *without evidence*, Chief Super-intendent Vernon Laverne still manages to hound down a number of serious whackos and put 'em away. That fact is very interesting, both to me and to the "laughably self-important" organization I represent.'

Laverne had to smile. He couldn't help himself.

'Since I got here, you've done your level best to freeze me out. I don't exactly know why that is. I guess this visit was more your boss's idea than yours. Right?'

Laverne didn't answer.

'So you won't talk to me. Fine. Maybe you *can't* explain what you do. Lyn here believes you act purely on instinct. Well, in that case, I'd like to hang around and see those instincts at work. Who knows? It might be worth the wait. And along the way, I might actually learn something.'

There was a silence while the women waited for Laverne to make some kind of conciliatory gesture. But Laverne, rightly or wrongly, was unwilling to apologize for telling the truth. As a compromise, he beckoned the waitress and ordered another round of drinks.

Moments later, Detective Chief Inspector Ed Holebrook arrived. He was a tall, angular-faced man in his forties, with a sharply pointed nose that gave him a triangular profile. His mud-coloured hair, combed back to form a widow's peak, looked as if it hadn't been washed since his last appearance on *Crimewatch*. The face underneath the smooth brow was genial but the eyes were alert and calculating. Laverne thought Holebrook looked exactly like the Identikit portrait of a rapist that had been hanging on the main notice-board back at headquarters in York since Christmas.

Holebrook was accompanied by a younger man, Detective Sergeant Mowart, whose dark features, high cheekbones and narrow eyes reminded Laverne of an American Indian. Holebrook laughed at most of Mowart's jokes, and Mowart returned the compliment. Laverne guessed that the two men trusted each other, preferring to work closely whenever possible. It was the kind of relationship that he enjoyed with Savage: not based on rank, or expediency, but on mutual respect.

But there was something about the new arrivals, a certain cool self-containment, that roused Laverne's curiosity. They made no apology for their late arrival, and it crossed his mind that they thought they were doing him a favour by turning up at all.

Holebrook ordered champagne, a bottle of iced Taittinger, and filled their glasses to drink to Laverne and his companions. 'To our guests from deepest Yorkshire,' said Holebrook. 'May they succeed where we've failed.'

Laverne accepted the tribute, but thought the toast a strange one. The Martin family had been dead for less than a month. Rather too soon, by anyone's standards, to start talking of defeat. 'Can things really be as bad as all that?' he wondered aloud. 'It took us two years to find the Animal. By my reckoning, you've hardly had time to get started.'

Holebrook tilted his head to one side as he gazed ruminatively into Laverne's eyes. 'There are three main kinds of murder. I call 'em "the three As". Murder by anger, avarice or appetite.'

And there are three main types of policeman, thought Laverne with a sinking heart: the ill-bred, the half-dead and the should-have-stayed-in-bed. At that moment, he placed himself firmly in the latter category.

'Most of the killings we all see fall into the first two categories,' continued Holebrook in a pompous monotone. 'Silly little murders prompted by greed or malice; malice that's either accumulated over a long period of time, or flares up suddenly as a result of drink or drugs, or some pointless argument. Then there are the kind of criminals you specialize in, Chief Superintendent: people with a genuine taste for the taking of human life.'

'Oh, I wouldn't go so far as to call them people,' offered Laverne sourly.

'Quite.' Holebrook attempted a smile, but only succeeded in producing a constipated grimace. 'But what we've seen at the Martin house confounds all these theories.'

Roth took a deep breath. Oh God, here she goes, thought Laverne. 'In the FBI, we recognize five categories of murder.'

Holebrook and Mowart turned to her with amused incredulity on their faces. Having secured their attention, Roth poured herself a cup of coffee from a stainless steel pot. There was a certain admirable insolence in the slowness with which she performed this simple task. When she'd returned the coffee pot to the centre of the table and taken two sips from her cup, she spoke again.

'One: felony murder; takes place during robbery, kidnap and so on. Two: suspected felony murder. Three: argument motivated murder, which you describe, sir, as "silly little murders". Four: other motives . . . literally any killing that doesn't come under the first three headings. For example, the guy who wants to make a mark, or the grudge-bearer who feels that being infamous beats the hell out of being nobody. Also under this heading come most of the sick bastards you read about.

'The fifth category we have is "unknown motives". As in the case of Wayne Maroevic, who happened to live two blocks away from my grandparents in New Haven, Connecticut. Maroevic held down

44

a job as a school janitor, raised two well-balanced children, but one day drove his eldest son out to a lake and beat the kid's head in with a wrench.

'It took the state police five years to pin the killing on Maroevic, because no one, Maroevic included, was prepared to accept that he could really have done such a thing. When we gave him the third degree, there was none of the usual shit about "disembodied voices" or "an Arnold Schwarzenegger video made me do it". Wayne Maroevic was just an ordinary middle-aged man with no history of violence, no criminal record. Not so much as a parking fine. Weeping with sheer terror because he couldn't begin to explain to us or himself why he'd done what he'd done.

'Neuroscientists have come up with the theory that crimes like the Maroevic killing are explained by a malfunction of the limbic system.'

'Limpid what?' asked Mowart.

'Limbic system. It's the part of the brain that deals with emotion and motivation. The phrase "limbic storm" has been coined to describe what happens in the brain before one of these killings. We're talking about sudden, random explosions of violence, usually triggered by bad memories.'

Mowart gave a guarded nod. 'And you think that's what might have happened at the Martin house?'

'No. Hear me out. What I was about to say is that to me personally, the most disturbing murderer comes under the "other motives" section. I'm talking about the "irrational rationalist". The guy who commits utter mayhem with the unshakeable conviction that he's doing society a service, or undoing social wrongs. Terrorists come under this heading. So, occasionally, do politicians. But so, also, do men like Bomford, your Bolton Strangler, who was under the impression that killing juveniles was what Christ had in mind when he said, "Suffer little children to come unto me".'

She glanced at Laverne. 'Am I right in thinking that Bomford wasn't insane?'

Laverne frowned. 'The psychiatrists say he wasn't. But then, they didn't have to look at what he'd done.'

Savage showed her agreement with a solemn bow of the head.

'Even so,' resumed Roth, 'I'm afraid Bomford wasn't an unusual case. He wasn't a sadist, he wasn't mad, he killed because he basically couldn't think straight. Not exactly a new phenomenon. The military have been led by men like that for centuries. From what I know about your murder here in Glastonbury, it wasn't a random killing. It was practically a blood sacrifice.'

Holebrook sniffed. 'Well, it's certainly an interesting theory.'

Roth shrugged. 'It's not exactly a theory. Call it a professional evaluation.'

Holebrook turned to Laverne. 'Looks like you and me can go home. The US Cavalry's arrived.'

As well as being impressed by Roth's speech, Laverne had been amazed to discover that her initial suspicions tallied closely with his own. Consequently, he found himself in the unlikely position of siding with Roth against Holebrook. His only response to Holebrook's remark, therefore, was an inflexible stare.

'Well,' said Holebrook dismissively. 'Words are easy. We can talk 'til the cows come home. All I can say is, come to the Martin house tomorrow. You might get a better idea what we're up against.'

Laverne's hotel room was situated on the top floor of the Abbot Whiting, overlooking the High Street. Savage and Roth were sharing a room two doors down the corridor. After Holebrook and Mowart had departed, he had retired to the hotel bar for a nightcap with Savage and Roth. A tacit truce had been declared, mainly because all three agreed that the red carpet that had been extended to them was decidedly threadbare. If this was an example of West Country hospitality, then their stay was destined to be a short one.

For some unknown reason, Laverne's single room contained a spacious four-poster bed. Worse still, the bed's drapes and counterpane were decorated with a pretty floral motif that matched the curtains. Had the overall colour scheme been plain brown, he might have felt more at home. But lying in a flowery four-poster was not, in Laverne's opinion, fitting behaviour for a grown man.

Once in bed, he tried to reassert his manhood by browsing through the latest edition of *Fast Car Monthly*. But the sight of all those beautiful automobiles that he couldn't possibly afford merely served to depress him. There were some books on a small locker beside the bed: a Jackie Collins novel, a paperback with a corpse on the cover and a Gideon Bible.

Distractedly, he picked up the Bible and opened it at random. But what he read troubled him, and he swiftly put the dusty volume down.

Perhaps, after all, there was nothing left to do with the day but end it. He pressed a switch on a cord to extinguish the lamp above his headboard and closed his eyes. Rest, however, was delayed by the memory of the lines he'd chanced upon in the Bible: 'Listen, I tell you a mystery: we will not all sleep, but we will all be changed.'

Laverne was no theologian, but he had endured enough windy sermons to recognize this as an allusion to Judgement Day, when the faithful will arise from sleep to occupy their newly perfect bodies. Yet from somewhere, the idea came to him that the passage spoke instead of the restless dead who disguise themselves in order to prey upon the living.

In the street below, a party of drunks were meandering by, singing 'Tie a yellow ribbon round the old oak tree'. There was an ugly crunch of breaking glass, followed by suppressed childish sniggers. Any more of that, my lads, and you'll be accompanying me to the station.

Eventually, he slipped into an uncomfortable doze. His rest was disturbed by the suspicion that one of the drunks had broken into the hotel and was pacing up and down outside in the passage.

As the suspicion solidified into conviction, Laverne struggled to rouse himself, but for a long time was unable to open his eyes. Neither asleep nor awake, he was like a diver who swims up to the surface, only to find that it has iced over.

With a sudden effort of will, Laverne snapped awake and turned on the light. Then he sat up in bed and listened. For a long time, he heard nothing more. Water gurgled in one of the pipes, and somewhere far away a lavatory flushed. Then silence, apart from the hotel sign outside the window, creaking gently in the wind. Reassured, Laverne turned over in bed, plumped up his pillows and reached for the light switch. At that instant, he heard another noise outside the door: a great rustling, like locusts descending.

Laverne hauled himself out of bed, stepped into his slippers and crossed the room to investigate. As an afterthought, he retraced his steps to the wardrobe, opened the door and selected a black brogue. Holding the stout shoe aloft, he unlocked the door to the corridor as noiselessly as he could and, coiling his hand firmly around its handle, wrenched open the door.

There was no one out there. The hotel was sleeping. He thrust his door key into his pyjama pocket and took himself and his shoe out into the empty corridor. A faulty light bulb blinked and buzzed at the end of the passage. Laverne, being something of a home improvement enthusiast, walked towards the bulb and flicked it with his fingernail, hoping to correct the fault. Instantly, the bulb fizzed and died.

Laverne shrugged. So much for his skills as a handyman. There was a noise in the corridor behind him, like a door closing softly. He turned, saw the carpet yawning into the distance.

He was now level with the main staircase. He glanced down the stairwell, seeing no sign of movement below. Rain pattered lightly on the black mullioned window above the stairs. He heard a faint burst of whispering from the floor below. A key rattled, a door closed with quiet finality. Perhaps the mystery insomniac had finally retired to bed?

On the way back to his room, he paused to listen at Savage's door, and heard the sound of snoring. Probably Roth, he guessed. She struck him as the kind of woman who couldn't even keep quiet in her sleep.

The door to his own room appeared to have blown shut. As he fished for his key, there was another noise behind him. To Laverne, it sounded exactly like the sharp crack of a human knee joint. He swivelled round to confront his stalker, only to be left glaring accusingly at the scarlet fire extinguisher hanging on the opposite wall. Feeling relieved and slightly absurd, Laverne backed into his room and locked himself in.

After returning his shoe to the wardrobe and himself to bed, the Chief Superintendent turned out the light. And while the hotel sign creaked, the rain tapped on the window and the ancient timbers murmured all around him, he drifted gratefully towards sleep.

In his early teens, Laverne had revelled in horror stories. Now, approaching the time of life that was so often chillingly described as 'maturity', he found such stories banal, even vaguely insulting. He had seen far too many mutilated corpses to be amused by the macabre. He now viewed sudden death as something lonely and pathetic, not a source of entertainment.

Yet he still vividly recalled the racy vocabulary of the tales he'd formerly relished and how, at the advent of some particularly ghoulish manifestation, the protagonist's blood invariably 'ran cold in his veins'. Hitherto, he had judged this unlikely image to be a colourful literary device, not the objective description of an actual physical sensation. Yet when the Chief Superintendent felt something stir in the bed beside him, his blood, regrettably, ran cold in his veins. It was embarrassing, it was hackneyed, but there it was.

Slowly, he opened his eyes. He held his breath and waited. Nothing. But as soon as he had convinced himself that the movement that had awoken him was no more than the involuntary jerk of a loose bedspring, he felt something icily cold pressing against the small of his back. With a grunt of alarm, he turned over and looked behind him. At the same time, the bed sheets flew up in his face and the mattress jerked violently. Something heavy and very much alive had rolled out of the bed and on to the carpet.

Laverne reached for the overhead light switch but, in his agitation, merely groped the air. A streetlight outside the window, invading the room through a chink in the curtains, had thrown a thin wedge of yellow radiance on to the wall by the door. Unfortunately for Laverne, it gave enough light to see by.

And this is what he saw: something long and black, its arched back upraised, scurrying past the door at nightmarish speed, then plunging into the black shadow in the corner of the room. Whatever it was darted by in a second, and Laverne had no time to identify its true nature. All that he knew was that the thing was huge, that it was crawling on its knees, and that it rattled as it moved.

When he eventually found the light, the room was as before: comfortably twee, reassuringly empty. His visitor had departed. Laverne went to the bathroom and mopped the sweat off his face and chest with a hotel towel. Then he splashed his cheeks with cold water and tried to smile at the lined face in the mirror in a devil-may-care manner. First night away from home, and he'd already had a guest in his bed. Now, *there* was an interesting story to tell the wife.

Most people in Laverne's situation would have resorted to a brandy from the mini-bar and a sleepless night spent in an armchair. But there was no mini-bar in his room, and no armchair. So he lay awake until the dawn broke and the first birds began to sing on the rooftops of High Street. Then, pacified by the dim light seeping through the thin floral curtains, he finally fell asleep.

3

THE KILLING HOUSE

It was a pleasant family dwelling, built in the early seventies, with brightly painted shutters and fine, high gables in the Scandinavian style. The surrounding two acres were ruled by evergreens: spruce, Scots pine and Douglas fir. The trees augmented the story-book quality of the house, making Laverne think of woodcutters, witches and golden-haired children with whimsical names. But not the massacre of four human beings. Certainly not that.

It was a warm afternoon, but he was unable to suppress a shudder as he viewed the Martin home from the trees at the southern edge of the garden. He hadn't discussed his troubled night at the hotel with anyone, mainly because he felt that to do so would have invited ridicule. But the experience had left him feeling tense and fatigued. Perhaps that was why he now felt that there was someone watching him from one of the upper windows of the house.

Unwilling to surrender to timidity, Laverne inhaled the moist sweet air and waved his arms about vigorously to free the tension from his shoulders. Then, whistling tunelessly and rattling a set of keys labelled PROPERTY OF AVON AND SOMERSET POLICE: DO NOT REMOVE, he strolled up the long garden and unlocked the side door.

On the first floor there were four ordinary-sized bedrooms, two lavatories and one bathroom. The triangular room at the top of the house belonged to Tess, the girl who'd survived. This was where Laverne commenced his search.

51

This room's tiny window provided a view of the front garden, and a worn drive leading over a ramshackle bridge. The rain that had fallen overnight had passed, and the cobalt sky was cloudless. The tower on Tor Hill peered dimly through the uppermost boughs of the wood beyond the bridge. Laverne guessed that the familiar landmark would be completely veiled from sight by midsummer.

He imagined Tess sitting by her window, smoking the secret cigarettes that his keen nose could distinguish from the cheap scent and the fabric softener. Here she had listened to music on her modest CD player and cast herself as the romantic lead in numerous adolescent fantasies. And, like any teenager, she had almost certainly brooded on the gross unfairness of her life. An unfairness that, in her case, was no longer imaginary.

At nine a.m. that morning, Holebrook had provided Laverne, Savage and Roth with a guided tour, punctuated by the kind of gloomy, negative pronouncements that had so endeared him to Laverne the night before. Nothing that was said or proposed added to what Laverne had already gleaned from the original report. Over a pub lunch in town, Holebrook, affecting magnanimity, had reminded Laverne that he had unlimited access to all files, data and witnesses pertaining to the case. 'Don't feel that you have to answer to me. Imagine you're conducting an independent inquiry. That's what the Chief Constable wants. That's what I want, too.'

Laverne had promptly wiped the smile off his host's face by asking for the keys to the Martin house. 'What'd be the point of that?' protested Holebrook. 'We've just been there. You've seen everything there is to see.'

'If that were true,' retorted Laverne, 'this case'd be closed. We've seen nothing, Chief Inspector. Not yet, at any rate.'

Sulkily, Holebrook had sanctioned the request and Laverne was now exploring the site of the homicides. Savage and Roth, meanwhile, had accompanied Holebrook to the police station at Wells to check out possible suspects on the Police National Computer.

Laverne popped an extra-strong mint into his mouth and moved away from the window. A felt rug, embroidered with a leaping gazelle, dominated the centre of the room. He crossed the rug and surveyed an old walnut dressing table, covered in dust. A collection of dolls, teddy bears and stuffed animals of every description had been carefully assembled on either side of the dressing table mirror.

Between the dolls stood bottles of cheap perfume, a cassette tape with a hand-written scrawl on its spine: 'Happenin' Soundz Vol Two'. Laverne recalled the 'BEANZ' in the York café and wondered primly if illiteracy was now taught as part of the National Curriculum.

A couple of postcards were jammed into the mirror's frame. One was from Nice and showed a smiling topless model reclining amidst a montage of Riviera images. Laverne turned the card over and read the message: 'Dear TT, Nice is great, lots of v. nice garcons. Actually, the French are tres vile, but have met a very nice German boy who looks like Marky Mark. (DON'T SHOW THIS TO MERCER!) Love from Gudrun.'

The second card bore the less obviously enticing image of a woman in traditional Welsh dress. On the reverse face was an address and a few lines, all rendered in a neat, rounded child-like script. 'Dear Tess, by the time you read this, you'll be at home and the best holiday of your life will be over. Love T.' The card was postmarked ABER, and dated last August.

Laverne sank down on to the low bed and re-read the card, checking that he'd understood it correctly. Then, with quiet respect, he shook his head. Unless he was greatly mistaken, this was a thirteen-year-old girl reminding herself of the mutability of all things. Such a child, he mused, might be worth knowing. Carefully, he removed a slim diary from the inside pocket of his jacket, slipped the card between the pages and replaced the diary.

There was a drawer built into the side of the bed, which he crouched down to open. Within lay a tell-tale box of Swan Vesta matches, an elderly, half-empty box of Bassett's jelly babies (kept, he guessed, to mask the tobacco on her breath), as well as bracelets, scarfs and a puzzling profusion of dusty two-pence pieces.

Above the bed hung a blown-up photograph of Tess in a boat with her arm around a Mediterranean boy. She looked bright-eyed, pretty and contented, although Laverne found it difficult to say how much of the prettiness was due to youth and how much to bone-structure. It seemed to Laverne, glancing at his creased, weathered face in the dressing table mirror, that practically everyone under thirty was better looking than him.

A book-case by the door contained mostly paperbacks: *Moondial*, *The Borrowers Aloft*, *Prince Caspian* and *The Owl Service*. There was a Patrick Moore guide to Astronomy, a *Child's Encyclopedia of Science and Nature*, and several *Brownie* annuals.

In a chest of drawers, Laverne found a photograph album: the two eldest children as babies, the whole family on a foreign camp site, eating eggs and greasy sausages around a circular table. On a page of its own, a tiny black-and-white snap of a proud-faced old woman holding hands with a small girl in a sunhat.

Overleaf, Dr Richard Martin on holiday, surprised by the camera as he emerged from the waves, thin strands of hair plastered to his scalp, a shy, boyish smile flashing in a brown, broken-nosed face, unaware that his swimming trunks had abandoned his waist and were heading for his knees.

Then a crumpled picture of Mrs Martin adrift on an inflatable lilo, in beautiful shape for a woman of forty, apart from the way her mouth hung open as she slept. Laverne imagined that Tess's mother had made sundry attempts to hide or destroy this snapshot, only to see it returning, with wearisome regularity, to its rightful place in the family album.

Faced with these carefree images, Laverne was suddenly beset by the kind of emotional involvement that professionals are not supposed to feel; a gloom that seemed to enter his body via the crown of his head, and then advance implacably earthwards, exorcizing what remained of his strength and good humour and forcing it out, out through the soles of his feet.

Then he descended to the first floor and realized that the feeling of depression did not originate from him, but from the house itself. It was everywhere: in the walls that needed painting, in the homely, threadbare carpets, in the awful stillness of the bright, untidy rooms. He'd come across this atmosphere before, in the dwellings of other murder victims, but had never felt it as strongly as he felt it here. He could only define it as a sense of *outraged disappointment*. It was as if the very walls were sickened by what they had witnessed.

Descending the stairs to the ground floor, his attention was immediately drawn to some letters lying on the mat by the front door. His trouser belt creaked as he stooped to gather them and he reminded himself to go on a diet. He sat on the stairs while he perused the mail.

There was a plain blue postcard, reminding Mrs Patricia Martin that she was due for a dental check-up. Then two junk letters, something from a bank and an invitation from an insurance company, printed with the words 'A Policy That Might Just Save Your Life!' Laverne scowled. Now that *would* be a bloody miracle.

He walked to the kitchen and added the mail to a mound of correspondence on the table. Sunshine glared through the kitchen window, fanning out across the red-tiled floor. Laverne stepped into the golden glow, like a performer taking the spotlight; while he warmed himself he considered what little he knew.

Minutes before the carnage, Tess, the eldest daughter, had entered the house via the kitchen door. As if to re-admit her, he unbolted the door and held it open. The sad and heady smell of narcissi in bloom washed over him. On the night of the murder, this door had remained unlocked. Why? His own parents hadn't

55

bothered much with keys or bolts, and nor had their neighbours. But that had been York in the fifties. Times had definitely changed. Had the Martin family been naively trusting? Or just careless?

Thoughtfully, he closed the door, and took one stride over to the pantry. It was dark inside the narrow closet, and at first he couldn't locate the light switch. But he instantly noticed an unpleasant smell. When he turned the light on, he looked down and saw the cause of the odour: a mouse rotting in a trap. The rodent had been dead for days, its snout crowned by a blue-black crust of dried blood.

Squirming inwardly, Laverne stepped over the trap and glanced around vaguely at the half-empty shelves. Then he stared back through the open door into the kitchen. According to her statement, Tess Martin had made herself something to eat before leaving the kitchen. Was this the moment, he wondered, when the murderer had opened the kitchen door and walked past her into the house?

Laverne left the pantry and returned to the hall. The door to the front room was open; he walked through, adjusted his tie and coughed. The cough bounced from wall to wall as if he was in a church. The dark bloodstains on the walls were extravagant enough to have been applied with a bucket. There was a faint smell of ninhydrin, with which the forensics team had sprayed every available surface in a desperate quest for latent fingerprints. Their search had been fruitless. The only prints in the room had been made by the Martin family.

The main floor-area was fenced off with tape, reminding Laverne of the time that Dawn had dragged him off to look at the Brontë Museum at Haworth. But the barriers at Haworth were only intended to deter weary visitors from taking a nap on the sofa where Emily Brontë died. In this room, their purpose was altogether more earnest: somewhere, ingrained in the fibres of the sofa, wedged between the floorboards, might lie the merest atom of hair, clothing or skin; the meanest, most ephemeral trace of the human beings responsible for this vile crime. Laverne knew that the forensics team, under enormous pressure to produce a result, would keep returning to scour and re-scour this room until such a trace was found.

The floor was covered in yellow chalk drawings: comic characters with spread-eagled arms and legs. There was even a speech balloon: a bright orb at Laverne's feet which contained no caption, yet managed to be chillingly eloquent. The balloon showed where Mrs Martin's head had come to rest after its separation from her body.

This meant that Laverne was standing on the precise spot where Tess Martin had remained for eleven hours until a friend's mother, calling to collect her for school, walked in to find her huddled in a ball, eyes tightly closed, in a state of nervous exhaustion. She had sweated so much that she was almost completely dehydrated.

She had once had a family, and here lay their yellow ghosts. A 'V' shape between the legs of the baby grand piano marked the resting place of Dr Martin's amputated right arm. The outline of his son adorned the lid of the piano itself. The boy had been held down by his throat, the only member of the family to be touched by hand. Then, with one almighty downward thrust, he had been skewered through the heart. The tip of the weapon had left a dry oval scar in the dust-coated wood.

The father's corpse lay under the fireplace. He had been the first to die. The boy had followed. Then Mrs Martin, calling in to remind Andrew that it was past his bedtime, had been instantly decapitated. The baby in her arms had been the last to perish.

The strangest detail of this strange case pertained to the final positioning of Mrs Martin's disembodied head. The experts agreed that after the fatal blow, Mrs Martin's body had reeled into the centre of the room and fallen on to its back. Her head had landed under the window. But before Tess Martin entered the room, someone had deliberately rolled, or perhaps even *kicked* that head back towards the door. According to the girl's testimony, her mother's head was still in motion as she entered the room. But whoever – or whatever – had cast that head before her feet was nowhere to be seen. Laverne could only draw one conclusion from this baffling fact.

It was a conclusion that he didn't much care for.

After leaving the Martin house, Laverne took the A39 and drove eight miles north-east, to the city of Wells. For some reason, he had imagined that Holebrook would work within pealing distance of the cathedral bells. He didn't know why he'd imagined this, because his own headquarters in York were nowhere near the minster.

Whereas the offices of county councillors and town planners are often to be found in listed Georgian buildings, the British police invariably operate from ugly square office blocks in seedy city outskirts. Wells Police Station, being no exception to this rule, was situated in Keward, south-west of the city, in easy retching distance of the local sewage works.

Wells was Detective Chief Inspector Holebrook's patch. He was the undoubted star of the local CID Department. A few years previously, he had gained a reputation for himself by catching a brutal serial rapist who had been terrorizing Wells and its outlying villages. Although not quite in Laverne's class – not on paper, at any rate – he was generally considered to be the brightest detective in the region. As far as Holebrook's superiors were concerned, there could have been no question of his eminent suitability for the present investigation.

It was with this thought in mind that Laverne knocked on the door of Holebrook's office shortly after four that afternoon. The room was in the basement, a temporary measure like the large incident room next door. Laverne's own temporary office, sus-piciously, was located on the second floor. After a moment's silence,

Laverne heard a sniff from behind the door. He knocked again and, this time, Holebrook answered.

'Hello, sir.' The accompanying smile was tight, unwelcoming. 'We were just talking about you.'

As Holebrook opened the door wider, Laverne saw that there was someone sitting in front of the desk. Even from behind, he recognized the angle of Roth's head, the dark hair shorn close to her neck. As he entered, she packed that over-familiar black notebook of hers away into her shoulder bag and turned to smile at him. He gave her a perfunctory nod and matched Holebrook's platitude with another.

'Nothing good, I hope?'

Holebrook grimaced. 'I'm afraid so. We were chatting about your extraordinary career, as it happens.'

Laverne was not pleased to hear this. There was an awkward silence.

'Could I have a word?' he said finally. 'In private?'

With unexpected tact, Roth smiled, eased past Laverne and walked away down the corridor, leaving a faint trail of a scent that smelled suspiciously like Old Spice aftershave. Holebrook pointed an outstretched palm towards the seat she'd vacated.

'The girl . . . Tess Martin,' Laverne began clumsily. 'Where is she now?'

Holebrook frowned. 'With her grandfather.'

'Does he live locally?'

'Why do you ask?'

'I need to see her.'

Holebrook looked alarmed. 'Why? What's happened?'

'Nothing. I just want to talk to her.'

Preparing to defend himself, Holebrook straightened his back. 'Well, she's distraught, as you'd imagine. We've already been over that whole night with her several times.'

By way of reply, Laverne opened his briefcase and took out a plain blue folder, which he passed silently over the desk to Holebrook. The folder contained Tess Martin's statement, which in Laverne's judgement was nothing more than an attempt to put insipid police jargon into a child's mouth. The final paragraph actually commenced with the phrase 'I then proceeded into the living room.'

Holebrook looked baffled and pushed the folder back across the desk to Laverne. 'I've already seen this.'

Next, Laverne passed Holebrook the postcard he'd taken from the girl's bedroom. 'Notice a certain difference in style? To my mind, the postcard was written by a sensitive, intelligent kid. Whereas that statement's the work of a particularly stupid copper.'

Holebrook's forehead swelled with annoyance. 'I took that statement.'

Laverne laughed. 'How unfortunate.'

'Chief Superintendent, that girl either saw nothing, or she remembers nothing. Either way, she's one deeply disturbed individual. I suggest we leave her in peace.'

Laverne hated it when people 'suggested' things to him. In his experience, the phrase 'I suggest' invariably meant 'I insist'. Staring Holebrook squarely in the eye, he said, 'You resent me, don't you?'

Holebrook reddened. 'No. Not at all.'

'Yes, you do. You resent my presence here, because you're a dedicated detective who's probably more than capable of handling this case without outside interference.'

Holebrook's jaw tightened.

Laverne raised his right arm and scratched the back of his neck. 'What you perhaps don't realize, Chief Inspector, is that I was under the impression that you wanted me here. Not just your Chief Constable, but you, personally.'

Holebrook neither denied nor confirmed this. With cold politeness, he merely said, 'We're all very happy to have you here. And we hope your stay with us will be more than fruitful.'

'More than *fruitful*?' repeated Laverne, wondering why this word sounded so outrageously insincere. 'In that case, why ask me to conduct an independent inquiry, then question my movements?'

Holebrook shook his head. 'No, no, Chief Superintendent. You're reading too much into this. I was merely trying to save you some time. We've spent many hours with Tess Martin. I'm convinced that she's told us all she knows. Why go over old ground?'

Laverne had been about to offer to buy Holebrook a conciliatory drink. But he knew that Holebrook was the epitome of a career policeman. As such, he was unlikely to drink during working hours, or to tell the truth at any time.

Laverne stood, closed the blue folder and thrust it into Holebrook's hands. 'Thanks for your opinion, Ed. But I still want to talk to Tess Martin. Just tell me where to find her.'

4

TESS

Laverne leaned out of his car window and spoke his name into the gatekeeper's intercom. After a few seconds, a portly man in an immaculate uniform emerged from the lodge and bent down to peer at him.

'I'm afraid the Major isn't expecting you, sir.'

Laverne admitted that this was true, but explained that he had come all the way from Yorkshire to hunt down the murderers of Major Blackmore's daughter, son-in-law and grandchildren.

The gatekeeper looked sympathetic. 'Wait a minute, sir. I'll see what he says.'

While the man ambled back to the lodge, Laverne drummed out a samba rhythm on the steering wheel. After what seemed like a ridiculously long time, but was actually no more than two minutes, the gatekeeper returned, his step invigorated by the good news he was bearing. 'You're in luck, sir. The Major will see you.'

Two wrought-iron electric gates whirred open and Laverne swept the Rover's wide bonnet into the crescent-shaped drive that led to Paradise House. Built in the reign of Queen Anne, this was the home of Major Aden Blackmore, Tess Martin's grandfather. The tall redbrick dwelling and its sprawling, uncared-for gardens lay to the east of Glastonbury. Several generations of Blackmores had successively bastardized their birthright with Doric columns and stucco before the present owner had lovingly restored it to its original form, thus turning a bogus Grecian temple back into an austere country house with restrained classical features.

Laverne had been surprised to learn that the Martins were so well-connected. Their home had been comfortably middle class, no more. Its worn carpets and home-made curtains evoked an air of cheerful bravado in the face of ever-encroaching impecunity. Perhaps that bravado owed something to the rich relation living on the far side of the Tor.

At the front door, Laverne was forced to undergo another vetting. A young, fair-haired bodyguard asked the Chief Superintendent to raise his face to a security camera on the wall. Then the guard closed the door, leaving Laverne outside on the step. After another infuriatingly long wait, the door opened again. Laverne tried to enter, but the same guard barred his way.

'Wait, sir.' The accent could have been Swedish. 'Let the Major get a closer look.'

Laverne was puzzled. From where he was standing, the dark entrance hall looked empty. But as he watched, a grey shape separated itself from the prevailing gloom; the figure of a man, with a pale domed head and eyes so deep-set that at this range, they looked like empty sockets.

'Major Blackmore?'

As he drew closer, the stranger gave the barest of nods. He was wearing a silk cravat above a white shirt, unbuttoned at the neck. His grey trousers had been pressed meticulously, and the black patent leather shoes shone.

He was well built and of middle-height. His thin white hair had been razored to the scalp. For a man in his seventies, Major Blackmore seemed to be in remarkably good condition. The heavy shoulders and deep chest hinted at great physical strength, and even the sagging belly below was oddly impressive.

'Fine. Let him through,' ordered Blackmore.

With an air of thwarted malice, the bodyguard waved Laverne

over the threshold, and then walked briskly away. Once inside, Blackmore subjected Laverne's hand to a fierce clasp that was more like a challenge than a greeting. When Blackmore turned his face to the light, Laverne found himself looking into a pair of unblinking eyes that were curiously devoid of light or warmth, with pupils the colour of dried blood.

'I'm Aden Blackmore. You can call me Aden. Or you can call me Blackmore. But please, please never call me Major.'

Blackmore laughed, and Laverne responded with a thin forced smile, knowing full well that despite this well-rehearsed show of humility, here was a man who expected respect and usually received it.

For a few moments, the two men stood in the dark, polished entrance hall, silently assessing each other. The sound of a Chopin nocturne, haltingly played, echoed in a distant room. By the stairs stood an impressive ivory carving of a dancing Hindu deity. Blackmore noticed Laverne's appraisal and said, 'Beauty has its price.'

'Pardon me?'

Blackmore smiled. 'You were feeling sorry for the elephant.'

Laverne was taken aback. 'Yes. Yes, I was actually.'

'Come.'

Pleased with himself, Blackmore led the way into his study. It was dark and exaggeratedly masculine, with a low timbered ceiling, red leather armchairs and military prints on every wall. No ornaments or souvenirs of eastern travels here. A well-stocked drinks cabinet and a seductive aroma of pipe tobacco proclaimed that this was the refuge of an old-fashioned English gentleman, a room consecrated to the serious pursuit of idleness.

Blackmore strode over to the drinks cabinet. 'What do you drink?'

'Well . . . I was hoping to speak to your granddaughter, really.'

''Fraid she's having a piano lesson. Didn't you hear the hatchet job she was doing on Opus 72, Number 1?' Blackmore lifted an almost barbarically thick wrist and studied his wrist-watch. 'Should be over in ten minutes. Why not have a drink?'

Conceding defeat, Laverne pinched his trousers at the knee to protect the creases and sank noisily into a chair. Looking up, he caught Blackmore eyeing him with unqualified approval. 'I'll bet you're a whisky man.'

Laverne nodded cautiously, unsettled by the amount that his host already appeared to know about him. Blackmore grabbed two stout crystal glasses and reached for a bottle. 'I've got a cracking twenty-year-old malt. The Old White Stag. Ever heard of it?'

Laverne shook his head. 'Very old company,' boomed Blackmore. 'Myles McQuire of Loch Lomond. A tiny little family distillery that never turns out more than six thousand bottles a year. How's that for quality control?' Blackmore unscrewed the cap and poured out two generous measures. He crossed the room to Laverne, then hesitated before offering him a glass. 'You don't take ice, I hope?'

Laverne shook his head firmly. 'What? And ruin a good malt? You must be joking.'

'Ha!' Blackmore slapped his own thigh to show his appreciation. 'Thank God for that. They've sent me a man this time.'

Laverne was unable to suppress a smile. Blackmore saw the smile, and laughed with gleeful triumph. Occupying the chair on the opposite side of the fire-place, he sniffed his drink and sipped it slowly. Then, as if calling a dog, he shouted, 'Holebrook!'

Laverne sniggered in a distinctly schoolboyish manner, and immediately regretted his unprofessional lapse. He took a mouthful of malt, finding it as indecently memorable as he had feared. It was so smooth and fragrant that it almost brought tears to his eyes. Now, having sampled perfection, he knew that the less-esteemed brand he kept in his drinks cabinet at home would never taste the same.

'Holebrook,' repeated Blackmore. 'If you ask me, he's the kind of man who'd piss his pants under fire and swear he'd spilt his cocoa. Know what I'm saying? Man wets himself and owns up, you can respect him. But a fella who's scared and won't admit it? No good. No bloody good at all. What's your name?'

'Laverne.'

'Laverne? Bugger of a name. Woman's name, isn't it?'

Laverne recognized that he was being tested, but refused to rise to the bait. 'It's only my surname.'

'Don't care. Still a woman's name.'

'The name "Aden" doesn't exactly strike me as virile.'

The riposte fell on deaf ears. Blackmore gazed around the room with a bewildered air, as if he'd suddenly awoken to find himself in unfamiliar surroundings. 'I'm surprised you're here, really. Surprised I let you through the door. Thought my Tessy'd be left in peace, now.'

Laverne explained that he was present in Glastonbury to assist with a difficult inquiry, carefully adding that if either Tess or her grandfather wished him to leave the premises at any time, he would respect their wishes.

Blackmore sat in silence for a while, scanning Laverne's face with his hard old eyes. 'She may talk to you. She may not. Wouldn't talk to Holebrook. He annoyed her too much.'

'Has Tess spoken to you about what happened?'

The question caught Blackmore by surprise. 'No. And I haven't asked. Know why?'

'No.'

'Because I used to serve in the parachute regiment. Lot of rough and ready men living too close to each other. Always made it my policy to respect the privacy of others. And in my opinion, grief ought to be a private affair.'

'I agree.'

'Not much chance of that, though. Not with all you bluebottles buzzing around. The police have been nothing but a bloody nuisance to us since this thing happened.'

Laverne gave a non-committal nod which Blackmore chose to interpret as an admission of guilt. 'Of course, you're paid to be a nuisance. Appreciate that. But I think the way you people deal with the families of victims is bloody insensitive. I had to identify the bodies, you see.'

'Ah.'

'Bloody stupid system. I saw them all in their own house, then I had to go to the mortuary for what they called a formal identification. In other words, had to go through the whole blasted thing twice. Is that the way the police usually treat people?'

'It's the law, I'm afraid. I don't happen to agree with it either.'

Blackmore refused to be mollified. He gulped down his whisky aggressively.

'I'm sorry,' said Laverne. 'I can't begin to imagine what all this has been like for you.'

'No,' snapped Blackmore. 'You can't.'

Realizing that the man had wearied of his company, Laverne took another mouthful of malt and, with regret, left the remainder of his drink in the glass. They both stood. Blackmore opened the door for Laverne and in a hoarse voice said, 'Of course, nothing ever dies.'

Laverne began to wonder if Blackmore was slightly crazed and grunted in acknowledgement, hoping to shut him up. But the old man gripped him by the arm. The strong fingers dug into Laverne's bicep like pincers. '"As the Spirit of our mortal body wanders on in childhood, and youth and old age, the Spirit wanders on to a new body: of this the sage has no doubts."'

Laverne saw that there were tears in Blackmore's eyes and was momentarily lost for words.

'Know where that's from, Chief Superintendent?'

'Sounds like the Bible.'

'Close. *The Bhagavad Gita.*'

Laverne gently extricated himself from the Major's grasp. 'I wouldn't care to be born again, myself.'

Blackmore slapped him boisterously on the shoulder. 'Ha! Scared of coming back as a cockroach, eh?' With a grunt, Blackmore dismissed the subject. 'Let's see what Tess is up to.'

They found her in a long, bright drawing room that looked out on to a small, neatly trimmed lawn. She was sitting at a grand piano that was so highly polished it mirrored her pale, sensitive face. Her music tutor, a tall nervous man with thin white hair and a pronounced stoop, was gathering up sheet music. The tutor turned and, at the sight of Blackmore, literally vibrated with self-consciousness.

Blackmore gave him a strained smile which resembled the rictus of a fox in a snare. 'Finished for today, Mr Briscoe?'

'Yes, Mr Blackmore. Sorry for taking so long.'

Blackmore walked over to the man, augmenting his discomfiture by linking his arm. 'Before you go, my dear fellow, might I have a little word?' Mr Briscoe bobbed his head overenthusiastically. Blackmore faced his granddaughter. 'This is Chief Superintendent Laverne, Tess.'

Laverne gave the girl a winning smile that won nothing. She dismissed him with a glance and returned her attention to the piano keyboard.

As soon as they were alone, she said, 'I don't know what you're here for. I've already told the others everything.'

Laverne sank down on to the stool that Mr Briscoe had vacated, finding it distastefully warm to the touch. He realized that the photographs he'd seen of Tess Martin had failed to do her justice. She had shoulder length auburn hair that blazed in the late afternoon sunlight, and the kind of waxen pallor that usually complements such colouring. But her most striking feature was her eyes: large and almond-shaped, with sea-green irises that glittered with intelligence and life. Only the dark shadows around those eyes betrayed the nightmare she was living through.

'I'm not with the others,' said Laverne quietly. 'I've come all the way from Yorkshire to talk to you.'

She laughed harshly.

He frowned quizzically. 'What's so funny?'

She shrugged, and Laverne realized that the laugh was a direct response to his patronizing tone. This is a bright kid, Laverne. Make the same mistake again, and you'll have lost her completely. 'I'm sorry about what happened to your family, Tess.' (She was already nodding sceptically.) 'The truth is, none of us have a bloody clue who killed them.'

'Do you really think I hadn't worked that out for myself?'

He could tell that he was already boring her. She played a brief snatch of Chopin on the piano, almost defying him to continue. But the music, intended as an assault, flooded him with an overpowering sense of melancholy beauty. He waited for the silence to settle again. Then he said, 'That was nice. You played that with real feeling.'

She gaped at him in utter astonishment. Laverne, misunderstanding, thought that he'd offended her. 'No ... I meant it as a compliment. All I'm saying is, some people just play the notes, if you understand me. And other people put a bit of feeling into it. Like you just did.'

Still staring at him, she quietly closed the piano lid and turned her whole body towards him. Fearing her imminent departure, Laverne came straight to the point. 'Anyway, I was explaining why I'm here. I've been lucky in the past, Tess. I've caught one or two pretty nasty characters. Some people seem to have got it into their heads that as far as policemen go, I'm not too incompetent. But to be honest, petal, what I've seen at your mum and dad's house makes no sense to me at all. You'd be well within your rights if you told me to clear off. But if you'd just go over what you did and what you saw that night, just one more time, I'd be very grateful to you ...'

She took a deep breath and recited a bitter mantra that she'd learned by heart, 'Six forty-five, Dad drove me to St John's church. Seven o'clock, choir practice with Mr Snape. Nine o'clock, choir practice ends. Some of the kids stay behind for coffee with Mr Snape, I go to Gudrun's house . . .'

'Why didn't you stay behind for coffee?'

She frowned, needled by his interruption. 'Couldn't. Gudrun's dad was picking us up.'

'Do you never have coffee afterwards?'

She shrugged moodily. 'Sometimes.'

'Bit boring, is it?'

'Sometimes.'

'What time did you get to Gudrun's house?'

''Bout ten past nine, maybe. We stopped for chips on the way. I've already told them all this.'

'But you haven't told me, Tess.'

She left the piano stool and began to walk around the room. 'We got chips, went to Gudrun's, ate our chips with a cup of tea, they drove me home, my family all got murdered, then I went to bed. And we all lived happily ever after.'

He gave her a gentle smile. 'Come on. Don't be like that. Talk to me.'

She leant against the door and slipped her hands into the pockets of her jeans. 'I am talking to you. Opening my mouth, aren't I? Words are coming out of my mouth, aren't they?'

An overweight ginger tom slinked into the room and made straight for Laverne, purring loudly and rubbing itself against his legs. 'Blast,' he complained. 'Hairs all over my trousers.'

Tess half-smiled at the sight of Laverne shuffling around the room in a vain attempt to escape the animal's attentions. Then she picked up the cat and began to stroke him. 'Poor Harrison. Does nobody want you, den?'

Without much hope, Laverne brought his dreary sales-pitch to a conclusion. 'I don't like asking you to talk about what happened. Not one little bit. But all I'm looking for is one detail that the others may have overlooked, something that may not seem important in itself but which might point the way towards the identity of the person we're looking for.'

Still holding the cat, she sank down on to the carpet with her back against the wall. 'It wasn't a person.'

'Sorry?'

'I said it wasn't a person.'

'What do you mean? Tell me what you mean.'

She shook her head as she averted her eyes. Laverne walked over to her, crouched down and gently raised her chin, obliging her to look at him. 'Come on.'

But she turned her face to the wall, and refused to say another word.

5

BLOOD SPRING

The desk sergeant at Wells Police Station was about to give Laverne a friendly greeting when he saw the visiting detective's face and thought better of the idea. No point wasting a smile on such a miserable bastard.

Laverne, in fact, was disgusted with himself. He'd read the girl's statement, so recognized that her recent admission had been a gift, meant only for him. But rather than holding back and allowing her to speak in her own time, he had been too pushy and scared her into silence. For a novice, such a blunder would have been understandable. But for a senior detective with three decades of interviewing experience behind him, it was unforgivable.

He descended the stairs to the basement, then entered the noisy incident room that had been set aside for the Glastonbury inquiry. Only a despot like Holebrook, he reflected darkly, would arrange his workplace in such a way. It was like stepping into a classroom.

Parallel rows of desks equipped with cheap computers, printers and telephones faced towards a full-sized table at the head of the room. This table clearly belonged to the head teacher, for it boasted two phones, a fax machine, a laser printer and an Apple Mac computer. A large white message board and a series of maps and murder scene photographs hung on the wall behind. The back-to-school effect was completed by a large round clock with an audible tick. Detective Sergeant Mowart was now seated directly under this clock, his back to the wall, tapping data into the computer.

Most of the men on duty (and they were mostly men) seemed to be passing the time by drinking coffee and indulging in desultory conversation. They looked jarringly unlike any of the detectives in Dawn Laverne's favourite television programmes, being neither handsome nor hideous, glamorous nor seedy. They were merely ordinary. Crushingly ordinary.

Mowart turned as Laverne approached, and grinned expansively. 'Hiya, there.'

Laverne glared at Mowart. 'Why are you looking so pleased with yourself?'

The Sergeant refused to be dispirited. 'You'd better ask your American friend.'

'I'm asking you.'

'Angela . . . the FBI lady? She's done us a psychological profile of the murderer.'

Laverne groaned in disgust. 'It doesn't surprise me. Where's DI Savage?'

'Both she and, er, Officer Roth have gone to have a chat with Gudrun. Gudrun Sweet, sir. Tess Martin's friend.'

'I don't remember asking them to do that.'

'No, sir,' said Mowart, an amused glint in his narrow eyes. 'I believe they were using something called initiative.'

Laverne scowled. 'What about Chief Inspector Holebrook?'

'Sir?'

'Where is he, Sergeant?'

Mowart glanced up at the clock. 'Shepton Mallet.'

'What's he doing there?'

'He lives there.'

'You mean he's gone home?'

'That's correct.'

'It's not even six.'

73

'He usually goes home after the five o'clock meeting. You know, unless something urgent crops up . . .'

'And, of course,' sneered Laverne, already walking away, 'catching maniacs who wipe out whole families isn't urgent at all. No more pressing than, say, hunting down a stolen bicycle . . .'

Angela Roth had never been inside an English council house before. The Sweet family's home on Pendragon Avenue was, to her, little more than a slum dwelling. The living room in which she now found herself was enough to induce claustrophobia. A cheap frosted glass door, now closed, led through to a kitchen that was like something from a model village. And to think that, as a child, she had believed that all English people lived in castles.

'Say "leisure",' urged Gudrun. She was an exuberant girl with short fair hair and glasses.

Roth smiled, shook her head. At her side, Lyn Savage smiled also and sipped her tea.

'Aw, go on,' pleaded the thirteen-year-old. She was sandwiched between her parents on the threadbare sofa. 'Say it.'

'Leisure,' repeated Roth, giving the word its English pronunciation.

'Aggh, no!' cried Gudrun, miming a sudden heart attack. 'You're cheating. She's cheating, Dad. I meant say it the way Americans say it. Lee-zure!'

Roth grinned slyly. 'Ah. But that's not what you asked me to say.'

'Can't get her that easy, Gudge,' said the girl's father, nudging his daughter playfully. 'Tricky, these Yanks.'

He laughed again. Reg Sweet was a farm labourer in his early forties and a life of hard manual work showed in the deep, entrenched grooves that lined his face. His eyes twinkled with an almost naive warmth. Lyn Savage thought him one of the least suspicious-looking characters she'd ever come across. His wife

Brenda, dowdy, overweight and shy, was possibly intimidated by the presence of these two smart career women. Father and daughter did most of the talking.

'OK. We'll try to be brief,' said Savage brightly. 'Just a few questions.'

She switched on a small portable AIWA tape recorder, and the effect was like throwing cold water over embers: the good humour in the room was instantly and brutally extinguished. Beside her, Roth opened the small black notebook that Laverne loathed so unequivocally and removed the top from a golden Sheaffer fountain pen. In the corner of the room, beneath a black and silent TV screen, a video recorder whirred into life, pre-programmed to tape an episode of Mrs Sweet's favourite soap. Next door's television blustered and blared through the paper-thin adjoining wall. To Savage and Roth, the TV was offensively loud. The Sweets, however, didn't seem to notice.

'So, Gudrun, we're talking about Thursday, February the twenty-ninth. The night of the murder.'

Gudrun nodded sombrely. Reg interrupted to shake his head and say, 'I still can't reckon it.'

His wife shushed him. 'It's true, though,' he reiterated. 'Can't reckon it at all.'

'Gudrun,' said Savage. 'That night you went to St John's church. For choir practice.'

The girl nodded. Her father nudged her, to remind her that a nod could not be detected by a tape recorder. 'Yeah,' she said. 'Seven o'clock.'

'The choir meets every week?'

'No. Depends what's going on. But we had a concert coming up. Easter.'

'An Easter concert?'

'Yeah.'

'And Mr Snape was arranging this concert?'

75

'Yeah. He always does.'

'And while you rehearsed, you and Tess stood together?'

'Yeah. We always do. Me and Tess and Gaby.'

'Gaby?'

'Gabrielle Town,' interrupted Mr Sweet. 'She's a year-and-a-half older. Goes to the convent.'

'A Catholic?' confirmed Roth.

'Yeah,' said Reg Sweet. 'We're not prejudiced.'

'She's a Catholic and she sings in a Protestant choir?'

'Yeah. Her mum don't mind. They're not religious.'

'Did you notice anything unusual about the night? Anything that Tess said or did that struck you as out of the ordinary?'

There was a silence. Reg Sweet decided to give himself the role of official prompter. 'What the officer means is, did Tess seem different in any way?'

The girl adjusted her glasses. 'No. She was just the same as always.'

Roth said, 'Excuse me. What exactly does that mean?'

Another pause, followed by Reg Sweet saying, 'In other words, Gudrun, what is Tess like normal?'

Then his wife spoke. 'Not "normal". What is she like "normal-ly".'

'Bit quiet,' mused the girl. 'Not dead quiet. Just a bit. Then she suddenly comes out with things, funny things, that really get you laughing.'

Savage smiled. 'Like what?'

The girl pondered, then grinned in recollection. 'Yeah! I know. Trevor . . .'

'Mr Snape,' explained Reg helpfully.

'We were rehearsing the harmonies for "There is a green hill far away" and it wasn't the sopranos' turn so we were talking a bit and Gaby said about Trevor's hair. He'd just had it cut, see, and it looked a bit daft. And Tess said, "I'll bet that cost him a pretty penny". And we all cracked up.'

She giggled at the memory, then was sobered by the polite answering smiles on the faces of the two detectives. 'It was funny at the time, anyway.'

'Anything else happen?'

'Nothing. The vicar came in, had a listen, then went after five minutes. Just like he does every week.'

Roth said, 'Pardon me, but what's the vicar called?'

'The-Reverend-Len-Small,' said Mr Sweet obligingly.

Roth recorded the name in a fine, flowing hand.

'Tell me about Mr Snape,' said Savage.

This seemed to throw the girl into confusion. 'What? What about him?'

'Do you get on with him? Do you like him? Do you have any doubts about him? That sort of thing.'

'Trevor's all right,' said Gudrun. 'He's just a bit lonely, we think.'

Mr and Mrs Sweet nodded sagely.

'I think that's why he does the choir,' added Gudrun. 'He hasn't got much else.'

There was a soft whispering sound from the direction of the kitchen. The Sweet family laughed. 'Oops! Careful. He's in there, listening,' joked Reg.

'What *is* that noise?'

'I expect it's the taters boiling over,' said Brenda Sweet. She hauled herself upright and lumbered into the adjacent room.

'What kind of relationship does Mr Snape have with Tess, would you say?' asked Savage.

'He likes her,' replied Gudrun simply.

Roth said, 'Meaning that he's just friendly towards her, right?'

'Yeah.' Gudrun's eyes glinted as she added, 'We all know who he's *really* keen on.'

'Now, now,' cautioned Brenda Sweet, returning from the kitchen.

Savage held out a hand to deflect another unwanted interruption. 'Yes, Gudrun? Who's that?'

'Gaby. Everyone knows it.'

'Now, now. No one knows nothing of the kind,' admonished Reg.

'Yes, they do! You never saw his face when she said she was leaving . . .'

Mr Sweet was about to argue when his wife prodded his leg. 'Reg, be quiet. They're asking Gudrun, not you.'

Reg started to sulk.

'Gudrun?' prompted Savage.

'When Gaby told him she was leaving, Trevor looked like he was going to burst into tears.'

'She told him this on the night in question?'

'No. A week before, I think. Yeah. Maybe two weeks. She said she'd stay for the Easter concert, and that'd be the end of it.'

'And you believe that Mr Snape was upset by this news?'

'Oh, yeah. We all saw it. His eyes went all misty when he talked to her. He even told her that her boyfriend wasn't good enough for her.'

'Mind you, he's right about that,' remarked Reg. He looked to Savage and Roth for support. 'One of these motorbike yobs.'

'There's nothing wrong with him,' protested Gudrun crossly.

'And after choir practice, what did Gaby do?'

'Her boyfriend picked her up. Dad fetched me and Tess and bought chips and came back here.'

Savage fell silent. Roth wrote something down, then took over. 'And you, Mr and Mrs Sweet: how did Tess seem to you that night?'

Reg and his wife agreed that Tess had seemed fine.

'On the drive home, nothing out of the ordinary took place?'

'No.'

'When you stopped near the Martin house, you saw nothing unusual?'

78

'No. Tess got out, I watched her go over the bridge. Then I drove off.' He sighed. 'Believe me, since it happened I've thought about bugger all else. Brenda'll tell you.'

Brenda nodded. 'He even dreams about it.'

Roth sighed in sympathy. 'That bad, huh?'

'Oh, yeah,' confirmed Reg. 'I wake up and can't get back to sleep, thinking "what if I'd walked her to the door instead of driving away?" Would an extra man being there have scared off the nutters who did it? 'Cause they must have seen me drive up, mustn't they? Whoever did it saw me drive up and drive away again. Makes you shiver just thinking about it . . .'

'You don't know of anyone who might have had a grudge against Tess and her family?'

'No. They were nice people.'

'OK, sir.' Roth closed her notebook.

An idea occurred to Savage. 'And what about the journey home?'

'I beg your pardon?' said Mr Sweet.

'Did you or Gudrun see anything or experience anything unusual on the drive back?'

Hugging her knees, Gudrun said, 'Not unless you count the dog.'

'Oh, yeah.' Reg Sweet chuckled. 'Nearly ran a dog over.'

Savage stifled a yawn. 'Where was this?'

'Driving away from Tess's. Five hundred yards down the road. Nearly squashed it flat. Came straight out of the woods, passed in front of the bumper from left to right. Swish! Straight across. Nearly hit a tree because of it.'

'What kind of dog?' quizzed Roth.

'Dunno,' said Gudrun. 'It happened too quick.'

'A bloody big black one,' laughed Mr Sweet.

His wife reached over to dig him in the shoulder. 'Hey! they don't want your swearing on their tape.'

Roth raised her voice to secure their attention. 'That stretch of

79

road bends round to the right, forming a loop around the woods. Right?'

Mr Sweet and his daughter nodded.

'Then something crossing the road from left to right could conceivably have been heading in the direction of the Martin house?'

Reg spoke up. 'Yeah, but it wasn't a dog that killed 'em, was it?'

Savage smiled. 'Seems unlikely.'

Roth thanked the Sweet family and Savage turned off the tape recorder. They all shook hands, and Mr Sweet led them down the hall to the front door. 'Anyway, I hope you catch 'em, whoever did it. I've lived in this town all my life, and bad things have happened here before. But nothing as terrible as this.'

He unbolted the front door, letting in the smell of the dusk and commenting on the dreadful state of the world. The two women thanked their host again, then Roth fumbled in the pocket of her jacket. 'Uh-uh. Think I left my pen behind.'

She moved back into the hall, but chivalrous Reg halted her with an upraised finger. 'I'll get it.'

He hurried down the hall and disappeared into the living room. Savage and Roth waited outside on the narrow path. A teenage boy, riding by on a mountain bike, leaned over and spat briskly into the gutter. Across the street, mean gardens crouched in front of identical cherry-red corporation doors.

'You don't really think the family was murdered by Lassie?' said Savage.

'No way. But, y'know, if I got an interrogation technique it's this: ask enough stupid questions and finally you might, just might, arrive at an intelligent answer.'

'But not today,' said Savage.

They both laughed.

Twenty seconds passed by. Mr Sweet did not return. Roth

rummaged in her bag, and extracted a golden fountain pen. 'Shit. It was here all the time.'

They both turned towards the house. Roth leaned into the hall through the open door and yelled. 'Hello? Mr Sweet? We got it!'

Her call met with no response. Savage felt an unpleasant cold sensation at the back of her neck. Roth tried again. 'Hello, you guys?'

There was a silence like falling snow.

Roth and Savage exchanged worried glances and hurried down the hall. Roth, leading the way, rapped vigorously on the living room door. Without waiting for an answer, she pushed the door open. 'Hey! Everything all . . .'

Something skidded under her feet. She raised her foot and, squinting, glanced down. At first, she thought she was looking at some kind of jelly fish. Then she remembered that jelly fish don't have fingernails. Gasping for breath, Roth slumped against the wall. She had trodden on a severed human hand.

Savage pushed past her, into the room. An ocean seemed to roar in her ears as she spun around the room. The once-plain walls were now running with human gore. Reg Sweet lay on the rug at her feet, his headless body quivering in an oozing mire of blood. His amputated hands and feet were strewn across the carpet. His head lay inches above his spouting neck and had been split into two halves, both of which were now laid open like the twin cups of an Easter egg.

Gudrun and Mrs Sweet were still seated on the sofa, staring straight ahead, rigid with shock. Although motionless, they looked intact and unbloodied. Approaching the mother and daughter, Savage heard someone far away saying, 'Oh God, oh God, oh God . . .'

There was a burst of movement and a loud clatter to her left. Angela Roth had recovered sufficiently to barge through the kitchen and out into the yard, searching for the killer.

Lyn Savage stepped over a foot encased in a bloody tartan slipper and squatted down in front of the sofa. Then she touched Gudrun's right knee and shook it gently. As she did so, the girl's head toppled from her shoulders, rolled down her chest and landed in Savage's lap.

6

'A' FOR ANALYST

Savage met Laverne at the garden gate of 17 Pendragon Avenue. She was trembling and the whites of her eyes were tinged with blood, but her voice was calm and controlled. Her white blouse and sensible grey skirt were covered in dark-brown stains.

'Lyn? You're not hurt, are you?'

She shook her head. 'They must have already been in the house. Must have been.'

Expressionless, he nodded and placed a reassuring hand on her shoulder. Behind him, the patrol car that had ferried him, siren wailing, from the Abbot Whiting to the scene of the crime, skidded diagonally across the road to block the path of a long white van with a blue BBC logo on the side. The uniformed officers within, two young constables who had broken the news of the murder to Laverne with positive relish and were obviously delighted, for once, to be doing something more exciting than harassing New Age travellers, promptly launched into a ferocious argument with the van driver and the bearded director sitting beside him. Across the road, two small boys and a labrador puppy squatted on the pavement, watching the commotion with great interest.

In the narrow hallway, Roth was in conversation with Holebrook and a small neat man with a sallow, hairless skull. She looked tense and strangely young. Her normally cool and watchful eyes were wide, bewildered, startled into new life by the shock of the killing.

83

Well, she had wanted drama. Now she'd got it. Seeing Laverne, Roth stopped speaking and nodded to him. 'Vernon? Have you met the Chief Constable?'

The bald stranger turned his face towards Laverne. It was not a particularly likeable face, and Laverne recalled seeing its owner once on television, outlining a three-pronged-plan to keep trespassers (i.e. travellers) off private property in Somerset. His name was John Macmillan and he was Chief Constable for Avon and Somerset. His cold eyes were empty of emotion. In Laverne's opinion, only a condemned man or a police officer could have eyes as dead as that.

There were no hand-shakes. This was no time for niceties. 'Grateful to have you here,' announced Macmillan tersely, tilting his head to one side as if to show that in spite of appearances, he was actually taller than Laverne. 'What a mess, eh? What a terrible, upsetting mess.'

The mess, such as it was, came as no surprise to Laverne. The Sweets' living room had already been appropriated by a forensics team, so he was unable to get close to the bodies. But the room was small, and he could see enough to know, beyond the ghost of a doubt, that whoever had claimed the lives of four members of the Martin family had struck again here today.

His attention was drawn to the headless body on the sofa. A pathologist was in the process of binding plastic bags around the corpse's small, delicately boned wrists in the hope of preserving any evidence. Laverne could see that the body had belonged to a young girl and knew, without seeing the gift-wrapped hands, that the fingernails would probably be bitten, broken and coated with cheap varnish. For some reason, that thought depressed him greatly.

'Name?'

A female scene of crimes officer holding a clip-board took a neat step sideways into Laverne's path. Her expression was grave and businesslike. His first impulse was to chide her for impudence. Didn't she recognize the great Laverne, the most illustrious detective in England? He quickly checked himself, knowing that it was her job to be pedantic. Quietly, he answered her, feeling the merest ripple of embarrassed realization pass through his questioner as she jotted down his rank and his unlikely story-book name.

Savage took his arm and led him through the cramped kitchen to a small garden, now lit by glaring spotlights. The lawn was being systematically combed by a line of overalled officers, crawling slowly forwards on their hands and knees. There was a modest greenhouse at the bottom of the garden, also occupied by white-suited spacemen.

Behind the greenhouse lay a tall, dense hedge and the narrow garden was flanked by identical wooden fences. A small man in a flat cap was leaning over the right-hand fence, insisting on his rights and being studiously ignored by the kneeling officers. 'I know these people. When they go on holiday, I water their tomatoes. If anything's happened to them, you have a moral duty to tell me . . .'

Laverne turned to Savage. 'And you think they came this way?'

Savage made a low noise in her throat, something between a grunt of assent and a despondent sigh.

'Did you see anything?'

With a measured shake of her head, she said, 'It was Angela who came out here. I didn't see a thing.' By way of confession, she added, 'To be honest, I completely lost it for a while. I just stood in that room and shook like a leaf. Didn't know what had hit me. Sorry.'

'Hey . . . don't worry. It happens to everyone. What did Angela see?'

'Nothing. Whoever did it had already gone.'

'Gone where?' Laverne looked at Savage, then peered out at the darkening rooftops. 'There's nowhere to go to.'

She shrugged, defeated. He placed a comforting hand on her shoulder and guided her back into the house.

*

While Roth and Savage were being interviewed by Holebrook's people, Laverne accepted a lift back to his hotel in the Chief Constable's Jaguar. Laverne was unlikely to be needed again that night, and callous as it would have sounded to anyone but a CID officer, he was also ravenously hungry. He'd been dining in the hotel restaurant when news of the homicide had reached him. After ordering asparagus soup followed by roast leg of lamb, he had abandoned his table without tasting so much as a bread roll.

Macmillan stared aggressively into the distance as he drove, as if hoping that the killer would oblige him by running blindly out into the road ahead, thereby denting the bonnet of a costly car but saving the rapidly sinking reputation of the Avon and Somerset constabulary.

'Is Holebrook giving you everything you need, Chief Superintendent?'

Laverne's hesitation was eloquent.

'Not having problems with him, are you? He's a good man, but he's temperamental.'

'Aren't we all?'

'I'll be straight with you. I've heard a little rumour that you and Holebrook haven't been getting on very well.'

Laverne squirmed slightly as a brown Volvo came hurtling round the bend on the wrong side of the road, missing the Jaguar by inches. The incident provided him with a neat excuse to sidestep Macmillan's question. 'Dear me ... there are some idiots on the roads ...'

'Anything you want, you can have.' Macmillan handed over a dainty white card. 'That's my direct line. I'll fix you up with anything you need.'

'That's good of you.'

'It isn't goodness, Chief Superintendent. It's pure self-interest. You're a brilliant detective, and I want to keep my job. You help me, I'll help you. Any idea how it feels to have my job at this precise moment?'

'I think we all feel more or less the same, don't we? We're the police. We're meant to protect people. When we fail to achieve that aim, we feel useless and, frankly, to the world at large, we look useless.'

Macmillan nodded, then nailed Laverne with his cold mortician's gaze. 'Exactly. At times like this, it's vital that we co-operate with each other fully. So I'll ask you again, Mr Laverne. Is DCI Holebrook obstructing your investigation?'

Laverne looked at Macmillan, at his drooping mouth and the thick black hair curling out apishly from the cuffs of his ostentatiously white shirt. He inhaled the man's musk-based cologne, which had been applied so extravagantly that Laverne's own clothes were destined to stink of it until they were dry-cleaned. And he decided that he was not going to tell tales out of school. Particularly to a man as charmless as this.

'Actually, DCI Holebrook's been more than helpful,' said Laverne, his eyes shining with evangelistic sincerity.

Macmillan's mouth fell open.

Laverne should have stopped there, but he was enjoying himself. If you're going to tell a lie, might as well make it a big one. 'Did I say helpful? No ... that isn't quite fair. Since we arrived, he and DS Mowart have been kindness itself.'

Later that night, Laverne knocked on the door of Savage and Roth's hotel room. Roth, still dressed, answered.

'Lyn feeling any better?' he asked.

'Nah. Not really. She's pretty shaken up.'

Not knowing what to say to this, Laverne declared the purpose of his call. 'I've spoken to the hotel manager,' he explained. 'He says he'll keep the bar open an extra half-hour for us. Don't know about you, but I could use a drink.'

'Sounds good.' She stepped back into the room, took a jacket from the back of a chair and slipped it over her wide, angular shoulders. Laverne, waiting on the threshold, thought he could hear Savage retching in the bathroom.

'Do you think it's all right to leave Lyn?' he wondered guiltily.

'Sure. Matter of fact, I think she'd prefer to be alone.'

The hotel manager, a fatherly Irishman called Briarley, awaited them in the deserted bar. It was eleven thirty-five. The slaughter of the Sweet family had become national news. Laverne was glad to see that Mr Briarley wore a sickened expression on his full, wine-red face; glad because he knew anyone who was sickened by the very notion of murder was unlikely to ask prurient questions. Laverne had always detested ghouls.

Mr Briarley placed two glasses, a bottle of scotch and a carafe of water on the bar. Then he removed a napkin from a plate, revealing a small mound of sandwiches. 'Chicken or cheese and salad,' he announced in a subdued voice. 'Take your pick.'

Laverne slipped a hand into his jacket, reaching for his wallet. 'What do I owe you?'

Briarley grimaced, his head quivering in refusal. 'No, no, no. I'm not charging you. Not after what you've been through today.'

'It's our job,' said Laverne, producing the wallet. 'We do get paid, you know.'

But Mr Briarley was already edging away. 'Please. I've got a son who goes to the same school as Gudrun . . .' He paused awkwardly, unsure of his grammatical tenses. He tossed a fat set of keys on to the bar. They skidded down the counter and stopped in front of Laverne, making him feel that he was in a Western. 'Lock up when you've finished. I'll make sure no one disturbs you.'

When they were alone, Laverne and Roth exchanged resigned smiles. Laverne snapped the cap off the whisky and began to pour. 'Say when.'

Roth let him fill the glass, took a mouthful of scotch, then scouted around for ice. Finding what she sought in a black covered container that resembled a funeral urn, she spooned transparent chunks into her drink and turned to Laverne, who had poured himself a rather more modest measure. 'That it?' she laughed. 'Am I getting drunk on my own, here?'

They chinked glasses. 'When things get as bad as this, I have to watch myself,' said Laverne. 'The way I feel now, I could drink this bar dry.'

'Why don't you?'

'And spend half tomorrow walking round with a hangover? No thanks.'

After a long, reflective silence, Roth said, 'There was no way anyone could have got out of that house without me seeing them.'

'I know,' he said, staring at a row of upturned bottles on the opposite wall.

'Mind if I smoke?' she inquired, taking out an unopened carton of Marlboro and a Zippo lighter bearing a stars and stripes insignia.

'No,' he said absent-mindedly. 'In fact, I'll have one too.'

'I didn't know you smoked.'

'I don't. But I used to. Long time ago,' he admitted. 'Used to believe that smoking helped me think.'

'Did it?'

'Did it hell.' He took a cigarette, flipped it into the air and caught it in his mouth. Roth applauded. They lit up, and Laverne, feeling the smoke rasping in his throat, instantly remembered why he'd given up in the first place. The smile disappeared from his face as he turned to Roth and said, 'I believe you've been doing some thinking of your own.'

For a few seconds she was confused. Then she nodded in realization. 'Yeah. You mean the profile? Yeah.'

Under other circumstances, he might have lectured her about treading on his toes. But next to the deaths of three human beings, his own professional pride seemed unspeakably trivial. 'Is that what you do in the FBI? Work out the profile, then go after any unsavoury bastard who fits the bill?'

'I actually don't "go after" anybody.'

'No?'

She swallowed some scotch, clicked her teeth in satisfaction. 'No. Not any more. I'm with the 'A' team, now.'

'What? Like "Mr T"?'

As soon as the words had left his mouth, he regretted them. He could tell by the way she snorted smoke down her nostrils that she'd heard the joke too often, and hadn't found it funny the first time. '"A" for analyst. We spend all our time researching violent crime. We're considered, with good reason, to be the backbone of the Bureau. At noon, I took the liberty of sending a description of the Martin killing down the Internet to PROFILER. PROFILER is the world's first attempt to profile murderers by computer. As the Sweet family were killed in exactly the same manner as the Martins, the profile that comes back to us may well prove to be invaluable.'

Laverne regarded her evenly. Her customary arrogance had all but disappeared. The blue-grey eyes that always seemed to be calculating when and how to offend him now looked sad, defence-less, almost child-like. 'And this computer of yours?' he said quietly. 'Will it tell us how anyone can enter a house in daylight, or at least twilight, wipe out a whole family in absolute silence, then vanish without leaving a trace, while two experienced detectives are waiting round the corner?'

She smiled grimly. 'You noticed that too, huh?'

After phoning her husband, Savage climbed into bed and tried to sleep. But the terrible events of the preceding hours plagued her, and, try as she might, she could not rest. In the course of her career, she had seen many dead bodies. Too many. She had literally lost count of the number of times she had seen matter-of-fact morticians open refrigerated cells to wheel out naked corpses in varying shades

90

of green, grey, brown, blue and putrified black. If there was one sight that summed up these frequent and malodorous calls of duty, it was the image of a dead man, seen in profile, lying on a slab, his belly dipping sharply beneath his jutting ribs. Viewed from this angle, the deceased always looked as if they were thrusting out their chests in one last gesture of foolish pride, when in fact their chests were at absolute rest. The unlikely slump under their breastbones was created by the emptiness of their lungs. This grotesque hollow, this arc of resignation, was a shape never seen in the bodies of the living and, for Lyn Savage, encapsulated the finality of death far more eloquently than all the writhing worms and grinning skulls of folklore.

She saw this vision now, every time she closed her eyes. The same male carcass of unsavoury hue, the same sunken abdomen. Only this time, the corpse kept turning its head towards her and its face always had the twinkling, unassuming eyes of Reg Sweet.

When this unpleasant little drama had played itself out for the seventh time, Savage opened her eyes and turned over in bed. She found that she was suddenly freezing cold. Her teeth were chattering and her limbs were shaking so violently that she couldn't control them. First the vomiting, now this. She was clearly suffering from shock. She'd often seen the symptoms in others, and now it was her turn. She sat up in bed, wondering what to do.

There was no need to turn on the light. Her eyes were accustomed to the dark. She could discern the oblong of paler darkness that marked the window. A thin beam of light from the street had penetrated the room through a gap in the curtains and was reflected in the dressing table mirror. One of Angela's dresses, suspended from the wardrobe door by a hanger, would have been more than enough to frighten any children who happened to be present.

Sitting up, she saw a brighter, wider band of light under the door leading to the corridor. She crossed her arms and gripped her shoulders tightly with both hands in an attempt to stop herself from shaking. A faint glint to her right reminded her that there was a glass of water on the bedside table. She reached out for it, and Laverne, who was standing by the bed, smiled gently and passed the glass to her. Drowsily, she thanked him, turned over on to her side and immediately fell asleep. Only in the morning, when she awoke feeling strong and refreshed, did she wonder what on earth Laverne had been doing in her room and how, in the dark, she could possibly have known that he was smiling.

7

A FIGURE IN THE FLAMES

The following day, Laverne, Savage and Roth travelled to Wells in
Laverne's car. The journey was predominantly silent, apart from
the odd murmur of discontent from Roth whenever Laverne braked
suddenly or drove over a bump in the road. The night before she
had consumed three-quarters of a bottle of whisky and now she was
paying for it.

At the police station, Holebrook cleared the basement incident
room of all officers apart from himself, Mowart, Laverne, Savage,
Roth and a female secretary to take notes in shorthand. The phones
were unplugged and an emergency meeting was held. Holebrook
was now exhibiting the dazed indecision of an accident victim. To
his credit, the Chief Inspector was probably aware of his own
disorientation. Why else would he have asked his junior partner to
chair the meeting?

'Right,' Mowart began. 'On the subject of witnesses ... unfortunately, none of Mr and Mrs Sweet's neighbours saw anyone
escaping through the back gardens, something we're naturally very
disappointed about. But because the murderer or murderers got
away so quickly, we have to work on the assumption that they
didn't have far to run to.

'As of now, practically every CID and uniformed officer from
Bridgwater and Portishead are shelving what they're doing to come
here and help us. Today we're conducting a full house-to-house

search of the Glastonbury area, starting on the Albion estate and working out to every building in a ten mile radius. We're looking for people who can't account for their movements yesterday evening, and we're searching for the murder weapon, which the coroner assures us was some kind of heavy sword.'

'Tell them about Arthur,' mumbled Holebrook.

Mowart grinned. Laverne noticed that a small black shred of food was wedged between his two front teeth. 'Oh, yeah. It's perhaps important to point out that we do already know of one individual living locally who carries a sword, in fact carries one most of the time. He's a traveller, lives on Five Oaks Farm.'

Roth lowered her cup of strong black coffee to interrupt. 'What? A traveller who owns a farm?'

Mowart smiled. 'No ... perhaps I should explain. He lives in a crappy old van, in a field. The farmer got so sick of travellers trespassing on his land that he donated a field for their exclusive use.' Holebrook sighed to show his opinion of this charitable act. 'Even built wash-basins and toilets for 'em, although I shouldn't imagine they know how to use 'em. Anyway, that's where Arthur lives. In a knackered van in a field.'

'Does he have another name?' queried Savage. 'Apart from Arthur?'

Mowart smirked as he answered. 'Pendragon. Arthur Pendragon, the once and future King of all England. Reincarnated in the body of one Terry Claypole from Derby. Funnily enough, Lancelot and Merlin sometimes park in a lay-by across the road. We've just brought Arthur in for questioning. He's waiting in Interview Room One and he's got Excalibur with him.'

This announcement was greeted by general laughter. Then Roth, who wasn't amused, ruined everything by asking a question. 'Does he live alone?'

'No. He lives with Guinivere and seven hungry little knights.' More laughter.

'Then he can't be the man we're looking for,' she asserted.

Holebrook raised his head sharply. 'Why? Why do you say that?'

Roth patted two sheets of fax paper on her lap. 'When I got in, the profile from Quantico was waiting for me. According to PROFILER, these killings are the work of someone who lives alone.'

Watching Holebrook's face, Laverne said, 'Like Major Blackmore, for example?' But Holebrook failed to react. Perhaps he hadn't heard. Perhaps he was dead.

'Major Blackmore lives alone,' Laverne expounded. 'And as far as I can see, is the only person who had anything to gain from the death of Tess Martin's family.'

'Like what?' snapped Mowart. 'What did he gain? Apart from a huge funeral bill?'

'Tess herself, of course. The old boy's obviously fond of her. He must have been aware that in the event of anything happening to his daughter and her husband, she'd become his responsibility.'

Mowart looked interested. 'You're probably right. The Martins made a will, naming the old boy as her legal guardian. He must have known about that. Mr and Mrs Martin must have asked his permission . . .'

Holebrook broke out of his trance to swivel his chair in Laverne's direction. 'So a highly respected member of the community would kill his daughter, his son-in-law, grandson and one granddaughter, just so he could live with the other?'

Laverne raised an eyebrow to indicate that his theory, however wild it might sound on first hearing, was not beyond the realms of possibility.

'And why would he have murdered Gudrun Sweet and her parents?' asked Holebrook, who appeared to have made a miraculous recovery. 'What did he have to gain by that?' It was a perfectly reasonable question, to which Laverne had no ready answer.

Having silenced the opposition, Holebrook moved in for the kill.

'Major Blackmore was a credit to his regiment. He's also over seventy — statistically far too old to be turning into a serial killer. Far too old for a lot of things, I shouldn't wonder. But that isn't the main reason why we've left him alone.'

Holebrook waited for Laverne to ask him for the main reason. But Laverne would sooner have lowered his backside into the flames of hell than defer to DCI Holebrook.

'The Major is a recluse,' sighed Holebrook, defeated by the long silence. 'He retired in the seventies, and since then, he's never left Paradise House.'

Mowart nodded. 'Maybe recluse is the wrong word . . . he's more of an agoraphobic. Either way, Aden Blackmore is not a suspect in this inquiry. The people we're after are definitely mobile. Frighteningly mobile. Blackmore couldn't make it to the end of his drive without suffering a panic attack.'

Laverne smiled. 'He may not be one of your suspects. But he's one of mine.'

Roth, who had demonstrated surprising patience during this argumentative interlude, was poised to resume her reading of PROFILER's character sketch. Before she could open her mouth, Mowart jabbed a ball-point at Savage. 'I believe your conversation with the Sweet family was recorded.'

Savage agreed that this had been the case.

'Then we'd better get that cassette analysed. We need to know exactly what was said, and what was going on in the background. Have you got it on you?'

Savage had been searching frenziedly through her bag. With a loud sigh, she zipped up the bag and placed it on the floor. 'It's still in the tape machine. Which is back in my hotel room. I'm sorry, everyone.'

She caught Laverne's eye. He gave her a cheery wink, knowing that this was unusually lax of his partner. Normally he was the one who forgot things, forcing Savage to cover up for him and act as his personal organizer. Yesterday's murders must have affected her deeply.

Roth, determined to establish herself as the classroom swot, reached into her own bag and extracted the little black book that Laverne knew and loved. 'Lyn's forgetting that I took a few notes of my own.' She flicked her way through to the appropriate pages. 'Before I run through them, I want to clarify something. There are about seven thousand people living in Glastonbury. Do we all agree that the link between the two sets of victims – i.e., the fact that Tess Martin and Gudrun Sweet were friends – cannot be put down to coincidence?'

'Could be coincidence,' said Laverne, voicing the opinion of the majority. 'But it's bloody unlikely.'

'OK. Good. Now, maybe it'd be possible to link Gudrun and Tess with any number of other individuals or groupings. But in the choir, the choir both girls attended on the night of the first murder, Gudrun and Tess always stood with a girl called Gabrielle Town. Gudrun, Tess and Gaby. Three girls together. One of them's dead, the other's lucky to be alive. At this stage, shouldn't we be thinking of protecting Gabrielle, and maybe Tess as well?'

Holebrook snorted. 'This is old stuff. We've talked to Gabrielle Town. There's no link there. Outside the choir, she never saw or thought about either of the other two girls. They were acquaintances, not friends. Haven't you got anything new?'

Roth pursed her lips. 'OK. If Gabrielle's family is the next to get hit, do you promise to resign, asshole?'

Subjected to this insolent outburst, Holebrook could only splutter. Savage choked back a laugh and made it sound like a cough. Mowart, anxious to avoid any further unpleasantness, patted the air with the palms of his hands. 'All right . . . We're all under a great deal of pressure . . . Let's take a vote on it. Who thinks we should place a guard on the Town girl's house?'

Everyone except Holebrook held up their hands. 'Right,' said

Mowart. 'Consider it done.' He smiled ingratiatingly. 'Angela, you said you had something to read to us . . .'

Roth shuffled the papers on her lap. 'It's a bit wordy . . . but I'll edit it as I go along. Basically, the man we're looking for is white, educated, lower middle class, about thirty years of age, of average appearance. He's a sex killer, attracted to young pubescent girls, but so far, he hasn't had the time or the courage to interfere with his victims sexually. This personality is essentially a fantasist. He's a paedophile and an introvert. He may have a previous conviction for sexual offences against minors. The computer rates him as seventy-five per cent organized, twenty-five per cent disorganized. The guy's disorganized because he depersonalizes his victims and leaves their bodies in full view. I'd say anyone who could kill a whole family in under a minute and get clean away is fucking frighteningly well organized, but what do I know? I'm not the computer. This man is lonely, and won't have many friends or close personal relationships. He'll be a virgin, an only child. His father is dead. He used to live with his mother, but PROFILER thinks his mother is dead. He's unemployed. He's probably getting psychiatric help for a mental disorder. He lives in the same house he grew up in, unwilling, unable to leave. He's a loser who dreams of having power over others. He's the type of loser who tries to manufacture a social life for himself by running shitty societies like the boy scouts . . . if anyone present is involved with the boy scouts, accept my apologies. This man is a paedophile because he's afraid of adults. So afraid of them that he wants to destroy them. He probably murdered Gudrun Sweet by mistake. That mistake will have sent him into a state of complete panic. He's out of control, ladies and gentlemen, and he's likely to kill again within twenty-four hours.'

PROFILER's character study had silenced everyone in the room. Holebrook and Mowart were staring into each others' eyes with the intensity of lovers. Roth, confident as ever, sat back and smiled. 'Sound like anyone you know?'

Mowart and Holebrook were astonished. As one, they turned to Roth, eyes shining with excitement. In unison, they said, 'Trevor Snape.'

Since his birth in 1963, Trevor Austin Snape had lived in Magdalene Street, above the same shop that his grandfather had opened in the thirties. According to Glastonbury's oldest residents, Snape's Bakery had once sold the finest bread in Somerset: iced buns that boys would trade in their catapults for, muffins that had to be eaten while hot for their true glory to be appreciated.

At eight in the morning, six days a week, an aroma would drift out of the bakery that made the mouth water and the belly pine. Before the shop door opened, a queue of regular customers used to form, stretching to the corner of High Street.

Dickon Snape the baker started trading in 1932, the same year that a Welshman called John Cowper Powys published an evocative, rambling novel called *A Glastonbury Romance*, a book that signalled the interest that artists and intellectuals, as well as Christian mystics and Arthurian scholars, were beginning to show in the town.

By the mid-sixties, the intellectuals, embarrassed by their mistake, had already abandoned Glastonbury to the pagans and the psychedelic dreamers. In three decades, an old West Country market town had turned from a quiet place of pilgrimage into a psychic Disneyland, the source of mythogenesis on an outlandish scale. It was now a UFO observation centre, the lost Isle of Bliss, Avalon, Fairyland or even Paradise itself.

It may be mere coincidence, but Snape's Bakery browned its last loaf in 1967, when the first hippies arrived by the commune-load. From that year on, Glastonbury would never again belong to the people of the town, many of whom still resent the fact. Even today, there are quaint tea-shops in Glastonbury where people wearing denim and leather are firmly turned away, or, at best, served without a hint of human warmth.

Trevor Snape's father, Dickon Junior, was a staunch Christian and refused to sell his wares to men with long hair, perhaps forgetting that Christ himself hardly sported a short-back-and-sides. This desire to pick and choose his customers may have contributed to the failure of the business he'd inherited. Snape was forced to sell his premises to a concern called Seven Miles Out, catering for the new taste in beads, amulets and Brigitte Bardot posters.

The family continued to live on above their old shop, occupying three dark rooms. While Trevor grew into a silent, nervous boy with a keen aptitude for the violin but little personal charm, Snape Senior developed cancer of the throat and died. Thereafter, Phyllis Snape always blamed the incense fumes wafting up from the drug-den below for her husband's fatal illness.

In the eighties, young Trevor had a brief moment of glory, winning a scholarship to the Royal College of Music. When he arrived home from college five weeks into the first term, never to return, family friends assumed that the boy had been missing his mother. Others concocted less charitable explanations. There was an unsubstantiated rumour about harassment, a female student being driven to the verge of suicide by Snape's unwelcome and unremitting attentions.

After a period of unemployment, Snape trained as a librarian and secured a job at Wells Public Library. He had few friends, and fewer still after he was officially cautioned by the police for exposing himself to a twelve-year-old schoolgirl from West Pennard. The incident took place outside library hours, but soon became common knowledge. Trevor himself felt that the lingering stigma of his indiscretion was responsible for the death of his mother, as well as the enforced redundancy that came his way in 1992. If you have to fire someone, why not fire the flasher?

The former site of Snape's bakery was now occupied by an antiquarian bookshop that was rarely open. Snape, his faith in God unshaken in spite of his utter solitude and his continuing joblessness, still lived in the flat above. He had become active in the local church, where he found some degree of tolerance, if not quite forgiveness. The vicar of St John's, the Reverend Small, was that rare commodity in the modern Church: a clergyman who believed in God. Braving the prejudices of his parishioners, it was he that placed Snape in charge of the choir, believing that only those without sin could throw stones at his choirmaster.

That was four-and-a-half years ago. Since then, Snape had done nothing to shake Len Small's faith in him. The children he taught were not aware of his past misdemeanour. (Snape always referred to the incident as 'his mistake'.)

Some of his choristers laughed at his haircut, or his ancient spectacles, their broken frames swaddled in sticking plaster. The expansive sweat stains that often appeared under the arms of his sports jacket were also the source of much merriment. In spite of his oddness, both senior and junior choirs had won many prizes for Mr Snape. It made no sense that a thirty-two-year-old man who had climbed from ignominy to a position of respect should suddenly resort to mass murder. But Laverne knew from experience that murder seldom makes sense.

When he wasn't engaged on choir business, Snape was reluctant to stray from his dark apartment. On the day that the police came for him, they fully expected to find him at home. His flat was reached by a door on the ground floor of the shop, facing a squalid little yard. They knocked and knocked again, obtaining no answer. Then they quizzed neighbours about his likely whereabouts. No one had seen him for days. Nor had he visited the church. But there was a light shining on the stairs above the back door.

Finally, impatient for a result, the CID officers, led by Holebrook and Mowart, smashed down the door and searched the flat. Snape was out, but everything within looked tidy, clean and well-kept. No blood-stained samurai swords or grisly mementoes. However, the investigating officers made one puzzling discovery. Snape's famous broken spectacles were sitting on the kitchen table. When questioned, the vicar of St John's agreed that Snape was chronically myopic. If he was in hiding, he was also virtually blind.

After the morning meeting, Mowart asked Laverne if he wanted to interview King Arthur while they went into Glastonbury to collect Snape. Laverne declined, feeling that another chat with Tess Martin might prove more profitable. Laverne asked Savage to accompany him, hoping that meanwhile, Roth would check that Gabrielle Town and her family were safe. Roth curtly reminded him that she was in England to observe Laverne, not to carry out tasks that were best handled by officers of a junior rank.

During the car journey to Glastonbury, Roth sat beside Laverne. Savage sat in the back. Laverne drove in silence, unwilling to engage in argument with Roth about the obvious inadequacy of the FBI computer's profile. Trevor Snape may indeed have exhibited classical characteristics of the serial killer. But could he walk through walls? Laverne was inclined to doubt it.

At Paradise House, Laverne faced the same delays as before: first at the gate-house, then at the front door. A different bodyguard – a grave, taciturn Indian – held all three of them at bay while Blackmore lumbered into the hall and peered out, his white, round face suspended in space like a baleful moon. Laverne introduced the women.

The familiar strident voice barked out a command. 'Rahul, step aside.'

The bodyguard dutifully complied, allowing Blackmore to survey Savage and Roth. There was a prolonged silence. Blackmore's eyes glittered coldly and the door slammed shut. Confused, Laverne rang the bell again. When the Indian reappeared, Laverne attempted a smile. 'Could we come in please?'

Rahul the bodyguard was tall and lean, with an almost western complexion. Laverne guessed that he was a high caste Hindu. 'You, sir, are welcome to enter. But the women must remain outside.'

Roth protested. 'But I've come all the way from America to observe this gentleman at work.'

Rahul shook his head. 'I'm sorry, madam. But the Major will not allow any female near him or allow any female to enter his house.'

'What are you talking about?' protested Savage. 'What sex do you think his granddaughter is?'

Rahul held up a long forefinger. 'This is the Major's decision. I am merely carrying out his orders . . .'

Annoyed but resigned to their fate, the two women opted to wait in the car. Laverne entered the hall, where Blackmore was standing. He was trembling with emotion. 'She's in her room, Laverne. And I warn you, that child is extremely disturbed. If her doctor knew you were here, I'm sure you'd feel his boot on your rear-end. But I think you're probably a decent man. So I'll grant you five minutes with her. Five minutes. After that, I don't want to see you here again. Rahul – show him the way.'

Laverne wanted to question Blackmore but had barely opened his mouth before the Major turned and marched across the hall to his study. Laverne tried to conceal his embarrassment with a cough. The tall Indian guided him up the stairs to a gallery that traversed the breadth of the house. At the top of the stairs, they turned left. Tess's room was at the end of the gallery. Rahul knocked on the door and spoke aloud.

'Miss Martin? There's a policeman here to see you.'

No answer.

Rahul shrugged, fixed Laverne with his sad stare. 'As the Major said, you have five minutes, sir. No more.'

Lest Laverne should misunderstand his meaning, Rahul raised the face of a bejewelled wrist-watch to his eyes and started counting.

Laverne entered the room. Tess was lying in a single bed, underneath the window. The curtains were closed. There were few personal possessions on display. An old rag doll reclined on the dressing table, attempting to look casual. A couple of magazines and a portable TV rested on a low table at the end of the bed. Otherwise, there was little to suggest that this was the girl's new home. It crossed Laverne's mind that his surroundings were more like a cell than the bedroom of a teenage girl.

He crouched beside the bed. She was wearing pyjamas, lying on her side, her face turned to the wall. Her red hair covered the pillow, burning through the gloom. She clutched a flowered duvet to her chest with both hands.

'How did you find out?'

'Television.' The girl's voice sounded lifeless. She was possibly drugged.

'Tess,' he said simply. 'I need to know what you saw that night. The night you lost your family. We don't want anyone else to die. Not if we can help it. Now, do we?'

She snorted at the absurdity of the question. Laverne found this encouraging. If she was well enough to subject him to adolescent sarcasm, perhaps she was well enough to tell him the truth.

'We believe there's a link, you see. A link between your family, and what happened to Gudrun's family ... to Gudrun. And we need all the help we can get if we're going to catch those responsible. Now, last time we met, you said you saw something. Something that wasn't human. It might help if you'd explain what you meant by that.'

Slowly, she half-turned her head towards him. 'Take me away from here.'

'Excuse me?'

'Please. He's keeping me prisoner. At night, he locks me in. Locks the door from the outside. That must be against the law, mustn't it?'

'Tess, I haven't got much time. Please . . . tell me what you saw.'

She rolled over in the bed. Yesterday, her face had been pale. It was now the colour of ivory and, like ivory, it shone. Her eyes were dark with reproach. 'First of all, before I even went in the house, I saw a light in the woods. It moved fast, like someone running with a lantern. Then I lost sight of it. I went in the house and when I was in the kitchen I saw another light flash past the window. So I went out to see what it was.'

'And?'

'I don't know why I'm bothering. You won't believe me. The other police didn't believe me.'

'Tess, I will believe you. In fact, I already believe you.'

She contemplated him for a few seconds. 'And you're sure you're a real policeman?'

He smiled. 'As far as I know.'

'No, I mean a proper policeman who tries to solve crimes.'

'This may surprise you, but sometimes I don't just try. I actually succeed.' He took out his ID and allowed her to brood over it. 'I've been a policeman for thirty-three years this autumn. Which should give you a clue as to how incredibly ancient I am. Why? Don't I seem like a real policeman to you?'

'No.' There was a hint of scorn in the observation. 'You seem more like someone's dad.'

'I am someone's dad. So are an awful lot of other policemen.'

'No . . . they're just policemen. Rachel Towan's dad is in the police. And you can tell just by looking at him that he isn't a real dad. The police have funny-shaped heads. Have you never noticed? Rachel's dad's hair is so greasy it looks as if it's been painted on to his head.'

She half-laughed and then started to cry. Laverne held her hand while she sobbed, wishing there was some indirect way to return her to the matter-in-hand without seeming pushy or contrived. But there wasn't, so he told her what was on his mind. 'Tess, love, I'm really very sorry to trouble you at a time like this. But seven lives have already been lost. We really don't want anyone else to die, do we?'

He passed her a paper tissue from a box beside the bed. She blew her nose loudly.

'Better now?' said Laverne.

A knock sounded at the door. Rahul leant into the room. 'Time's up, I'm afraid.'

Laverne stared back at him coldly. 'We're almost done.'

The bodyguard nodded uncertainly, darkly suspecting that his authority was being flouted. As Rahul withdrew his head, Tess shifted her weight on to one elbow and looked earnestly into Laverne's eyes.

'Whatever killed Mum and Dad and Helen and Andrew wasn't a person. I swear it wasn't. It was some kind of insect, and it was on fire. It had six legs and its mouth was open, like it was screaming, but no sound was coming out. I swear I'm telling the truth. It was screaming and dancing and it was on fire and it had the ugliest face I've ever seen.'

'Where is it?' Laverne asked simply. He tapped the photocopied form he was holding. It was his personal copy of Tess Martin's statement. 'Where's the information that I've just been given?' He shook the statement, as if to empty Tess's missing eye-witness account on to the floor.

He was facing Holebrook. Roth and Savage, to whom Laverne had already related his latest findings, were standing behind him. They were in the bedroom of Trevor Snape's flat, while around them, Holebrook's officers rifled through the choirmaster's belongings.

In the last hour, Holebrook had recovered most of his self-possession. For the first time since the death of the Martins, he knew what to do. Snape was their suspect, and now that suspect had vanished. Bringing him in, therefore, had become Holebrook's plan. So far, Laverne had been unable to come up with a plan of his own. Laverne's opinion, therefore, was of infinitesimal importance to DCI Holebrook.

In a patronizing voice, Holebrook answered, 'We passed Miss Martin's description on to a distinguished child psychiatrist, who assured us that a little girl who was so deeply shocked is more than likely to have been hallucinating. I happen to agree with that assessment. Red lights . . . balls of fire. It's textbook stuff.'

Laverne struggled to contain his temper. 'But she saw what she saw *before* she knew what had happened to her family. Are you suggesting she was suffering from shock in advance?'

'After an ordeal like that, could you seriously expect Tess Martin or anyone else to recall the exact chronological course of events?'

Mowart, overhearing the dispute, wandered in from the other room.

'So you falsified a statement,' said Laverne, wishing to clarify the matter. 'You listened to what our only witness had to say, then edited out the bits you disapproved of.'

Mowart joined forces with his boss. 'Oh, come off it. All statements are edited. They have to be. We all know that. Otherwise we'd just get a long list of what people were watching on telly, or what they ate for their tea.'

'Yes, of course,' interrupted Savage impatiently. 'Ordinary things, yes. Digressions and repetitions, certainly. But not an eye-witness account that might prove to be vital.'

Mowart glared back at them all stolidly. 'So what would you have done? Assembled a Photofit and circulated it to all available officers? "Wanted: A Giant Daddy-Longlegs. Do Not Approach. This insect is known to be dangerous."'

'John . . . Ed,' said Roth equably. 'We all accept that Tess couldn't have seen what she thinks she saw. It's our job to put our heads together and work out what she actually did see. How the hell do we do that if you censor her statement? I'm sorry. I'm with these guys on this one. Since we got here, you've been blocking Chief Superintendent Laverne every step of the way. Maybe you get off on this power trip you're on. Fine. I'm happy for you, really. In the meantime, people are dying because of your mistakes. You guys have screwed up. Maybe it's time you faced that fact.'

Laverne turned to leave, and the two women followed him. Holebrook called after them. His voice contained a thin note of misgiving. 'Where are you going?'

At the doorway, Laverne glanced back, malicious humour twisting the corners of his mouth. 'Your Chief Constable asked me to carry out an independent inquiry. Well, that's what I'm doing, Ed. I'm rediscovering my independence . . .'

8

EVERY CREEPING THING

After sharing a moody and virtually silent lunch, Laverne, Savage and Roth drove down the old Wells Road and turned right into Holywell Road. Lammas Farm lay at the end of a winding track, an attractive eighteenth century farmhouse enclosed by seven acres, every strand of its intricately thatched roof visible in the glare of the afternoon sun.

The house's latest owners had enlarged its windows and white-washed its stone walls. There were ivy-laden trellises around the doors and windows. A decorative fibreglass cat, crouching on the roof, added a note of absurdity to the proceedings.

There was a large field at the back of the house, where a few sheep and goats grazed, and an enclosed yard where chickens irritably pecked the ground and each other. A garage had been built on to the side of the house, its colour and contours carefully complementing the farmhouse. Outside the garage sat a new white BMW, recently washed and waxed, the gravel beneath its wheels still damp.

'Old England,' said Roth approvingly as Laverne locked the car.

'Correction,' said Savage. 'New money.'

As they approached the front door, a lone figure rounded the house from the left. It was a young uniformed police constable, his soft stubble-free cheeks shining. He was holding his unsightly domed helmet underneath one arm. Recognizing Laverne, the constable stood to attention and saluted. Laverne was surprised by this. It had been so long since anyone had saluted him that his first impression was that the constable concerned was deliberately mocking him. Choosing not to draw attention to the man's inappropriate behaviour, he asked the officer who he was and what his business was at Lammas Farm, home of Gabrielle Town and her family.

'PC Kevin Childs, sir. I've been instructed to guard the premises until ten p.m., when another officer . . .'

Roth interrupted him sharply. 'Another officer? You telling me you're alone, here?'

PC Childs nodded. Laverne, Roth and Savage grimaced in unison. Childs blinked in hurt surprise, wrongly thinking that his effectiveness as a police officer had been called into doubt. Savage saw the look and promptly corrected him. 'And we're sure you're doing a fine job.'

While the constable resumed his patrol, the three visitors walked over to the entrance, the sun casting their shadows before them. 'I can't believe that Holebrook only sent one guy,' said Roth.

'He's doing it on purpose,' scowled Laverne. 'He must be. Just to score points off us.'

The front door was ajar. A soft feminine voice drawled within. Laverne knocked and gently pushed the door open.

'Hello?'

They peered into a cool, low-ceilinged living room. A small dark-skinned woman was crouching on the uncarpeted floor, laying newly laundered clothes into an old leather suitcase. She glanced up sharply at the three strangers crowded in her doorway. When she spoke, her voice was breathless with nerves. 'What? What is it?'

Savage acted as spokeswoman, briefly explaining that they were CID officers, that Trevor Snape was suspected of involvement in the Glastonbury killings and that Snape had gone missing from his home.

'We're aware of that,' replied Mrs Town. 'That's why we've been given police protection.'

'Then you'll understand why we fear your daughter's life may be in danger.' Laverne softened the unpleasant words with a regretful smile.

'Of course I understand. Why do you think we're packing? Tomorrow we're leaving for London. And we're staying there until you've caught him. Whoever it is.'

Roth stepped into the cool shade of the room. She was at least eight inches taller than Mrs Town. 'You don't believe it was Snape, then?'

She shook her head vigorously. 'Not from what I've been told. He used an axe, didn't he?' The officers stared back at her unhelpfully. 'That's what I read, anyway. Well I know for a fact that poor Trevor couldn't swing an axe.'

'Why's that?' demanded Laverne.

'Rheumatoid arthritis. He has a lot of pain in his joints. Some days he can hardly lift his arms above his head.'

'I thought that only affected older people,' said Savage.

'Trevor's old before his time,' said Mrs Town. 'He always has been.'

Laverne waited for the woman's words to settle before asking, 'How do you conduct a choir when you can't lift your arms?'

Someone spoke at the far end of the room. 'With difficulty.' A young girl was standing in the low arch that led through to the kitchen. She looked about fifteen, her hair long and dark, her bearing bold and faintly pugnacious. The girl moved into the room like a dancer, sullenly aware of her own beauty. Laverne could see at a glance why she'd been Snape's favourite, although his own initial impression was that the girl was a cheeky young madam who needed a stern talking-to.

'These people are police officers, Gaby darling,' said Mrs Town, her fawning tone more than accounting for the girl's imperious demeanour.

'I've got nothing to say to them,' snapped Gabrielle. 'My friend's dead because of the law.'

Mrs Town simpered apologetically. 'I'm afraid the police aren't Gaby's favourite people at the moment. Her boyfriend's in trouble with you lot.'

Roth was staring in unequivocal horror at a set of white porcelain figures on the mantelpiece which, judging by their flared trousers, appeared to date from the early seventies. Mrs Town's words snapped her back into the unflared present.

'Yeah? What's he done?'

Uncomfortably, Mrs Town fidgeted with the top button of her blouse. 'Drugs. Possession. Only cannabis, but . . .' She lowered her voice and leaned forward. 'I'm not happy about the relationship. But what can you do? She's fifteen. Did you listen to your parents when you were fifteen?'

'As far as I recall, I had no choice,' replied Laverne severely.

Mrs Town suddenly remembered her manners. 'Please. Sit down, why don't you?'

Laverne and Savage sat side-by-side on a two-seater sofa. Roth eased herself into a pine rocking chair by the window, rocking gently, legs outstretched, her long feet in their sensible shoes hovering above the tiled floor.

Mrs Town cleared her throat. 'Would anyone like some tea?'

Laverne and Roth accepted the offer with enthusiasm. Savage demurred somewhat, feeling that Mrs Town ought to continue with her packing. But Mrs Town insisted, and the tea was duly made, arriving in bone china tea cups and accompanied by a mound of chocolate digestive biscuits. Mrs Town then perched on a high stool which drew attention to her short, plump, evenly tanned legs.

'Has Gabrielle gone out?' asked Laverne, suddenly aware that she had left the room without him noticing.

Mrs Town looked surprised. 'She's not allowed out, is she? We were told . . . advised . . . to stay on the premises.'

Roth spooned sugar into her tea and stirred it daintily. 'Makes sense. No one knows where Snape is, right now. So we need to know where your daughter is.'

Mrs Town was not in the habit of asserting herself. Nor could she contain her scepticism, so she sniffed to demonstrate her heart-felt belief in Snape's innocence, unaware that this belief was secretly shared by everyone in the room.

Laverne dipped a chocolate biscuit into his tea. 'I take it Mr Town isn't home?'

His host wriggled on her stool. 'Mr Town is never home, I'm afraid.'

What exactly did this mean? Was Gabrielle's father a commercial traveller? Or was he dead? Had he run off with a younger woman? No one had the heart to ask. With a jolt, Laverne remembered that his biscuit was submerged in hot tea. Too late, he raised his hand. A molten chocolate digestive sank to the bottom of his cup.

Laverne hastily invented a question to divert attention from his mishap. 'So there's just you and Gaby living here, is there?'

'No. I have one son. Anthony. He's at college.'

'He doesn't live here, then?'

'Yes. Yes. But he's staying with his girlfriend at the moment. Keeping out of the way, you know?'

'I take it he hates the police as well, does he?'

She confirmed his suspicions with a tight, pained smile. Laverne took Delia Town in with a glance, saw the end of her marriage in the dark shadows under her eyes, felt how desperate she was to meet someone decent and kind, and to meet them soon, today, before she grew too bitter and too old.

He had always loathed his ability to look at people and drink them in, taste their vices and dream their dreams. It is not always comfortable to know what others are thinking. But Laverne's aptitude for empathy was part of the greater gift that made him different and gave him the edge over his plodding colleagues.

Unprompted, Mrs Town began to talk. 'The worst thing is, this has always been such a lovely place to live. So peaceful. Sometimes in the day, you can just sit here, in this lovely old house, and not hear a sound. Nothing. I love Glastonbury. I've always loved living here. We local people can't believe that such terrible things could have happened in our town.'

During a long, eventful career, Laverne had heard many variations on this particular speech. Quite so, my dear, he thought. None of us believe in tragedy until it comes to our door. It's our faith in life's goodness that keeps us strong. But that same faith lends us the courage to take the short-cut home, down the dark alley, across the moonlit playing field, under the tree where the murderer waits. It's our faith in life that gets us killed.

'We don't often watch television. Gaby listens to music, I like to read. We had no sense that anything was wrong until we saw the light.'

The police officers looked blank. Diffidently, Mrs Town scanned each of their faces in turn. 'Last night . . . before midnight. We saw a light moving in the field at the back of the house. Like a big searchlight. That's how we knew something was wrong. Then we turned on the radio and heard about Gudrun . . . well, need I go on?'

Laverne, Savage and Roth sipped their tea in silence. A few moments later, while Mrs Town questioned Roth about America and whether she was visiting England or hoping to live here permanently, Laverne ambled out to his car and contacted the incident room at Wells on his police radio. When the call was over, he took two standard issue police flashlights out of the Rover's glove compartment. As an optimistic afterthought, he picked up a pair of shiny handcuffs and slipped them into his jacket pocket.

Stepping out of the car into the yard, he saw Savage and Roth approaching from the house. Laverne was then able to confirm what the two women already suspected: that the light Mrs Town had seen from her window had not been cast by officers of the law.

The police search of Holywell Lane and its environs was not scheduled to begin until the following morning.

They re-entered the house, where Laverne informed Mrs Town and her daughter, quietly but forcefully, that it would probably be best if they spent the night in the living room, in full view of the three detectives, who would be sitting up until dawn to guard them. He expected Gabrielle to argue with this suggestion, but there was a limit to the girl's rebelliousness. Of course, she sighed and grumbled and made a great show of outward discontent. But she was afraid, and like everyone present, sensed that her life might depend on following Laverne's instructions to the letter.

The evening was dull beyond belief. Mrs Town moved a small portable television into the living room. Mother, daughter and the three officers gathered around it, mesmerized with boredom by the dismal pap on offer. For supper, everyone had a Chinese takeaway, ferried from the town by a delivery boy on a moped. The food and the boy's tip were paid for by Laverne, who was careful to take a receipt for the full amount. He probably didn't stand a chance in hell of putting the bill on expenses, or of claiming the night's vigil as overtime. But there was no harm in trying.

When Mrs Town or her daughter left the room, one of the female officers accompanied them. This inevitably led to tensions, particularly when Craig arrived. Craig was Gabrielle's boyfriend. Laverne thought he was rather too old for her. He was about seventeen, clad in leathers, carrying a dented motorcycle helmet. His otherwise pretty face was marred by a riot of overripe pustules. Forced to collude in public, the teenagers drank tea, sniggered and whispered while their reluctant chaperones stared at the cracks in the wall. When Craig had left, Gabrielle approached her mother and pointed at Savage.

'Craig's seen her picture in the paper. She's useless. She was with Gudrun when she got killed. If she couldn't protect Gudrun, what makes you think she can protect us?'

Savage reddened slightly. Gabrielle appealed to her mother for support. 'Mum, I'm scared. Why don't we leave now? The cases are packed. Let's just go.'

Roth cleared her throat. 'Gaby, we can't guarantee your safety if you leave here. I'm not trying to scare you, honey, but we think the man who killed Gudrun might want to hurt you, too. That's why we're sticking close to you.'

Hearing these comfortless words, Gabrielle sank on to the sofa and commenced a marathon sulk. A knock sounded on the front door. Laverne answered it. Two figures stood in the darkening yard. He recognized the nearer of the pair as PC Childs, now wearing his helmet. Childs grinned and shone a torch into the face of a slightly older man with a thin ginger moustache who was wheeling a bicycle. 'Sorry to disturb you, sir. Thought you might like to meet the night shift. This is PC Underwood. We call him Understain, because of his disgusting personal habits.'

Laverne grunted unaccommodatingly. Childs and Underwood stopped grinning. Underwood coughed. 'Anyway, right you are, sir. I'll be on duty until eight tomorrow morning.'

Laverne nodded dismissively. 'Fair enough. We'll be up all night. Give us a shout if you need a brew or anything.'

He closed the door, walked past the four women, through the narrow kitchen and out into the back yard. There was a barn facing him, and beyond that a large ploughed field. The sky above was streaked with bands of blue-black, like ink in water. A breeze flew into his face, bearing with it the warm smell of manure and the sweet, cold perfume of open meadows. A sense of space and freedom swelled inside him, which was instantly quashed when he saw something moving near the black mouth of the barn.

He tensed, charged with the exhilaration of excitement and fear. Then he heard a lazy champing sound, and realized the shape by the barn was nothing more than a goat. He heard footsteps and saw the thin beam of a torch dancing round the yard from the left. Not wishing to engage in further pointless banter with Underwood, he closed the back door, went to the sink and filled the kettle to prepare the day's umpteenth pot of tea.

At eleven, Mrs Town and Gabrielle bedded down for the night, mother settling on the sofa, daughter occupying a camp-bed that took all of Laverne's strength and ingenuity to assemble.

While Roth kept watch, Laverne and Savage toured the house. The living room was adjoined by a large dining room containing a winding staircase. Overhead, there were three bedrooms, a small landing and a bathroom. Laverne switched on the landing light and followed Savage into the main bedroom, where Mrs Town slept. The room faced towards town. The dirty orange glow of street lamps muddied the distant horizon. Directly under the window, a vague light swept past as Underwood continued his lonely patrol.

'Shouldn't we bring him in?' said Savage. 'I don't like the idea of him out there all on his own.'

'Don't get sentimental. He's got a job to do. And so have we.' He checked that the window locks were secure, all the while conscious of her unease. 'More to the point, do you really imagine that we're any better off than he is? Nobody's safe tonight.'

'Don't,' she said, hugging her shoulders for warmth.

They visited the back bedrooms, Laverne repeating his ritual with the locks. In the larger of the three rooms, Gabrielle's room, Laverne surprised Savage by peering into the wardrobe and then looking under the bed. 'Good God,' she laughed. 'You really are expecting the bogey man . . .'

He gazed at her seriously. 'Do you mean to tell me you're not?'

As they reached the foot of the stairs, a Georgian carriage clock chimed the half-hour. Laverne nodded to a framed photograph above the fireplace. It was a picture of the choir, taken the year before. Tess Martin and Gabrielle were standing at the back, beaming at the camera. Gudrun Sweet appeared to be missing from the photograph altogether. Trevor Snape sat in the centre of the front row, pale and myopic, his lank hair severely parted. He had small eyes and a comically jutting chin, reminding Laverne of Stan Laurel without a sense of humour.

It was a better likeness than the blurred mug-shot that DCI Holebrook had supplied, and lent solid credence to Mrs Town's view that Snape was not the stuff that murderers are made of.

'What do you think, Lyn? Would you leave that man alone with your children?'

She shrugged. 'I wouldn't leave many men with my children.' Then she took his arm and squeezed it. 'My husband and present company excepted.'

They both felt slightly queasy as they opened the living room door, half-expecting to find another gathering of fresh corpses behind it. But all they saw was Roth idling back and forth in the rocking chair, her shadow thrown high above her by the single lamp at her feet. Nearby, Gabrielle wriggled uncomfortably on the narrow camp-bed. A soft snore sounded from the direction of the sofa. Mrs Town was already asleep.

The three detectives sat down and waited. Smiling mischievously, Roth produced a leather-covered brandy flask from her bag and offered it round, like an officer in the trenches preparing for the final push. Laverne hesitated. What the hell. What harm could a little drink do? And what possible advantage could there be in staying sober, knowing as he did that the Butcher of Glastonbury might already be in the house?

They each took a few mouthfuls of the warming spirit, and, thus comforted, sank back into their own sombre thoughts. Laverne was sitting under the window, facing Savage and the archway that led through to the kitchen. There were no blinds on the kitchen window. Every minute or so, light washed over the glass as PC Underwood passed by. Laverne smiled faintly to himself, remembering the constable's nickname. Was it true about his disgusting personal habits? Probably not. Police nicknames usually erred on the side of gross exaggeration. After all, his own sobriquet at training college had been 'misery-guts'. Now, really, what could have been further from the truth?

He closed his eyes and drifted for a while, half-aware of Savage and Roth whispering. The clock in the next room struck twelve. Someone nudged his arm, and he looked up to see Roth's face above his own. Mischief glinted in her eyes. She leaned over to whisper in his ear. 'How about a smoke behind the gym?'

He sat up sharply, and signalled to Savage that he and Roth were about to check the house again. Savage nodded, a wry smirk on her face. Gabrielle protested incomprehensibly in her sleep. Laverne and Roth tiptoed into the dining room and closed the door behind them.

'Neat house, huh?' she remarked, turning on the light.

Laverne answered with a nod, guiltily accepting the offered cigarette. Was this really it? The end of twenty years of abstinence? A return to clandestine, stolen smokes in his own house, with Dawn, always a fierce campaigner against tobacco, once again drawing his attention to the sad, limp cigarette butts floating in the lavatory?

'You're the devil, do you know that?' he said as she held up the Zippo lighter.

She blew smoke out of her nostrils like a fire-breathing dragon. 'Not me, pal. I'm just the support act.'

They sat together on the stairs. Roth said, 'You know, when we met a couple of weeks ago, I thought you were the most arrogant man alive.'

He laughed. 'And what do you think now?'

'I think you have a right to be arrogant. Because you're smart. It's all intuitive, too. You don't think things through at all, do you, baby? You do what you feel, what you feel is right, which is why we're here, doing what we're doing.'

'Wasting our time, you mean.'

'No. Because if this was my investigation, I'd be here too. Everything you do and say contradicts everything my beloved "A" team holds to be right and true. But shit, I think you're on the right track.'

'Is that so?'

'No doubt about it. The link between Tess and Gudrun and Gabrielle is a set-up. Someone wants us to think that Gabrielle is at the centre of all this. Someone wants us to think that so badly that they're willing to murder her, just to prove the point. But we both of us know that it all goes back to Tess Martin.'

Laverne said nothing, merely sucked on his cigarette and listened.

'Don't know how. Don't know why. But both you and I know that these killings are connected to the Martin family. Ain't that so?'

'Stop agreeing with me. It's making me nervous.'

She then alarmed him by reaching under the left arm of her jacket and extracting a handgun. 'Like it? Smith & Wesson 9 millimetre. Semi-automatic. Carries thirteen rounds. I hope you're not superstitious?'

Laverne shook his head gravely. 'Right. Hand it over. You're not authorized to carry that weapon in this country.'

Her mouth dropped open. 'Are you kidding? Christ alone knows what we're in for tonight. What are you planning to do when things get hot, Sherlock? Go in there with your baton?'

He sighed. 'Haven't got a baton. And incidentally, we call 'em truncheons. Except that I'm CID, and CID officers don't bother with truncheons.'

'And you don't bother with guns, either. Wow. Good thinking. The only people who bear arms here are the goddamned criminals. What a backward country.' She studied him for a while and her eyes lost some of their confrontational glare. 'So, whadya say. Wanna kiss me?'

'I beg your pardon?'

'I'm asking you. Kiss me, why don't you?'

He was aghast. 'Have you been drinking?'

'No. I just happen to like my men old and decrepit, you big dummy.'

Laverne tensed as Roth placed a coaxing hand on the back of his neck. He looked at her, but saw no warmth or affection in her face. A terrible coldness came over him, and for a second he felt that this moment had no bearing in reality. This woman, his visit to Glastonbury, the investigation itself, all seemed to be part of some deep and hellish dream. Aggressively, he yanked her arm away.

The door opened. Savage thrust her head into the room as Laverne hid his cigarette behind his back like a schoolboy. Savage signalled urgently with her eyes, nodding back into the living room. Roth and Laverne bounded off the stairs, stubbed out their cigarettes in the hearth and silently followed her. She led them past the recumbent women, into the dark kitchen. Mrs Town, perhaps sensing that something was wrong, raised her head from the sofa as they crept by.

'I'm worried about Underwood,' said Savage.

Laverne thought he'd misheard. 'Who?'

'The PC on duty . . . I haven't seen him pass by for about ten minutes.'

'Probably having a sly smoke on the job,' proposed Laverne, without thinking.

'He's not the only one,' retorted Savage, her nostrils flaring with reproach.

'Maybe we'd better check up on him, anyway,' said Roth.

Roth volunteered to stay behind, standing guard over the Towns, while Laverne and Savage picked up their torches and went out into the yard. Hurriedly, Roth bolted the door behind them.

The night was oppressively airless. Rain drops spat down irregularly from a dense, overcast sky. They stood in front of the barn, crossing torch beams as they scanned the dark terrain for PC Underwood.

'Maybe we should split up?' said Laverne. Savage's unwillingness was almost palpable so he quickly added, 'No. Let's not.'

Together, they walked round the house. The yard was deserted. They searched the barn, where the goats were tethered, and aimed their torches into the chicken coop, causing a nervous rustling in the darkness. They walked out of the farm, throwing light down the empty lane, over the hedges and high up into the drizzling sky.

'Know what I think?' said Savage. 'I think he's gone home.'

'What? For the night, you mean?'

'No. Just for a sleep and a cup of coffee and some toast. Maybe he'll be back.'

'He'll feel my boot up his arse if he does.'

They turned and walked back up the track, towards the house. The rain started to fall harder. The lone light shining in the farmhouse window looked cosy and welcoming, and they were both more than willing to accept that Underwood was playing truant from his post. But as they entered the yard, Laverne's flashlight chanced upon a lone black bicycle, chained to a drainpipe at the side of the house.

'If he's gone home, he must have walked it.'

'Shit!' exclaimed Detective Inspector Savage, who was not given to oaths.

They were about to knock on the kitchen door when something shrieked in the field behind them. They halted, afraid to breathe. Savage grabbed Laverne's arm. 'Did you hear that?'

Without answering, he turned and walked towards the sound.

The rain lashed their faces with insulting vigour as they stepped into Mrs Town's one and only field. The darkness was overwhelming. The meagre beams of their torches were swallowed whole by the black maw of night.

There was another scream, further away. It was a human cry, mingling fury, outrage, cold panic and excruciating pain. This time, the scream tapered off into a series of frantic pleas. Someone was being tortured.

They began to run, blindly, their flashlights dancing wildly before them, their shoes slipping on the muddy ground. Some kind of small, quick animal reared up before their legs and dashed off to the left. Laverne staggered, clung to Savage to steady himself, and sent them both crashing earthward.

As they hauled themselves up, panting, Savage made a hissing sound through her teeth. Laverne raised his eyes to see a cold light coming to life in the black void. It was like a single eye opening in hell. Savage saw it too, and murmured something inaudible. They were looking at a cone of white fire. From where they were standing, the blaze looked no bigger than a matchstick, but something told them that its actual proportions were considerable. As they watched, the fire changed colour, from yellow, to blue, violet and back to white.

Yet the strangest feature of this mysterious conflagration was that although it shone with piercing intensity, it gave off no radiance, making the dark night seem darker still. Then the fire began to move, at first inching forward hesitantly, then coasting like a great locomotive gathering speed.

Savage, who had forgotten to breathe, gasped sharply. 'It's coming straight for us.'

'Run!' shouted Laverne.

She needed no encouragement. They bounded back to the cottage, blinded by the rain, their hearts slamming against their chests, the charging inferno at their heels. Laverne's legs felt heavy and stiff, refusing to do his bidding. He seemed to be running in slow motion. His breath came in short, painful snatches.

Savage reached the yard before him. As the house came into focus, he glanced behind and received the fleeting impression of a firestorm with a grinning, blackened face in its heart.

The back door flew open before Savage could reach it. Roth stepped out into the yard, gripping her gun, legs straddled in a firing stance as Savage rushed past her. Laverne looked back, saw the vivid flame racing towards the house. As he drew level with Roth, she opened fire. Gunshots cracked through the dull air. There was no time to reason with her. If she wanted to play Annie Oakley, that was her own affair. Laverne knew what he had to do.

He stormed into the kitchen, diving for the mother and daughter who were now shouting and screaming in the middle of the living room. Savage, who had been trying to calm Gabrielle, listened to Laverne's short bellowed command and obeyed it instantly. The police officers pressed the two women together, then threw their own bodies around them, linking arms to form a human shield. Then they closed their eyes and waited.

They waited for disaster; a deafening roar, the swish of a sword parting the air, then the thud of impact, followed by blood, pain and unrelenting darkness. But nothing happened. All was silent. Nor was there another sound from the yard. Roth had not fired her weapon since Laverne entered the house.

Another twenty seconds passed. Gabrielle began to shout and struggle. 'What are you doing? Get off us, can't you? Just bloody ... get ... OFF!'

Laverne wondered whether anyone in history could ever have been so ungrateful to have had their life saved. As far as the girl was concerned, she had merely received an unwanted bear hug from two police officers who had rudely gate-crashed their way into her house. Laverne nodded to Savage and they released the Towns from their grip.

Now that the danger had passed, Laverne's first thought was for Roth. Unsteadily, sweating liberally from his exertions, he walked out to the yard. He felt certain that he'd find the American dead, hacked to bloody pieces. She was still standing where he'd left her, gun in hand, stoically watching the drifting darkness. Gingerly, he touched her arm, half-expecting her head to roll off her shoulders. She gave him a quick sideways glance.

'OK?'

'We're OK. What about you?'

She nodded slowly.

He laughed with relief. 'Nothing happened.'

'I know. When I fired, it turned and headed back out to the fields. It's still out there. It's watching us. Now, this minute. Can't you feel it?'

He wiped the sweat out of his eyes with his sleeve. 'I don't know. At this precise moment, I don't honestly know *what* I feel. But I think it's over. For now, at least. Come on, Angela. Come back inside.'

She resisted. He put his left hand on her shoulder and swivelled her in the direction of the house. What happened next happened so quickly that Laverne, when questioned, was unable to recall the exact order of events. There was a shriek and running footsteps, and Roth fell face downward on to the kitchen floor with something dark protruding from her back. But Laverne could not say whether the shriek preceded the footsteps, came from her assailant or was made by Roth as she fell.

Hearing the commotion, Savage rushed into the kitchen and tried to hold the American still. The thick black handle of a butcher's knife was wedged between her shoulders. Half of the blade was buried in her back. Laverne felt sick. It looked bad. Blood as dark and thick as oil was quickly spreading around the FBI officer's body. Mrs Town appeared, flapping her arms and dithering, and was ordered to ring for an ambulance.

With a jolt, Laverne remembered Roth's attacker and ran out into the yard to confront him. As confrontations go, it was something of an anticlimax. Trevor Snape was kneeling in the dirt, pale as a sow in the light from the kitchen door. Snape was naked, on his knees, dried mud smeared across his face and his emaciated

125

ribs. He was crawling about in crazed circles, jabbering. A sticky line of blood and dribble hung from his chin.

Laverne recognized Snape's face from the group photograph. The hair and the long chin were distinctive. The eyes that raised their gaze to Laverne were weak and unfocused, but brimming with defiant venom.

Laverne pressed a knee into Snape's back, and twisted his arms behind his back. Then he took the handcuffs from his jacket pocket, roughly snapping them shut over the choirmaster's narrow wrists. The prisoner, his face pressed into the dirt, mumbled incoherently.

'What was that?' snapped Laverne.

'I didn't do it.'

Laverne was angry. He could hear Roth groaning in the kitchen. For all he knew, she was bleeding to death in there. Harshly, he pulled the knifeman up by his hair. 'No . . . of course you didn't. I suppose it was one of the goats, was it?'

Laverne twisted Snape's face towards the light and was amazed. A transfiguration had taken place. The madness that had been visible moments ago had vanished, to be replaced by fear, despair and bewildered incomprehension. 'Please . . . I'm innocent,' slurred Snape. 'It wasn't me. It was someone in . . .'

The speech ended in a fit of wild snarling and shrieking as Snape, once again, wheeled about in the dirt like a dog chasing its own tail. Laverne had little sympathy for violent criminals, and no time at all for those who attempted to kill officers of the law. But faced with the sight of this scrawny, deranged man-beast, all his anger ebbed away and in its place, he felt an unexpected and entirely unwelcome surge of pity.

9

A WELL-REMEMBERED FACE

Savage accompanied Roth in the ambulance, while Laverne followed behind in his Rover P5. The victim was taken to hospital in Bridgwater, where she underwent an emergency operation. Roth remained in theatre for one-and-a-half hours. The two ashen police officers roamed the empty hospital corridors until five-fifteen, when they were informed that the patient's progress was 'satisfactory'.

The podgy, red-faced surgeon who came out to share this news was still wearing his green smock and Wellington boots. He opined that Roth had had a remarkable escape. She had lost a great deal of blood, but the knife had missed all of her vital organs.

Laverne and Savage ate a silent breakfast in the staff canteen, surrounded by nurses who were working the early shift. Afterwards, they drove back to Street, through dark and deserted country roads. On the way, Savage marvelled at Roth's extraordinary luck.

'Slightly more than luck, wouldn't you say?' asked Laverne, his face expressionless. 'Every other poor bugger gets dissected. Special Agent Roth escapes with a bloody flesh wound . . .'

After a few hours of excitable, unsatisfactory sleep, they showered, dressed and lunched in the hotel restaurant. There was a telegram waiting for Laverne at his table.

SOUNDS LIKE YOU DID IT AGAIN STOP YOU ARE A

When Laverne and Savage arrived at Wells Police Station, they were not unduly surprised to discover that Holebrook, with his usual sensitivity, had interviewed Snape in their absence.

'Thought it best to get him while he was hot ... unfortunately, all he's done so far is cry and bark like a dog. But you'll be pleased to know he's calmed down in the last few hours ... with the doctor's permission, we'll be talking to him again at three. And with any luck, the bugger'll be talking back to us.'

By three o'clock, a washed and clothed Trevor Snape reappeared in Interview Room One of Wells Police Station. Mowart and Holebrook asked the questions. Under the circumstances, Holebrook was showing extremely bad form by not asking Laverne to sit in on the interview. Laverne was an official guest of the constabulary, as well as the arresting officer. He would have been well within his rights to have kicked up a fuss. On the other hand, did he really want to spend hours, possibly days, in close proximity to a policeman for whom he felt no respect or affection? The answer was an emphatic 'no'. So he accepted the snub with good grace.

Snape had no solicitor and refused to be legally represented. Laverne and Savage watched the proceedings in black and white, on closed-circuit television in an adjacent room – the interview was being video taped. On the screen, Snape's face appeared so horribly white that it was almost luminous. There was no doubt in Laverne's mind that Snape had stabbed Roth. Perhaps, in spite of his unathletic appearance, he might also have wielded the weapon that had ended seven, possibly eight lives. (PC Underwood was still missing.) But watching the man, seeing him twitch and hang his head, Laverne felt another odd little tug of sympathy for him.

At six minutes past three, the grilling began. Holebrook activated the Neal Interview Recorder, supplying the time and the date. He named himself and Mowart as the officers conducting the interview. Lastly, he gave Snape's name and address, having forgotten to do this at the outset of the announcement. The effect of this blunder was to make Holebrook sound like an apologetic chat-show host, introducing a singularly unedifying guest.

From a technical point of view, Laverne knew that Holebrook had his work cut out for him. The biggest snag was the absence of a convincing murder weapon. Everyone realized that the butcher's knife that had been removed from Roth's back would have been incapable of creating the mayhem seen at the Martin house and 17 Pendragon Avenue. And there was absolutely no forensic evidence to link Snape, or anyone else for that matter, to the massacres at either address. All the police had was the butcher's knife, the handle of which bore Snape's fingerprints. So far, all they could hope to pin on him was the attempted murder of Angela Roth, a charge which any barrister with a brain cell could easily convert into a few years in a mental hospital. Naked men who bark like dogs are not generally judged to be responsible for their actions.

A young male constable came in, offering to fetch tea or coffee for Laverne and Savage. They gratefully accepted, and Savage reflected that maybe the police service was finally moving with the times. Once upon a time, only a WPC would have been allocated such a mundane task. But her optimism was short-lived. When the tea arrived, accompanied by a plate of rich tea biscuits, it was carried by a WPC.

The interview with Snape was not, actually, an interview at all. It was a monologue punctuated by the occasional dazed interruption from Holebrook. In police parlance, a suspect who confesses is said to 'cough'. Snape didn't so much cough as open his mouth and spew his entrails on to the table. His voice was mild, reticent, with a light West Country accent. He spoke in a halting, mechanical manner, sometimes lapsing into an inaudible mumble. Every so often, Holebrook was forced to ask him to speak up.

'On the night in question, I went to the Martin house and hid in the garden.'

'How'd you get there?'

'I went by bicycle.'

'The Martin girl didn't mention seeing a bicycle.'

'I left it out of sight, round the back of the house. I hid in the garden until Tess came home. I watched her through the kitchen window. When her back was turned, I slipped into the house and killed them all.'

'Say that again.'

'I said I killed them all.'

'What with? What did you kill them with?'

'A katana.'

'A what?'

'A traditional Japanese combat sword.'

'Could you spell that for us, Trevor?'

'K-a-t-a-n-a.'

'Where's this sword now?'

'I don't know. I lost it.'

'You lost it? When did you lose it? Where did you lose it?'

'The night before last, when I was running away from the Sweet house. I dropped it in a garden.'

'Where do . . . did the Sweets live?'

'17 Pendragon Avenue.'

'Why did you go there?'

'You know why.'

'Tell me anyway.'

'I went there to kill them. But not Gudrun. Never Gudrun. That was a mistake. I don't know how it happened.'

'Back to the sword, Trevor. Where did you get it from?'

'Antique shop.'

'What shop? Where?'

Snape chose not to reply.

'Right ... right. We'll come back to that, shall we? Let's talk about the Martin family.'

'I killed the father first.'

'Pardon me?'

'I said he was the first to go. Mr Martin.'

'Go on.'

'I took the top of his head off. Swiped it right off. Like it was a boiled egg. He didn't die, though. He still came at me, trying to fight. But he must have been feeling dizzy, 'cause he walked straight on to the blade. Then I disembowelled him. Think I cut off one of his arms, too. I might even have cut them both off. I don't remember.'

'All right, Trevor. Don't stop now.'

'The boy tried to hide under the piano. I yanked him up and laid him on the piano lid. I stabbed him with the sword and pinned him to it like he was a butterfly. The mother came in and saw what I was doing. So I killed her next.'

'How?'

'Knocked her head off. Swish. In one. Made a noise like a coconut when it hit the floor.'

A long silence. 'Anything else?'

'The baby.'

'Yes?'

'I killed the baby, didn't I?'

'You tell me.'

'I think so. I'm pretty sure the baby was last.'

'Tell us how you did it.'

'The sword was sharp. All it took was the tiniest little cut on the side of its neck. Cuts the jugular, you see. He bled to death in about two seconds.'

Laverne and Savage, watching this on the screen, saw Holebrook and Mowart exchange anxious glances. So far, Snape had fulfilled all their expectations. Most of the details he'd imparted were known only to CID personnel. Yet now they were dissatisfied, and not merely because Snape had mistaken a baby girl for a boy. 'So,' said Mowart. 'You slashed the baby's neck? You didn't do anything else to it?'

Snape thought for a moment. 'Yes . . . yes. Nearly forgot. When he was dead, I cut him in half.'

Laverne saw relief appear on Mowart's face. How odd, to be actually relieved when a suspect admits to carrying out such an atrocity. Yet it was an emotion that Laverne had felt himself, many times, under similar circumstances. For a CID officer, a voluntary confession that tallies with the known facts is a result. It signifies kudos, a commendation, possible promotion. It means you were right. It means you can get drunk, or even go home.

'Tess Martin says you weren't in the room when she entered.'

'How would she know? She shut her eyes.'

'She saw what had happened to her family. Her eyes were open then.'

'Then she shut them. I was standing behind the door. She didn't see me. Mainly because her eyes were closed.'

For the next hour, the interview continued in this breezy vein. John Macmillan oozed in to congratulate Laverne, while simultaneously giving the impression that he, the Chief Constable, was the true hero of the hour. He watched the interview for a few minutes, was suitably delighted by Snape's co-operation, and promised Laverne a crate of champagne. Laverne coolly suggested that Macmillan donate the money he was willing to squander on champagne to the police benevolent fund. Vaguely aware that he was being insulted, and having impregnated the room with the disgusting smell of his cologne, Macmillan left.

When he'd furnished the police with details of the Martin murder, Snape moved on to the Sweets, describing their execution with the same matter-of-fact attention to detail. Snape claimed to have been in the Sweet house, hiding behind the sofa, while the family were in conversation with Roth and Savage. To verify this, he recounted snatches of dialogue that could have only been known to someone present in the house, and which would later be matched with Savage's tape recording of the meeting. 'I remember one of the women asking Mr Sweet if he saw anything suspicious on his way back from Tess's house. And he said he nearly ran over a dog...'

This seemed conclusive. For good measure, Snape even provided Holebrook with a passable modus operandi. 'They were my girls. Tess, and Gudrun and Gaby. I wanted to keep them together. I wanted to look after them. When I heard that Gaby was leaving the choir, I got scared. So I thought, if I could get rid of their families, it'd be easier to bring them to my house. And look after them myself.'

By now, Holebrook and Mowart were almost euphoric. 'Bit greedy, that, Trevor,' joked Mowart. 'Three girls in that little flat of yours? Where were you planning on putting 'em all?'

Snape failed to see any humour in the situation. In that same flat, robotic tone, he said, 'They were my girls. I wanted to look after them. That's all I've got to say.'

With this, Snape turned his head and looked directly into the camera in the corner of the room, creating the impression that his final statement of the afternoon was for the exclusive benefit of Savage and Laverne. Laverne experienced a sick jolt of surprise. The face that peered at him out of the TV screen was familiar, but it did not belong to Trevor Snape. Someone else was sitting where Snape had been sitting seconds before. At that moment Laverne knew, beyond a shadow of doubt, that despite his assault on Roth and his intimate knowledge of the local murders, the man in police custody was not the Butcher of Glastonbury.

While Mowart and Holebrook congratulated each other on their sound judgement and Snape was returned to his cell, Savage and

133

Laverne went for a walk on Glastonbury Tor. The trip was Savage's idea. 'Seems a shame not to visit the sights, as we're here.'

However, by the time Laverne had driven to the stile on Wellhouse Lane that marked the southern route to the Tor, there was precious little to see. The hill and the surrounding fields were wreathed in white mist. It was as if the clouds themselves had descended.

'No point getting out of the car,' declared Laverne sourly. But Savage disagreed, and he felt obliged to escort her.

They crossed a field and reached a second stile, where a sign informed them that the tower on the hill was all that remained of St Michael's church, and that the Tor had been the scene of the execution of Richard Whiting, the last Abbot of Glastonbury.

'Guess how old he was when they killed him,' said Savage, who had been reading a guide book in her hotel room.

'Twenty-two?' ventured Laverne facetiously.

'Eighty,' said Savage. 'Henry the Eighth had an eighty-year-old man hanged, drawn and quartered.'

'What? I thought this was meant to be a holy place,' said Laverne.

They began their ascent. A narrow path, with concrete steps, zig-zagged all the way to the summit. The mist reduced visibility to about six or seven feet. The tower of St Michael's, normally manifest for miles around, was obscured by the drifting murk. Yet they could feel the tower's dark presence, five hundred feet above them.

Half-way up, Laverne had to stop to catch his breath.

'That'll teach you to start smoking again,' commented Savage.

'Sod off.'

'Snape's innocent,' she added quietly.

Laverne nodded, taking deep breaths.

'Did you notice the way he was talking?' she continued. 'Like an actor in an amateur dramatics production who has to concentrate to remember his lines. Or someone who's been hypnotized. It seemed completely artificial.'

Laverne agreed. 'And all that nonsense about the sword. Even if it exists, which I personally doubt, those weapons are bloody heavy. I'd struggle lifting one and I'm twice his size. You saw him . . . he's not a strong bloke. Even if he used to be strong, we've been told he's now got rheumatoid arthritis. You can't swing a sword if your joints are knackered. I mean, I've no doubt he'll go down for this. They've got enough to convict him. You saw Holebrook. He was almost wetting his pants. But no. It's all wrong, Lyn. Snape's not the one.'

They resumed their climb, and the mist deepened, dampening their hair and clothes. The silence was ominous and absolute. The fourteenth century tower came into view, first as a dark-grey shadow, then as a rectangular stone edifice, stark, impressive and unwelcoming. An arched doorway cut through the heart of the tower from east to west. Ruined statues and faded carvings clung to its castellated walls.

Laverne and Savage were alone on the hill.

A concrete path stretched from the tower's eastern door. The path ended in a circular concrete slab, crowned by a compass rose that pointed the way to all the major landmarks in the country.

'St Michael's Mount is thattaway,' said Savage idly, pointing south-west.

Laverne, lost in his own dark thoughts, failed to answer her. She nudged him gently. 'So what do we do about Snape?'

'I don't know about you, but I'm not prepared to see an innocent man go to jail. I'm going after the real murderer.'

They entered the tower. There were puddles on its floor and its stone benches. Looking up, they saw a square of pale sky. The roof of the tower had gone, exposing it to the mercy of the elements.

'You know who the real murderer is, then?' asked Savage.

He coughed to clear his throat. 'I don't *know* anything. But this afternoon, while they were grilling Snape ... I saw something on the VTR monitor. I was listening to Snape talk, but I saw Major Blackmore sitting there.' He glared back at her, anticipating scorn. 'Not that I expect you to believe me.'

Savage stared at the damp oozing down the wall in front of her. 'No,' she said. 'I believe you.'

Laverne hadn't expected this. He suddenly felt exhilarated. 'You do?'

Savage had known Laverne a long time. She respected him, mainly because he had always respected her. She had no idea how his mind worked. All she was sure of was that it *did* work. Time and time again, he had taken her aback with his errant disregard for procedure, only to astound her further by leading her straight to a murderer's door.

'I *do* believe you,' she reiterated. 'But I don't know what it means, or what the hell we're supposed to do about it.' After a pause, she turned to him excitedly. 'Just a minute ... is it likely to have been caught on video?'

'No,' he said, shaking his head. 'I very much doubt that. These things don't work that way.'

'What things?'

'I didn't really see Blackmore with my eyes. I saw him with this.' He punched his chest over his heart. 'Not the sort of thing you can photograph.'

She gave Laverne a searching look. This was by far the most revealing thing she had ever heard him say. Laverne, seemingly oblivious to her gaze, took a fruit lozenge from his pocket, ripped off the wrapping and slipped the sweet into his mouth. Automatically, Savage held out her hand. Laverne looked sheepish. 'Sorry. It was my last one.'

'Charming.' She shivered. 'But no, getting back to the point, I don't find it hard to believe what you're saying. Nothing you do surprises me. The night before last ... did I tell you I saw you in my hotel room?'

She saw him stiffen. He tugged at his gloves, affecting nonchalance. 'That so?'

'Yes. You weren't there, of course. Not really. But I saw you. You felt and looked as real as you look now.'

This appeared to alarm him. 'Felt? What d'you mean? I didn't touch you, did I?'

'No ... I mean you felt real in here.' She tapped herself on the breast, deliberately copying his own gesture. His only response was a low murmur of disquiet.

Laverne was clearly uncomfortable. But Savage, having gained so much ground, was disinclined to retreat to the trenches. 'It wasn't the first time that I've seen you where you shouldn't be, either. I also saw you the Christmas before last. You were in my house, that time. You didn't see me, but I saw you, all right. Even tried to catch you, but you got away. Scared me half to death.'

He respected her. This time, there were to be no denials. When he turned to look down at her, his eyes were tender, his face full of infinite sadness. 'The other night ... weren't scared then, were you?'

'No. Not in the least.'

'Good. I'm glad about that.'

'Well? Are you going to tell me what it all means?'

He patted her softly on the hand. 'Soon. I promise. I'll tell you everything soon.'

They both knew that she would hold him to his word. Feeling a gush of warmth for him, she linked his arm. 'OK. And what are we going to do about your prime suspect?'

He grimaced. 'Don't call him that. Please. We're not on television.' He flapped his arms, feeling the cold. 'You're fond of research, aren't you? Well, then. We're going to research Blackmore, find out everything there is to know about him, find out why he's so obsessed with his granddaughter and why . . .'

Laverne swallowed his words. Two dark figures were approaching. As they drew closer, he saw that they were cheerful young men with dreadlocks, sharing an ostentatiously large joint.

'Hey! That's against the law, that is,' he commented.

One of the youths beamed, revealing unfeasibly white teeth. Laverne and Savage moved away from the tower and commenced their descent. 'But even if you're right,' protested Savage, 'neither of us has a clue how Blackmore did it.'

'True.'

'We have absolutely no evidence.'

Laverne laughed and touched her shoulder affectionately. 'That's never bothered me before . . .'

10

INCIDENT ON THE PICCADILLY LINE

Geraint John smiled his mail order catalogue smile and raised a full beer glass to Laverne. 'To North Yorkshire's finest export. You've done us proud, Vernon.'

They were dining in The Boatman, a waterside restaurant that was renowned for its spectacular view of the Ouse and, in periods of drought, for the foul and fishy smells that drifted through its windows. Today, those windows were firmly bolted. Steady rain sliced the surface of the dark grey river. A dingy motor boat chugged past. In its wake, the craft left a trail like a guilty secret: yellow and brown scum dredged from the river's sick heart.

The Boatman's culinary reputation rested on its seafood, transported daily from Grimsby and Hull, but today, Laverne and Geraint John were throwing caution to the winds and sampling sirloin steak, allegedly flown in from Argentina.

'Of course, it'll still be contaminated,' Geraint had commented. 'Like everything else we eat in this factory-farmed fucker of a world. In fact, the Argentinians have probably poisoned it on purpose to pay us back for the Falklands.'

It was when the waiter had ushered in the main course that Geraint had toasted his friend's latest success. This compelled Laverne, who felt that he was being fed and watered under false pretences, to set the record straight. 'I've done no one proud, Geraint. Least of all the man who's been charged with the murders.'

With his mouth crammed full of beef, the Deputy Chief Constable demanded to know what Laverne was talking about. Laverne told him.

'Have you shared your suspicions with DCI Holebrook?'

'No. It would have been a waste of time.'

'Why?'

'Holebrook's an idiot.'

'Oh, very fair. A very mature assessment.' Geraint sighed. 'Well, we'll know soon enough whether he's an idiot or not. Snape's inside. He can't exactly kill from a prison cell, can he? So if the murders don't stop, we'll know Holebrook's got the wrong man. And so will he.'

'And what if the murderer doesn't kill again? What if he doesn't *need* to kill again? Serial killers can sometimes leave years and years between their crimes. We just leave Snape to rot, do we? I joined the police force to protect the innocent. Not to put them behind bars while the guilty roam free.'

'Innocent? Tripe and bollocks! Snape isn't innocent. He stabbed our American friend, didn't he? Could have killed her. Indirectly, that bastard cost me a small fortune in flowers and Belgian bloody chocolates.'

Laverne stood his ground. 'Snape was manipulated. He was offered to us like a sacrificial lamb. I'm convinced of it.'

'And you think this Major's behind it?'

'He's definitely involved. That's all I'm prepared to say at this stage.'

Geraint, shaking his head, dabbed at his chin with a napkin.

'You don't believe me?'

'Vernon, I don't even know what you're talking about. You were there when that bastard stuck a knife in her. You saw it happen.'

'No. I didn't see the stabbing. I saw a knife sticking out of Angela's back. Then I saw Snape a few yards away, crawling round in the muck.'

140

'Exactly. You caught him red-handed and he confessed. The end. Now shut up and eat your fucking dinner . . .'

'Geraint, I'm serious about this. I'd like your permission to carry on the investigation.'

'I'm serious, too. Fuck off, Vernon. It's not our problem. We're the North Yorkshire Police. Funnily enough, we're called that because we're based in *North Yorkshire*. This case is being handled by Avon and Somerset, who, mad as it may seem, work in the land of cider, tractors and educational sub-normality.

'It's a simple question of resources. The yokels down in Wells and Bridgwater have got to keep to a tight budget and so have we. While you were in Glastonbury, they were paying us for the privilege of your company. Paying your expenses and, in effect, paying your wages. Which was fair enough, seeing as we . . . you . . . were doing them a favour. Now, just from the point of simple economics, surely you see that it'd make no fucking sense for us to pay you to go there and help 'em out.

'At the moment, their Chief Constable thinks the sun shines out of your anus horribilis. OK. What if you were to turn up on his doorstep to tell him that he and all his good little police boys and girls are guilty of a king-sized cock-up? Do you think he'd thank you for it? Would he hell. He'd think you were a fucking killjoy and frankly, I wouldn't blame him.'

Laverne stared at the Deputy Chief Constable. Geraint stared stolidly back. As far as withering looks were concerned, the two men were more than a match for each other. Soon tiring of the game, Geraint downed his beer and ordered two more. 'Besides, I need you here. I've got a shortage of good officers as it is. Be happy for once in your life. Everyone's pleased with you.'

'Especially the real murderer.'

'It's not our problem.'

'It's *my* problem. It's been my problem since I agreed to go to Glastonbury.'

'Vernon, even if I said yes, Neville Wood'd say no. You know he's never liked you.'

Observing Laverne's unbelievably sulky face, Geraint suddenly threw back his head and laughed. 'Oh, give over. If you want to go to Glastonbury, you know very well you can go there any time you like. What do you need my permission for, eh? A man of your talents?'

Laverne pretended not to know what the Deputy Chief Constable was talking about. When he glanced up, Geraint winked slyly, like a music hall comedian directing a joke at the fat lady on the front row. Geraint was the only officer on the force who knew Laverne's secret.

Angela Roth recuperated from her injury in the Mary Piper Hospital for the Victims of Violent Assault. As hospitals go, this one was rather beautiful, an Edwardian mini-mansion in the heart of London's Bloomsbury. With its high white gables and its pastel pink walls, Savage thought Mary Piper's looked more like a gigantic doll's house than an establishment where the casualties of explosions, shootings and stabbings were cared for.

Officially, Savage was in London as an ambassador for the North Yorkshire Police, checking on Roth's recovery. In reality, she had spent most of the day in the British Library, following up a lead on Major Blackmore.

She had managed to uncover some useful information, and it was with a light heart and a keen sense of achievement that she took the elevator to the hospital's third floor. In her right hand, she carried a bag of fruit and groceries. In her left, a bunch of tulips.

Roth was sitting in an armchair, a listless expression on her face as she watched a low-budget cookery show on a small colour TV. She smiled wearily at the sight of her visitor. Instantly, Savage saw that her friend was still far from well. Her lips were tinged with blue, her eyes lustreless.

When Roth spoke, she sounded hoarse and exhausted. 'Four lousy channels. What do housewives do in the day, here?'

Savage kissed Roth's cheek and sat down on the bed. 'Housewives don't have time to watch television. And it's lovely to see you.'

Roth smiled, held Savage's fingers and squeezed them. 'Yeah. Same goes for me.'

The room was alive with scent and colour. A riot of crimson hibiscus blossom drifted in water on a table beside the bed. On the opposite side of the bed stood a locker supporting a jug of orange juice and a bunch of jasmine in a cheap vase. Savage leaned over to inhale their melancholy sweetness.

'These are a bit exotic, aren't they? Where did they come from?'

'John Macmillan's greenhouse. He's keen. Keeps tropical and sub-tropical plants.' She laughed drily. 'The Chief Constable of Somerset seems kind of embarrassed about the fact that I got hurt doing his dirty work for him.'

'Good. Anyway, you're looking better. How are you feeling?'

'Not great. A bit woozy. And I'll never wear a bikini again. Nothing wrong with me, really. They're just being cautious. Should be out of here in a couple of days.'

'That's great. Really.' Savage took two home-made cards out of her bag. 'From the children.'

One of the cards depicted a smiling face and the words 'GET WELL ANGELA'. The other, from Savage's youngest daughter, showed a rabbit that, for reasons unknown, appeared to be performing a jig on a mountain of steaming excrement. Roth made appreciative noises and passed the cards back to Savage, who added them to a row that were hanging on a length of string above the bed.

'Any news on Snape?'

'He's been moved to Wakefield Prison in Yorkshire. High security.'

'When's the trial going to be?'

'Don't know. Probably not for some time.'

'You don't suppose they got the wrong guy?'

Roth's question threw Savage on her guard. Laverne had pledged her to secrecy about Blackmore and her research at the British Library. Nor did she want to hinder Roth's convalescence by fuelling any doubts she may have nursed about the Glastonbury case. It was important that Roth should concentrate all her energies on getting well again.

Savage helped herself to a grape, bit through its skin and slowly drew the pulp into her mouth. 'I wouldn't waste your time worrying about Snape. He's no saint. And you've got the stitches to prove it.'

'Guess so.' Roth poured some orange juice into a glass, sipped it, pulled a face and pushed the glass away. 'You know, Lyn, I'd kill for a cigarette.'

'Now, that *would* be silly, wouldn't it?' she said, in that disapproving schoolma'am tone that her husband and Laverne frequently mocked, and that for years she had been struggling, unsuccessfully, to eradicate from her repertoire of intonations.

Roth, already tired by the visit, leant back in her chair and stared at the ceiling. 'I guess so.' Savage let Roth rest for a few moments and closed her eyes, savouring the stillness of the room. A car horn honked angrily in the street below.

A young nurse came in to record Roth's temperature and blood pressure. When she'd left, Roth spoke again. 'Any news of the missing bobby?'

Savage shook her head regretfully. When Snape had been questioned further, he had revealed no knowledge of PC Underwood. The police believed him. An extensive search of the area had provided no clue to his whereabouts.

Roth asked for some grapes. Savage passed her the whole bag. 'I'm still waiting for someone to take a statement from me,' mused Roth. 'Have they questioned you yet?'

Savage shrugged. 'They're not likely to. When they turned up at Lammas Farm, they found a victim and a crazed knifeman. A day later, the knifeman confessed to several murders. Somerset are more than happy with the way things have gone. What do they need to talk to us for?'

Roth ejected a stream of inventive obscenities, the gist of her invective being that the legal system in Great Britain was feeble and amateurish. Savage smiled cynically. 'Perhaps you're right. But at least we don't execute innocent people. Unlike you lot. We just put them in prison for life.'

Roth failed to see anything amusing in this remark. 'So no one's going to mention that fireball we all saw. Right?'

Carefully, Savage said, 'Possibly not.'

'Looked like ball lightning to me. That thing came within a monkey's spit of me, Lyn. I think I saw something inside it. A face, just staring at me. Not the kind of face you'd like to think about when you're alone. Now, I wouldn't swear to this or anything – my memory's kind of hazy. But it looked an awful lot like that old Major . . .'

Savage made no comment, merely promised to pass Roth's observations on to Laverne. Roth yawned ostentatiously and Savage, taking the hint, reached for her coat. 'I'd better start walking.'

'Where are you headed?'

'King's Cross.'

'You don't need to walk. Russell Square subway is just round the corner . . .'

Savage, deeply preoccupied, left the hospital at five-forty and walked the length of two streets to Russell Square. It was the rush hour, and the lift down to the Piccadilly line was crammed with tired, irritable commuters. When the lift doors opened, she was embraced by the uniquely vibrant atmosphere of the London Underground.

It was an odd sensation, at once stimulating and draining, as if the desires, dreams and disappointments of a century of travellers had become ingrained in the subterranean tunnels.

As she reached the eastbound platform, a train was just leaving. Its carriages were monstrously overcrowded, with resentful red faces squashed up against their windows. A man with an umbrella rushed on to the platform and slammed an accusing fist into the side of the train as it passed, willing it to stop.

She felt the vibration of the next train before she heard it. Moving away from the tunnel, she glanced back and saw two blinking eyes winding closer through the gloom. As the engine snaked into the station, a thin haze of light seemed to dance around the driver's cabin. Then, rumbling and clattering, the train whisked alongside the platform and slowly pulled to a halt. The people waiting on the platform surged forward, forcing the guard to broadcast a world-weary command over his intercom. 'Let the passengers off the train first, please . . .'

Savage found a seat in a half-empty carriage at the rear of the train. She hugged her bag and briefcase close as other passengers piled in to occupy seats on either side of her. As the train filled up, she became aware of an unlovely odour: like the breath of a pig that has been eating onions. This, she knew, was the distinctive aroma of too many people huddled together in a confined space.

She surveyed the faces of her fellow travellers, saw that they looked uniformly cold and despondent. She tried to evoke sympathy for all these strangers by playing a favourite game. She imagined them all as babies, small and vulnerable, unsullied by the world and its disappointments. This time, however, all she could picture was a train-full of cold, despondent adults wearing nappies.

The train stopped at King's Cross. Savage joined a solid stream of halting, hobbling bodies that oozed out on to the platform. She followed the signs for British Rail. Near the escalators, a young man was sitting cross-legged on the floor with his back to the grim tiled

146

wall. He held a cardboard sign that read 'HOMELESS AND HUNGRY'. Savage started to reach for her bag, then thought to look at the supplicant's face.

His eyes, set in a thin, wasted face, literally blazed with malice. Unsettled, she averted her gaze and moved on. As she merged with the throng of bodies waiting to mount the escalator, she heard a voice behind her murmur, 'Rich bitch,' and was glad that she'd hung on to her small change.

At the exit, she fumbled in her purse for her ticket, and was poised to use it when she noticed a well-built elderly man with a domed head passing through the barrier to her right. After an initial moment of incredulity, she realized that she was looking at Major Aden Blackmore. She stood still, stunned, her ticket hovering over the slot in the barrier. A man behind her griped impatiently and she stepped aside to let him pass, her eyes still fixed on Blackmore.

The Major was clad in dark trousers and an immaculate white short-sleeved shirt that displayed his brutishly thick forearms. Unaware of her attention, he took the escalator downwards and sank into the earth. Savage wavered for a few seconds, unsure what to do next. She was drained in the way that only London tires people: her head ached, and she longed for sleep and solitude. She had set her heart on catching the next train home.

Yet the man whose past she had been investigating only hours before, the man that Laverne was so suspicious of, had just walked past her. How could that be so? Ignoring the statistical improbability of such an encounter, what was Blackmore doing in London anyway? This, after all, was the man that Holebrook and Mowart had eliminated from their inquiries on the grounds of his chronic agoraphobia. Savage smirked. How many agoraphobics, she wondered, could bring themselves to travel alone on the London Underground at peak-time?

Yet not only had Blackmore seemed unperturbed; he had also looked as cool and relaxed as an elderly playboy on the deck of a yacht. No. This was a gift from heaven. Savage had no choice. She simply had to follow him.

Resolved, she rushed to the moving staircase and began to descend. Below, she could see the crown of Blackmore's skull. He was half-way to the bottom, relaxed and unhurried, content to ride at the escalator's pace. A cloud of blue smoke rose from his shoulders and drifted upwards. Savage thought she was hallucinating until a second cloud followed the first. She was appalled. Smoking was forbidden on the underground. Yet Blackmore rode down unchallenged, his head tilted at an imperious angle.

At the foot of the stairs, she lost sight of him. For a second she hesitated, and a procession of ruthless commuters crashed into her, knocking her out of the way. Rule number one for all visitors to London: never stand still during rush hour. Unless, of course, you enjoy being trampled underfoot.

Savage steadied herself and tried to think. Where could Blackmore possibly be going? North or south? Towards the City or away from it? The answer seemed obvious. Towards the City. She stepped on to the southbound platform.

She eased her way through the waiting crowd, looking for Blackmore. Then she saw him, his back to the track, nonchalantly reading a film poster. Another cloud of smoke wafted up from him. How infantile. Did he imagine that he was being discreet? He glanced in her direction and she stepped back, wary of being recognized, and took shelter behind a group of raucous French schoolchildren.

The monitor said the next train was destined for Rayners Lane, and would arrive in two minutes. Savage took a small bottle of mineral water from her bag, opened it and swallowed a few mouthfuls. The water was warm, but her dry throat received it gratefully. As she replaced the lid on the bottle, she looked up and found that Blackmore was standing next to her, his eyes slowly absorbing every detail of her appearance. The expression on his face could only be described as murderous.

Then he said, 'What do you think you're looking at?' She almost laughed. It was the kind of remark one expects from adolescent drunks, not retired army officers.

Savage was about to reply that she was looking at the contemptible sight of a grown man smoking at the very station where, not so long ago, lives had been lost in a fire caused by a discarded cigarette. Then she realized that the fumes she had seen were not emanating from Blackmore's mouth or nostrils, but from his entire body.

Before she'd recovered from the shock, the Major reached out, grabbed her by the shoulders and lifted her into the air as if she weighed no more than an infant. Both her bags tumbled to the floor. For a moment she hung in his grasp, his pale, pitiless face filling her vision. Then he hurled her at the wall. She hit her head and fell heavily.

She blacked out for ten seconds. When she came to, there was a harsh metallic taste in her mouth. Blood. She vaguely remembered that she had a CS spray in her bag. It was imperative that she reach it. But Blackmore was already standing over her, and the bag was behind him, its contents strewn over the platform. She heard a woman's voice, urgently saying, '*Allez! Allez!*' The French children were being shepherded away, out of danger. But many people remained. They kept their distance, silently watching, hoping not to get involved.

'I'm a police officer,' she slurred, addressing anyone who might be prepared to listen. Her mouth felt half-frozen, as if she'd been injected with Novocaine. 'Could I have some assistance?'

Blackmore stooped down, thrust his hands under her armpits and again launched her into space. It was clear to Savage that she had to act, and act fast. As he lifted her she grabbed his shirt with both hands, drew back her head and butted him in the face. For a small woman, not given to violence, it was a tremendously brave and powerful act. Leaning back to observe the damage, Savage saw that the bridge of her assailant's nose had been flattened. It had been a blow that would have floored any normal man. But Blackmore, despite the blood that was gushing out of his nostrils on to his white linen shirt, merely sneered and tossed Savage into the air.

This time, her fall was broken by a middle-aged clerk who had been attempting to hide behind the *Evening Standard*. He rolled to the ground, grunting, with Savage on top of him. Blackmore advanced and kicked the City gent out of the way. He seized Savage and, once again, tried to lift her. She fought frantically, knocking away Blackmore's arms and yelling at the top of her voice.

'For God's sake! Somebody help me!'

Those nearby responded to her request by backing away. Blackmore's hands found Savage's throat and squeezed. He was dishearteningly strong. She now recognized, her stomach lurching with fear, that he had not been merely attempting to maim her. He intended to kill her. As his grip on her windpipe tightened, she started to choke. The blood from his broken nose poured into her eyes, blinding her. In fear and desperation, she released her grip on his arms and allowed her fingers to climb his face. She found his eyes and dug in her nails. Instantly, he snatched back his head, simultaneously removing his fingers from her neck.

At first, Savage imagined that Blackmore had been deterred by her attempt to gouge out his eyes. The look of dreamy pleasure on his face forced her to reconsider this theory. The old man's head was cocked on one side, as if he was listening to a favourite melody. Savage, too, could hear the murmur and drone of a metallic voice.

A train was nearing the station and the noise of its approach had given Blackmore an idea. Savage read his mind, panicked and tried to scrabble away. Blackmore seized her by one foot and started to pull. She turned over, arched her back and kicked his hand away.

The heels of her shoes slammed into his arms, wrists and face. Apparently indifferent to pain, he braved the barrage until he had a firm grip on each of her ankles. Then, slowly, his back to the rails, he started to drag her towards the edge of the platform.

She now knew that Blackmore meant to destroy them both. She clawed at the concrete floor in a desperate bid to anchor herself. Blackmore tugged again and she slid six inches closer to the brink. The drone of the oncoming train became an intimidating clamour, punctuated by shrill stabs of static. Savage was dimly conscious of blurred faces and murmurs of concern from onlookers, but no one intervened. She opened her mouth and screamed, half petrified, half incensed. This was not supposed to happen. She was not ready to die.

Blackmore stood on the platform's edge and leant back, his face suddenly vacant, an unthinking, unfeeling orb of pallid, hanging flesh. Savage felt herself slipping. She swivelled her head, desperate to catch the eye of someone, anyone, who might be prepared to help her.

There was a commotion to her left. First she heard a shout. Then, above the heads of the crowd, she saw a man approaching. He was about fifty, with thin grey hair and a white moustache. It was Chief Superintendent Laverne, rudely shoving people out of the way as he rushed towards her. Her heart sang with hope. Laverne, Laverne. Everything was going to be all right.

At that moment, the train swung out of the tunnel, wheels grinding and sparking as the driver applied his brakes. The diesel whine resounded through the station. Savage screamed Laverne's name.

She looked at Blackmore, saw him re-secure his hold on her legs and tense, ready to yank her over the edge. Death was now three seconds away. Laverne stepped in between Savage and Blackmore, and slapped away the Major's hands. Blinking with surprise, Blackmore fell backwards into the pit. As soon as he hit the track, the train thundered over him. Instantly, blood exploded through the station, spattering the driver's cabin, the tunnel walls, the platform and the clothes of waiting passengers.

Laverne helped Savage to her feet and held her closer than he'd ever held her. She inhaled his comforting smell. She sobbed with relief, and he spoke softly to her and guided her to a seat. Soon, further down the track, at Covent Garden, Knightsbridge, Green Park and Hammersmith, passengers would groan in frustration as a voice announced over the tannoy that all southbound trains would be 'subject to delay. This is due to an incident on the line . . .'

Savage was about to ask Laverne how and why he was there when she looked up and saw that he was not, in fact, there at all. Not beside her, not on the platform. Nowhere. She heard raised voices. The transport police were on their way, marching towards her from the direction of the exit, shouting for everyone to remain calm and wait on the platform. But where was Laverne? In York, probably, while here in London Detective Inspector Savage accepted paper tissues and solicitude from kindly strangers. The same strangers who, moments before, would have stood by and watched as the wheels of a train sliced her in two.

11

THE BLACK GODDESS

Wakefield's high security prison is situated on the outskirts of the city. Trains pulling into Wakefield from the north pass, on the left, the towers of St John's church, the town hall and the cathedral. To the right, almost sensed before it is seen, lies the prison, a dark, skulking presence in an otherwise unremarkable city.

Laverne had visited this decaying fortress once before, years ago, when interviewing Bomford, the infamous Bolton Strangler. He remembered the building's interior as being squalid and depressing, even by prison standards. This morning, as he arrived for an early meeting with Trevor Snape, he saw that his memory had not deceived him. The prison stank of violence, misery and sweat.

The warder that led Laverne to Snape owned a stomach of gargantuan proportions, and, like others of his calling, presumed that a natural affinity existed between himself and the police. Laverne had encountered the same automatic camaraderie from fire-fighters, paramedics and soldiers, none of whom he bore a grudge. But there was something about prison officers and the extent of their powers over their caged charges that had always made him uneasy. It was a curious aversion, because Laverne had little time for criminals, either.

'He's been as good as gold,' Laverne's escort was saying. His name was Vic. ('Next to the governor, I suppose you could say I'm in charge.') 'Hard to believe he killed all those people. A lot of fellas in this place'd love to get their hands on him.'

Laverne made a 'hmm' noise in the back of his throat, which was meant to imply 'Is that so?' but came out sounding like 'Sod off'. They came to a reinforced steel door, which a smiling guard deftly opened, before guiding them to another door at the end of the passage. Vic rapped on a grilled window. A third warder, jangling keys, popped his head into the passage.

A few jokes were exchanged, and Laverne was admitted to a sparsely-furnished room that stank of disinfectant. Warder number three seated himself by the door and assumed an air of disinterest. The other two men waited outside. Snape was sitting at a long table, his starved face tinged with green by the harsh strip lighting.

Laverne took a chair opposite him. 'Remember me?'

Nervously, Snape shook his head. Laverne noticed that he had a large swelling over his left eye.

'I was at Lammas Farm on the night that Angela Roth was stabbed. That was when we met.'

A look of terror appeared on Snape's face. He seemed to shrink in his seat.

Laverne persisted. 'Don't you recognize me?'

He could hear the low voices of the guards in the passage, as they discussed beer, women and football. This mingled with a rapid tapping, which Laverne identified as the sound of Snape's teeth knocking together. The prisoner was shaking violently.

'Hey. Steady on, now,' said Laverne. Without thinking, he took off his jacket and moved to place it over Snape's shoulders. In seconds, the prison officer had bounded to his side. He was a youngish man with lank, bleached hair. 'I wouldn't advise that, sir,' he said, grasping a sleeve of the jacket. 'He might be sick on it.'

Laverne tugged at the sleeve. 'It's my jacket. I'll take the risk.'

'In that case, I'm afraid I'll have to search it.'

Patiently, Laverne explained that he had already been searched at the gate. The guard checked his pockets anyway, and handed the jacket back to Laverne, who draped it over Snape's shoulders. Snape, annoyingly enough, gave the jacket back to Laverne.

'Thanks. But I'm all right.'

'You don't look it,' said Laverne.

'I was frightened, that's all. Thought you might have been someone else.'

'Like who?'

Snape shook his head vigorously. Laverne replaced his jacket and formally introduced himself, outlining his role in the Glastonbury investigation and revealing the purpose of his visit. 'I believe you're still refusing legal representation.'

'The Lord Jesus represents me.'

'Not in court, he doesn't.' Snape lowered his eyes. 'It might interest you to know, Trevor, that a number of people, myself included, aren't happy with the case that's being prepared against you.'

Snape raised his long face and marvelled at Laverne. 'Really? You're not joking, are you?'

'No. I'm quite serious. One of those people is Angela Roth, the woman who was stabbed. And I, for one, would be prepared to testify to my doubts when your case comes to trial.'

Once again, Snape expressed his incredulity. Laverne reassured him. 'But you know, Trevor, there's one thing about that night that's been plaguing me. Something you said. You told me it wasn't you that stabbed Officer Roth.'

'No. That's correct. It really wasn't.'

'Yet you told DCI Holebrook a very different story.'

'No. I didn't tell him anything. That was someone else. That wasn't me talking.'

'I'm not with you.'

'It wasn't me that confessed. It was the thing inside me. It forced its way into me, the night before I turned up at the farm.'

Laverne thought he heard a tut of disdain from the guard standing behind him. 'How? How did it get inside you?'

'I was kneeling by my bed, saying my prayers, when I heard a knock at the door. I went downstairs and opened the door, and who should I see but my mother?'

'Your mother?'

'It looked just like her. She asked if she could come in. Of course, I had to let her. She was my mother.'

'But Trevor, isn't your mother dead?'

'Oh, yes. But she's still my mother.'

'So you let her in?'

Snape nodded. 'But when she'd followed me up the stairs, I realized I'd made a dreadful mistake. The room went icy cold, and when I looked round it wasn't her.'

'You mean she looked like someone else?'

'No. I mean she *felt* like someone else. Do you understand me? My mother was a gentle person. This thing may have looked like her, but inside it was evil. Evil.'

'So what did you do?'

'What would anyone do? I told it to go away, and it disappeared. Then I got into bed and it came back to lie on top of me. I couldn't move. It lay on top of me and stared at me. I could even smell its breath. Terrible. It wasn't anything like my mother.'

'What then?'

'I prayed and prayed for it to go away, but it didn't seem to fear God. When I spoke the name of the Lord, it actually laughed. That frightened me, I must say. The more I prayed, the more it laughed. It pressed its face against mine and I lay there for hours, trying to fight it. I couldn't move, I couldn't even cry out. It overpowered me, then forced its way inside me.'

'Inside your head, you mean?'

'Not just my head. My entire body. I couldn't fight it, you see. It was far too strong.'

156

'Is he inside you now?'

'Not a "he", an "it". And no. As soon as it had made its confession, it left me.'

'Ah. It could speak, could it?'

'It used my voice, yes. It used all of me. I was powerless against it. So much anger and hatred. But, thank God, I'm free of it now.'

'So this thing was sharing your body?'

'No. Oh, no. I'm sorry . . . I'm not explaining myself very well. I wasn't in my body at the same time as the demon. When it came in, it threw me out.'

'Pardon me?'

'It threw my spirit out, then used me for its own ends. I had to follow myself around while it committed blasphemous acts with my own body.' Snape sighed hopelessly. 'Just listen to me. Isn't this the kind of thing that schizophrenics say? No jury would believe a single word I've said.'

Laverne leant back in his chair, inspected the ceiling. Then he looked Snape directly in the eyes and nodded. 'Try not to worry about that for now. Let's take things a step at a time. This thing inside you . . . did it use your body to kill the Martin family or Gudrun Sweet and her parents?'

'No. All that happened before it took me over.'

'You're sure?'

'Of course. It was lying. It was a demon. Demons don't tell the truth.'

'OK. Now, Trevor, think carefully. This, er, demon . . . did it look like anyone? Anyone you know or might have seen somewhere?'

'Apart from my mum, you mean? Well, yes, as a matter of fact, it did remind me of somebody. Years ago, I worked on the post at Christmas. One day, I was trying to find somewhere safe to leave a parcel when I found this old man lying in his garage. Poor old soul

157

had been there for about a month. None of his neighbours had even missed him. Anyway, that's what it looked like.'

'What? Like an old man?'

'No . . . like a dead person. Someone who's been dead for a long time.'

'I don't want to hear about Snape, Vernon. I want to know about you. I've waited long enough. Tell me. *Now.*'

Startled, Laverne looked into Detective Inspector Savage's candid blue eyes. He had been describing that morning's visit to Wakefield Prison, when she had suddenly cut him dead with a groan of exasperation. 'What happened on Monday?' she went on to say. 'Come on. How come I saw you in the underground?'

Opening his mouth to speak, he suddenly found that his throat was clogged with sawdust. He had been planning to tell her this afternoon, but in his own time, which would inevitably have involved telling her at a later date. He knew that Savage could be assertive. It had not occurred to him that she might *demand* to be put in the picture.

They were sitting in Savage's living room. Laverne was drinking tea, while his companion sipped iced water. The day had turned drab and rainy. They were alone in the house. Ian was at work, the children at school.

Lyn Savage was still in her dressing gown. Her bloodshot eyes were ringed with black and the thumb prints of her attacker showed as oval bruises on either side of her swollen throat. She found it painful to swallow, hence the iced water and her inability to raise her voice.

The floor and sofa were littered with library books with curious titles: *Mysteries*, *The Unknown Guest*, *Journeys Out of the Body*, *Doppelganger* and *A History of Astral Travel*.

'You've been busy,' he observed.

158

'I wanted to know what was going on.' Her voice was little more than a whisper.

Laverne picked up *The Mechanisms of Astral Projection* by Robert Crookall and flicked through it gloomily. 'Looking at this, it strikes me that you've already got a pretty good idea what's been going on . . .'

'So it's true?' She winced, then paused to swallow some water and a few painkillers. 'I didn't imagine it. You were actually there? On the platform?'

He considered lying, or making some inane comment about the dreadful weather, then decided that further procrastination would not further his cause. 'OK. The answer's "yes". You didn't imagine it. I had a feeling you were in danger. I was driving home after six o'clock, and suddenly felt sick with worry about you. Felt so bad I had to pull over and turn off the engine. Next thing I knew, I was in an underground station, and a man who looked like Blackmore was about to drag you in front of a train . . .'

Her eyes widened. 'He looked like Blackmore to you, too?'

'Exactly like the horrible old bugger.'

Yet when the train had been jacked up, and the body parts retrieved, the deceased had been identified not as Major Aden Blackmore, but as Donal Thompson, the same young beggar who had called Savage a 'rich bitch'. To the Metropolitan Police, the facts spoke for themselves. The dead man was already known to them via a string of violent assaults. This, they decided, had been a mere grudge attack, prompted by Savage's failure to offer a donation. 'Don't feel bad, dear,' one of the investigating officers had opined. 'He was clearly a thoroughly unpleasant individual. Your only mistake was making eye contact with him . . .'

All that the bystanders on the platform had seen had been an attractive blonde woman in her thirties being attacked by a young homeless maniac, who had then slipped and fallen under a train.

159

None of the witnesses mentioned seeing a stocky old man with burning eyes, or, for that matter, the tall, middle-aged man who had pushed him to his death.

'So how could that be?' said Savage. 'We both know what we saw.'

'I believe they call it possession,' said Laverne regretfully. 'Blackmore's more powerful than I thought. Somehow, he took over that poor devil on the underground and made him attack you. He did exactly the same thing to Trevor Snape, as I was about to tell you before I was so rudely interrupted.'

'You believe that people can be possessed, then, do you?'

Laverne shifted uneasily in his chair. 'I'd rather not believe anything of the kind, Lyn. But in view of what I've seen and what I can do, I've got no bloody choice, have I?'

She smiled, relieved to hear him speaking openly to her after so many years of evasion and subterfuge. 'It might interest you to know that I've been reading all about what you can do ... it's called astral projection. The ability to be in two places at once. The American military tried it during the Gulf War. Except that they called it "remote viewing". Intelligence officers were actually trained to leave their bodies and travel behind Iraqi lines. Sometimes they met the astral bodies of Russian soldiers, coming the other way ...' She regarded him with wonder. 'Have I got it right, Vernon? Is this your secret? All those amazing arrests, those hunches that came from nowhere?'

He nodded, visibly embarrassed. To see his face, one would have assumed she'd caught him stealing her underwear off the washing line.

She felt herself trembling slightly, not in a fearful way, but in the way she used to shake when she was a little girl, waking up on Christmas morning to find that Santa had kept his promise.

The incident at King's Cross had plunged Lyn Savage into a deep depression. As a police officer, she had heard many stories about the extraordinary apathy of the general public. But experiencing that apathy at first hand had been a rather different matter. She had found herself doubting the wisdom of a career spent in the service of the public, and her entire universe seemed to contract into something dark, meaningless and claustrophobically small. But as the mystery of Laverne unravelled before her, her despondency gave way to a thrilling sense of wonder and inner expansion.

'Does Dawn know?'

'She's got an inkling . . . no more than that. She's seen my double once or twice. But I don't think she's guessed the whole story, and I haven't told her. Geraint John knows more than she does.'

'You're joking! I thought he didn't believe in anything.'

'He took a bit of convincing. But I paid him a home visit. Why do you think he went after the Animal with me?'

She was puzzled. 'Why tell Geraint and not Dawn?'

'Because Dawn doesn't like all this spiritual nonsense, and neither do I. To be honest, I'd been trying to give it up. This business in Glastonbury has forced me out of retirement. I'd sooner live in the real world, Lyn. I don't want to be different.'

'Well, it's very lucky for me that you *are* different. If you weren't, I'd be dead now.'

'True. So would a lot of others. Doesn't stop me resenting it, though. Before it happened, I never used to believe in life after death or any of that nonsense. But now I know it's all true. Spirits walk this earth. Some of them belong to the dead. Others belong to the living – like Blackmore and myself.'

'So that's what Blackmore is? The same as you . . . only evil?'

'I'd say that was a fair assessment of the situation.'

A pleasant calm descended upon her as the painkillers set to work. 'God. Just think about it. A man who can leave his body.'

'If you had a body like mine, you'd leave it, too.'

His witticism was wasted on her. She found the subject far too interesting to mock. 'Could you do it for me? Here and now?'

161

'Do what?'

'Astrally project . . . whatever you want to call it.'

'No.' The single word was emphatic. 'It's not a party trick, Lyn. Besides, it can be very tiring. I feel knackered enough as it is.'

'Yes, that rings a bell.' Eagerly, Savage consulted the index of one of her books, then turned to the relevant page. 'Here we are . . . Emilie Sagée, a young French schoolmistress, back in the 1830s. Her pupils used to see her in two places at once . . . when they did, the "real" Emily always looked really pale and ill.' Savage closed the book, afraid that she was being patronizing. 'Sorry. I expect you already know all about her.'

'Never heard of the woman.'

'Are you telling me you've never researched this? Vernon, you must at least have read about it.'

'Never. You're the one who's keen on research, Lyn. I left school with one O level to my name. It takes me all my time to understand a bloody road map.'

'So you don't know about the poet Goethe meeting his own double? Or Robert Monroe – an American businessman who not only left his body to explore this world but discovered other worlds as well? He was like you, by the way . . . when he left his body, his centre of consciousness travelled with him.'

'What's that supposed to mean?'

'It means that his soul or astral body was fully aware of where and who it was. As opposed to Emilie Sagée, who had no idea that people were seeing her double.'

Laverne grunted rudely. 'Listen to her. Half-a-dozen library books and she's a bloody expert . . .'

'I don't understand your attitude.'

'I dare say you don't. I'll spell it out for you, shall I? I don't like walking through walls, Lyn. Oh, I can do it, I just don't like doing it. I'd sooner enter a house by the front door, like everybody else.'

Having stated his case, and received no opposition, Laverne

started to relax. Lyn listened placidly while he told her how he'd first left his body after the death of his son.

'Yes. That fits,' said Savage. 'Most out-of-the-body experiences are linked to a crisis. That must be where the phrase "beside oneself" comes from.'

Laverne bowed his head in respectful accord. He went on to explain, in general terms, how the major successes of his career – the defeat of the Bolton Strangler, the Racecourse Rapist, the Animal and the Black Kahuna himself, Hugo Prince – had all been brought about, directly or indirectly, by his ability to be in two places at once. But when Savage asked for details, Laverne grew gloomy and taciturn.

'Lyn, you already know more about me than anyone else alive. Let's leave it at that, shall we?'

Savage voted that they should take a tea-break. It was two thirty-five; they only had an hour before Lyn's daughters came home from school. Laverne went out to the kitchen and filled the kettle.

By the time he returned to the living room to rejoin Savage, another ten minutes had been wasted. He stooped to place the crowded tray on the coffee table and Lyn realized that her dressing gown was half-open, exhibiting a vast amount of cleavage. She folded her arms to preserve her honour, then saw that Laverne, bless him, hadn't even noticed.

He passed her a china cup on a saucer. She apologized and pointed to her throat. 'Can't drink anything hot . . .'

'So I've gone to all this trouble just for myself, have I?' he grumbled. He added half a teaspoon of sugar to the cup and stirred it noisily. 'Over the phone, you said you'd found out something about Blackmore.'

She plodded over to two matching bookcases. Her briefcase was wedged between them. On her return to the sofa, she unzipped the briefcase and drew out a slim exercise book that reminded Laverne, horribly, of maths lessons at school. 'The first thing I did was to

163

check his entry in *Who's Who*, which states that he was born in West Bengal, North-East India, in 1925, son of the Reverend R. F. Blackmore and Sarah St Clair. Educated at Rugby and Sandhurst. A former Major General in the Parachute Regiment and published poet.'

Laverne lowered his tea cup and raised his eyebrows. 'I beg your pardon?'

'A poet. Thirty years ago, he won the Toni Derbyshire Medal for a book called *The Destroyer*.'

'A poet? But he seemed no more poetic than . . .'

'Yes?'

'Well, than I do.'

'It's true, nonetheless. He only had one book published, but it does exist. I've seen it. But . . . let me see . . . he married in 1951, his wife died twelve years later. They had one child, Patricia . . . he lists his hobbies as guns, eastern mysticism and military history. The book of poems is a series of hymns to Hindu gods, as far as I can tell. But when I was searching for him on the computer, I came across another Blackmore, name of Sarah. Having already noticed that Blackmore's mother was a Sarah, I thought it was worth a try. And sure enough, it was the same woman. Just two books: *The Black Goddess* and *The Black Goddess Reborn*.

'It appears that she worshipped the Indian goddess Kali. The books were heavy-duty mysticism, almost impossible to plough through in one day in a busy library. But a very helpful librarian pointed out that an American company publish them in one volume, so I've placed an order.

'I checked *Who Was Who* for Sarah Blackmore and found out that she died in 1960, in Dakshineswar, India, and was the high priestess of the Bhairavi Cult, which, and I quote "worshipped the goddess Kali in her most extreme form".

'I found more about Sarah Blackmore in a book called *Witchcraft in the Twentieth Century*. The Bhairavi Cult were considered heretical by orthodox Kali worshippers. Nothing was ever proven, but they were believed to torture and sacrifice children as well as animals.

'Sarah Blackmore herself was known and feared as the Jadugar of Dakshineswar – I can't even pronounce that. Jadugar is an Indian word for a kind of sorcerer who is believed to have the power to expel a person's soul from its body.'

Laverne interrupted to recount Snape's story of the creature that came to him in the form of his mother. 'He said it wasn't exactly possession . . . more like eviction.'

Savage paused to shake her head. 'You know . . . this is all a bit too much.'

'Now you know how I feel. It's been too much for me for the past twenty-odd years.' He grabbed a chocolate biscuit and devoured it wolfishly. 'Fancy having a mum like that. No wonder Blackmore won't allow women in the house.'

Savage shook her head. 'No. You're wrong. Before I went to visit Angela, I took another look at his book of poems. It's dedicated to his mother.'

Laverne whistled in awe. 'That settles it, then. Blackmore must be carrying on her work. Better find out what that work involves, eh?' He swallowed his tea and gave her a glorious smile. 'All credit to you, Lyn. You've done brilliantly.'

12

DEATH COMES HOME

On his return to Huntington, Laverne was pleasantly surprised to find his daughter's truck parked in the drive. It was an old Toyota Land Cruiser, painted funfair red and blue by Jennifer's own hand. Her husband, the actor Michael Berensford, regarded the vehicle as vulgar and refused to travel in it, preferring the BMW Estate he'd purchased with the earnings from his first film role. Laverne heartily disliked Michael Berensford. So whenever the Toyota arrived, as opposed to the BMW, Laverne knew that he was about to enjoy the company of his daughter and granddaughter without having to suffer the lingering horror of his son-in-law.

As soon as he entered the front door, Laverne knew that there was something wrong. This knowledge owed little to his psychic abilities and a great deal to the fact that Dawn was standing in the hall, facing him, with tears in her eyes. A suitcase and a series of bags, overflowing with toys and child-care accessories, lay stacked against the wall.

'What's wrong?'

'It's Michael.' She pulled a handkerchief out of the sleeve of her cardigan and blew her nose on it. He had never understood why she kept handkerchiefs up her sleeve, but thought that this was not a sensible time to draw attention to the habit. Dawn's hesitation made Laverne nervous. 'What? What about him?'

From the kitchen came the sound of the baby, burbling. Dawn

lowered her voice. 'He's left her. Just packed his bags and walked out.'

Laverne was relieved. If Berensford had been killed in a road accident, he would probably have regretted the fact that their relationship had been less than ideal, and that he'd never taken the trouble to conceal his contempt for the man from his wife, daughter or, for that matter, Berensford himself. But a Berensford who could abandon his wife and child somehow justified all the unkind thoughts that Laverne had been harbouring about him for the past two years. 'Let me guess: he's got a part in a new play. He's playing a man who dumps his wife, so he's doing it for real in order to find his bloody character.'

Dawn hissed at him. 'Don't. I'll tell you about it later.'

Seething, he walked through into the kitchen. Harriet was sitting in a pushchair, spooning rice pudding in the general direction of her face. Jennifer was seated at the kitchen table, pretending to read the *Yorkshire Evening Post*. Harriet smiled at Laverne in recognition. 'Misty ... Misty come.' Misty was the infant's pet-name for Laverne. He chose to believe that the word was an approximation of 'Mister'. Dawn swore that the child was trying to say 'Misery'.

Laverne ruffled Harriet's hair and patted Jennifer's shoulder. 'I believe you've come to stay with us for a while, Jenny-wren?'

She nodded, moved to tears by the warmth in his voice.

'Good. Good idea,' he said. 'You can stay as long as you like. Get yourself sorted out . . .'

That evening, he played with his granddaughter in the kitchen, leaving his wife and daughter to carry on their soul-searching in peace. It wasn't that he was too embarrassed to discuss emotional matters, rather that where Michael was concerned, he didn't trust himself to offer mature guidance. A woman who is pining for her wayward spouse does not necessarily want to be told that he was a vain little pillock and that she could do a lot better.

167

When Harriet was in bed, Laverne walked out to the pub in the village and downed two pints of Boddington's best bitter. Shortly before ten, he returned home to learn that Jennifer was taking a bath. Over tea and toasted teacakes, Dawn filled her husband in on the sordid details. While acting in an Anglo-American film at Pinewood, Michael had met a well-known American actress. They had embarked on an affair, and now she wanted him to join her in Los Angeles. Michael felt that this was too good an opportunity to miss.

Jennifer, meanwhile, still loved her husband and prayed that the American actress would quickly tire of him, thereby propelling him back into his wife's less-famous arms. Dawn had pointed out that a man who could fall from grace once might easily do so again, and that anyway, Michael possibly had no intention of returning to England. At which point Jennifer wept inconsolably.

In Laverne's opinion, the separation of Michael and Jennifer was typical of show business, where the terminally shallow (Michael) are led astray when they come into contact with money, glamour and cocaine for the first time. Jennifer was the archetypal first wife, the woman who had nurtured Berensford and mopped up his tears when he couldn't even get voice-over work. Now that he was rubbing shoulders (or worse) with international stars, Jennifer had become expendable. It was a sordid story and a very old one; perhaps the oldest story of all.

As he sipped his cocoa, Dawn searched for a more charitable explanation. 'What we have to remember is that Michael's still young. All right, he's had his head turned and he's made a mistake. But for all we know, he might already be regretting what he's done.'

Laverne was unwilling to comment, knowing that Dawn was looking to him for wisdom, not for speeches about how he'd like to kick Berensford's arse from here to Hebden Bridge. 'I think you should both go to bed.'

'No,' said Dawn. 'Jenny wants to talk. We're going to have a brandy and talk it over.'

He frowned. 'A brandy after cocoa? Seems like a funny way round.'

'The cocoa was for you.'

He drew back, taking offence. 'What makes you think I'm ready for bed? I'm going out to check something on the car. I'll leave you two to it . . .'

There was, in fact, nothing wrong with the car. He simply craved solitude. The tension in the house was suffocating. So he lay across the back seat with the radio on. It was peaceful in the Rover. He closed his eyes and felt himself sinking into the red leather upholstery.

Then he thought of Tess Martin, felt himself floating, and knew that he was about to leave his body. It was a peculiar sensation, simultaneously liberating and intimidating. Mostly, Laverne could control and limit his out-of-the-body experiences. Occasionally, as now, his spirit didn't seem to care whether it had his permission or not.

He found that he could see with his eyes closed. The darkness of the car assumed a reddish tinge. The air around him pulsed and vibrated with energy. Then he was rising above the rather tired-looking man on the seat below and rocking gently from side to side, like a leaf wafted by the wind. For a few delicious moments, he forgot his purpose and was content to bask in his own spiritual freedom.

He exited the car via the roof, and found, inexplicably, that he was still able to see his body lying on the back seat. His physical eyes were now open and seemed to be looking up at him, but he had no sense of being conscious within that living carcass below. Everything he'd known and knew himself to be was out here, embraced by the night breeze, floating under a heaven that was as black as despair.

Despair: a condition that other families may soon experience unless you get down to business, Laverne. With a determined jolt, he landed on his feet and assumed a manly bearing. He looked down at himself. Even in the dark, he could see that he was dressed in the same trousers, slippers, shirt and cardigan that his physical self was wearing. This was an aspect of astral travel that he'd never been able to understand. How could a Marks and Spencer cardigan have an astral double? Perhaps he ought to follow Lyn's example and read everything he could find on the subject. She had been right to ridicule him. After all, he wouldn't have dreamt of driving a new car without first reading the handbook. So why did he insist on leaving his body without any kind of groundwork?

He grimaced, knowing the answer. Denial. Analysing his ability would involve accepting it. And as a Yorkshireman, reared on common sense and hard-headed realism, he could never accept that spirits not only walk, but walk before their time.

He eased his way through the front of the house into the living room. The bricks, metal and glass that he passed through felt no more substantial than a warm vapour. Dawn and Jennifer were seated on the living room sofa, holding hands. Dawn was attempting to reassure their agonized daughter.

Neither of them could see him. That privilege was reserved for clairvoyants, the dead and people he chose to reveal himself to. He leant closer, heard Dawn say, 'I'm serious, Jenny. All relationships have problems in the early years. Your dad was bloody murder to live with when we first married.'

His daughter was as sceptical as Laverne. 'Dad? But he's lovely.'

'He is now. He wasn't then. He was awful. I nearly left him several times.'

Laverne stepped back in dismay. Awful? Murder to live with? Impossible! So much for eavesdropping. Silently, he passed into the hallway, then climbed the stairs and entered the spare room. He peered into Harriet's cot. She was lying on her belly across the breadth of the mattress, snoring, her head touching the wooden

170

bars. Gently, he lifted her and laid her lengthways, then rearranged her sheet and blankets.

Content that his own house was in order and his family safe, he turned his thoughts towards a certain house in Glastonbury. Then he launched himself at the bedroom wall and plunged into utter darkness. For an instant, he was engulfed by a roaring hurricane. Then he found himself in Blackmore's study, standing beside the drinks cabinet. The room was dark and unoccupied. Light poured in through the half-open door.

Laverne paused by the ivory god at the foot of the stairs, wondering where to look first. A noise from above made this decision for him. At first, he thought it was a dog, yelping frenziedly. After concentrating on the sound, he realized that he was listening to the shrieks of an hysterical child. Alarmed, Laverne rushed to the landing above.

The screams seemed to be coming from the girl's room. He started to run down the dark gallery towards her door, then halted abruptly. He had heard his own footsteps. The floorboards on the landing had definitely rumbled under his weight. So. He was invisible, but not inaudible. In two decades of astral travel, he had never before registered this fact. He was going to have to be more careful.

He peered over the rail at the lobby below, and noticed for the first time that the mosaic on its floor displayed a startling motif. The floor was deep crimson, or to be more accurate, the colour of crimson in a medieval illuminated manuscript. Across this red expanse stretched two coiled snakes, formed from semi-precious stones. As Laverne looked down, a man crossed the floor and looked up. It was the fair-haired security guard Laverne had met during his first visit. The young man swore under his breath. Laverne drew back, afraid that he'd been seen. Then he realized that the guard was more likely to be reacting to the harrowing cries coming from the girl's room.

171

This suspicion was confirmed moments later, when the guard appeared on the landing and bounded upstairs to the floor above. He returned, clutching a set of keys and moving so quickly that Laverne had no time to evade him. On his way to the girl's room, the guard walked straight through Laverne. For the Chief Superintendent, this experience, comparable to a mild electric shock, was not pleasant. The guard, however, seemed oblivious to Laverne, who followed behind at a safe distance until he reached Tess's room, unlocked the door and entered. Tess was on the floor, shouting and threshing wildly. She was completely hysterical. Her television set was chattering away inanely to itself. In a calm, business-like manner, the blond man walked over to the dressing table and, with his back to Laverne and the girl, rummaged about in a plastic container.

Laverne stood over Tess Martin. She was soaked in perspiration and her right ankle was bound by a strong leather shackle. This manacle was attached to a glittering steel chain, leading to a heavy duty steel plate securely bolted to the floor. The guard returned and spoke to her softly as he raised a disposable syringe and injected something into her arm. She struggled and fought, but he restrained her economically, without fuss or any hint of undue force. He was clearly a professional.

'There. Everything's all right now.' He wiped the pin-prick on her arm with a cotton wool swab. She swooned, her head lolling sideways. Then he picked her up as if she was a doll, took her over to the bed and as her cries subsided, covered her with a quilt. Something bleeped under his jacket. He unhooked a radio from the waistband of his trousers and raised its aerial. 'Kari speaking.'

A scrambled voice snapped out a handful of syllables. The man who had called himself Kari gave a superfluous nod, then left and locked Laverne in the room. Alarmed by what he had witnessed, Laverne stood by the girl's bed, watching her eyes flicker as the sedative pulled her under. She looked ill, drawn and about as haggard as a thirteen-year-old can look. She moaned appreciatively as he smoothed her fiery hair away from her brow. After making a silent vow, Laverne turned away and walked through the wall.

As he reappeared on the landing, he glimpsed the guard setting off up the stairs and rushed after him. On the floor above, he found Kari standing in the doorway of a room that faced the stairwell.

Laverne heard Kari say, 'You're just getting jumpy.'

'No.' It was a man with a celtic-sounding accent. 'See for yourself.' Southern Irish?

Kari plodded into the room and hung his keys on a nail by the door. Laverne tiptoed in behind him, attempting to synchronize their footsteps. The room was well-lit and functional. There were three TV screens above a computerized desk. The screens were linked to infra-red cameras which monitored the house and grounds from various vantage points. An obese man with a head of thick, dark curls was slouched before the desk in a swivel chair, a cigarette in his mouth, eyes squinting through the smoke. He pressed a row of buttons and the screen on the right switched to rewind.

'Here,' said the Irishman. 'What the hell is this?'

The screen showed the gallery downstairs, filmed from a high angle. Kari surfaced from the base of the picture and walked up the passage, towards Tess's room. Then there was a flash of light which shrank to a pinpoint and vanished.

Kari scoffed. 'Is that it? That's nothing.'

The other man shook his head. 'Look at it again.'

The scene was replayed, this time in slow motion. A pale ball of phosphorescence appeared behind Kari's head and danced down the gallery behind him, shrinking as he shrank until it became the size of a firefly. A rather cunning firefly that hovered behind the guard as he unlocked Tess's door, then followed him into her room. The man at the controls fast-forwarded to his partner's reappearance.

'That's the lot. But I think we should show the old man.'

The two men watched the scene again in silence, this time

freezing the tape at key moments. Laverne also watched, and was only slightly less subdued than they were. Was that really him? A fuzzy blob of light? Was that all his energy and spirituality amounted to – the cosmic equivalent of a thirty watt bulb?

More to the point, he had been mistaken to assume that he was invisible. Evidently, for reasons that he could not begin to fathom, his astral body could sometimes be photographed. Laverne considered sabotaging the tape, but decided against it. What did it matter? Blackmore would be unable to identify him. The ball of light looked nothing like him.

After watching himself being pursued by a will-o'-the-wisp for the third time, Kari said, 'OK. What the fuck is that?'

'Back in the bogs, we might say you'd been visited by the Shee.'

'A woman, you mean?'

'The fairy folk. Don't you have fairies in Kerava?'

'That's KE-rav-a. You stress the first syllable.'

Obligingly, the Irishman re-pronounced the word three times until his partner was satisfied. 'Tell me: are all you Finns such fussy fuckers?'

Laverne moved back towards the door. One of his knee joints cracked, but neither of the guards appeared to notice.

'Know what, Michael?' said Kari. 'I really hate this job.'

'Ah, your man's paying us well enough.'

'I don't care. What's he want with the kid anyway? I hate him. I hate him and I hate this house.'

The Irishman sucked his cigarette right down to the filter and crushed it into a saucer. 'Sure, he's a nasty old bastard. But we won't be here much longer. Pay-day's coming up. Later, if your conscience is still troubling you, you can always go to the law. But I'd wait for the cheque to clear first, if I were you . . .'

The conversation turned to more serious matters, namely the breasts of a barmaid at a well-known Glastonbury inn. Laverne searched the rest of the house. Blackmore's bedroom was a few doors further down the corridor. It was bare, almost spartan, apart from the floor, which was dominated by a huge, intricate and beautifully painted mandala, possibly of Tibetan origin. Not that Laverne was familiar with the full meaning of the word mandala; he had simply seen such designs in films and photographs of the east, and knew that they were always circular and had something to do with meditation. This mandala had an old camp-bed in its centre. Candles, incense burners and dishes of dried flowers spanned the circle's perimeter.

But where was the Major? Laverne found him downstairs, in the drawing room where he had first met Tess. Blackmore was sitting alone in the dark, dressed in an old-fashioned quilted smoking jacket, the like of which Laverne had only seen in Laurel and Hardy comedies. Yet there was nothing remotely amusing about Blackmore, or his demeanour. The old man was resting on the piano stool, staring out of the French window.

Standing beside him, Laverne read hard, unshakeable purpose in the old soldier's face. There was no capacity for compassion in that thin mouth or the dried-blood eyes. But nor were there any signs of dementia. The deep brow and the man's overall poise suggested reason and self-control. It therefore followed that if Blackmore was not insane, he must be congenitally evil.

Blackmore's attention was concentrated on a fixed point some-where out in the darkness, beyond the terrace and the tangled lawn. He was watching out for someone. Or something. Laverne looked at the man's thick, stubborn neck, and, thinking of Tess, was momentarily tempted to wring it.

Instead, he walked through the French window, crossing Black-more's line of vision. Blackmore showed no awareness of his presence. Laverne descended to the garden. A cold wind encircled him, but lacking the power to chill his blood, moved on. Laverne glanced back at the house. Blackmore's position remained unchanged. His white face shone like a shield in the darkness of the room. Laverne traced the Major's line of vision to a wooden arch set in a hedge at the edge of the lawn. He guessed it to be the entrance to an orchard.

He waited by the hedge, and once again looked back towards Blackmore. Laverne was now approximately two hundred yards away from the house. For a long time, he watched the dark drawing room window, unable to tell whether the Major was still sitting there or not. Then a shadow stirred behind the panes, and the Chief Superintendent thought he saw his enemy leave his seat and move away from the window. Laverne was on the verge of giving up and going home, when a flicker of light made him turn his head. Something large and bright was hurtling through the trees at the side of the house.

At first, Laverne thought he was looking at some kind of hideous low-flying bird or an enormous moth. Then, as the shape drew nearer, he was able to identify it as the upper half of a man's body. There were no legs. Only a trunk and a loathsome, glowing head.

The apparition flew at man-height, its arms making macabre swimming movements in the air as it skimmed over the lawn towards him. It resembled Blackmore, or Blackmore as he would have looked in hell, for on its face was written every conceivable vice and iniquity. The spirit's eyes were sulphur-yellow, and the shroud-like material that clothed its body trailed smoke. Perhaps the missing legs owed something to the accident at King's Cross, when the young man possessed by Blackmore was cut in half by the wheel of a train.

Laverne now saw the aim of Blackmore's vigil in the drawing room. He had been waiting for his own astral body to return to him. With a violence born of total revulsion, Laverne hurled himself at the creature. The two spirits collided in mid-air with an explosion of sonic intensity.

Laverne knew from experience that all spirits feed on mana, or life force, which comes partly from food, but is mainly created by the will. If the strength of Blackmore's astral body was anything to go by, his will was superhumanly strong. The force that emanated from the Major's phantasm sent Laverne spinning over and over, backwards through space. That should have been his cue to depart. But when he'd picked himself up, foolish Yorkshire pride made him stand his ground. Blackmore charged at him again, grasped Laverne by the temples and began to squeeze.

The effect of this was akin to slow electrocution. The heat was unbearable. As Laverne struggled to free himself, he felt his brain, or its astral equivalent, boiling in his skull. Tonight, Laverne had learned two useful facts about astral projection: the astral body can be heard and it can also be hurt. The agony he was experiencing surpassed anything he had ever known.

Screaming and reeling, he shook himself free. The entity before him surveyed his pangs with obvious relish. Then flames erupted from Blackmore's mouth and eyes, turning his head into a grinning Hallowe'en pumpkin. Without realizing what he was doing, Laverne started to back away. There was a terrific whoosh of ignition as the vision before him transformed, becoming the tower of infernal flame that he had seen at Lammas Farm. Laverne took another step backwards. In the core of the fire, something was stirring; a shape that brought to mind a deformed foetus twitching in its mother's womb.

Laverne had seen enough.

He flung himself into the ether and after a frightening few seconds of utter blackness and utter non-being, opened his eyes to find himself in his own body, in the back seat of his luxurious, uneconomical car. With an effort, he sat up. The car radio was playing something comforting and familiar: 'Stranger on the Shore' by Acker Bilk. The pain in his head was now no more than a memory, the fading vestige of a particularly vivid nightmare.

Breathing laboriously, he heaved himself upright and straightened his cardigan. He opened the car door, grateful for the cool air.

Then he bent over the front seat and turned off the radio. After locking the car, he sauntered up the drive towards the house.

Soft light shone behind the curtains in the front room. Dawn and Jennifer were still awake. Laverne glanced up at the moon and smiled, heartily relieved to be home and in one piece. Before the smile had faded on his lips, a hissing fireball burst out of the clear night air and launched itself at the front of the cottage, showering the living room windows with sizzling sparks before merging with the fabric of the house. Laverne cursed his own stupidity. Blackmore had followed him home.

The fireball had caused no damage. The living room windows were intact. Laverne's legs and hands shook as he fumbled for his door keys. He unlocked the porch, and the cat tore past him, hissing as it sped under the car. He stabbed repeatedly at the front door, trying to locate the lock. When he succeeded, and the door yawned open, he suddenly lost his desire to go inside. With a great effort, he mastered himself, stepped into the warm hallway, closed the door quietly behind him. It shut with a click.

A strip of light, two inches wide, showed between the living room door and the jamb. He listened. No sound came from within. Still shaking, steeling himself for what he knew he must face, Laverne climbed the stairs, walked into the bathroom and threw cold water at his face. Towelling himself dry, he deliberately turned his back on the mirror above the wash-basin. He had no wish to see how he looked at his weakest, at his most vulnerable.

On his way across the landing to the baby's room, he let out a low moan of dread. The door was wide open in order to catch the light from the landing: Harriet hated the dark. He stood on the threshold and peered round at the cot against the far wall. It was empty.

Please God. Not all three of them.

Stumbling like a drunkard, Laverne descended the stairs. Again, he waited outside the living room, listening to the silence, now knowing how Tess Martin had felt on that night in February. The hardest burden of all was the knowledge that this was all his own doing. He had led Blackmore straight to his family.

Fighting the urge to vomit, Laverne steadied himself, pushed the door open and walked into the room. Dawn was sitting on the sofa. Jennifer was kneeling on the floor in front of her, head in her mother's lap. The baby lay on the sofa beside Dawn.

They were all alive and unharmed.

Laverne began to laugh with boyish delight. It was the happiest moment of his entire life. Dawn shot him an angry glance. 'Shush!' She gestured towards Jennifer and Harriet, who were both dozing.

He walked over to her, sat on the arm of the sofa.

'Did I ever tell you that I loved you? Love all of you?'

Her dark eyes softened. 'No,' she answered. 'I don't believe you did.'

He reached over, his face solemn as he stroked her hair. 'Well, I'm telling you now . . .'

13

BLOOD OF THE BELOVED

For the first time in her life, Lyn Savage slept late while her husband gave the children breakfast and got them off to school. When she awoke, it was just after nine. She felt better, and immediately considered going into work. The only part of her body that still ached was her tongue, which she'd bitten accidentally during the attack on the underground.

She washed her face and went downstairs. There was a padded envelope waiting for her on the kitchen table. A sticker on the back of the envelope gave the sender's name and address: Watkins Ltd, Booksellers, 21 Cecil Court, London.

She ripped open the package and pulled out a weighty soft-covered book. It was *The Black Goddess* by Sarah Blackmore. A small heading beneath the title read, 'Incorporating *The Black Goddess Reborn*'. The cover bore a rather unnerving etching of the goddess Kali on a battlefield, beheading fallen warriors. The book was published by Weiss and Davidson Ltd, New York.

Savage prepared some tea and cereal, while on the radio, a scientist from Jodrell Bank Observatory enthused about some imminent celestial event. 'The Met Office predict clear visibility, so we fully expect a grand showing. It should be well worth staying up for.'

A record began to play: 'Moon River' by Andy Williams. Savage sat down to eat and peruse Sarah Blackmore's work. Inside the book's cover, there was a photograph of the author, a hard-faced woman with a mouth like a gash and staring eyes. Savage felt that those eyes were trying to tell her something.

Spooning muesli into her mouth, she skip-read a few pages in an attempt to extract the essence of Sarah Blackmore's philosophy. The literary style was both arcane and archaic. 'On Mount Meru, at the hour of sacrifice, there shall she descend, standing upon her divine husband Shiva, her right foot on his chest, her left foot on his right thigh. Then will the mountain bleed with the bliss of Satchidananda, and Shakti and Brahman shall unite, and death that is life that is death-in-life shall come again to the world.'

Maddeningly, there was no index or glossary to help unravel such obscure passages. Savage was forced to resort to a dictionary and, even then, emerged none the wiser. She learned that 'shakti' was derived from the Sanskrit word for power and meant 'the female principle or organ of reproduction and generative power in general'. Shiva was described as 'the destroyer; along with Brahma and Vishnu, one of the three principal deities of the later Hindu pantheon'. The word 'satchidananda' was not listed.

She turned to another chapter and read: 'Mount Meru may be taken to signify the axis of the inner body (Merudanda or Susumna), meaning that for each of us, the universe is a circle that emanates from our own axial centre. It therefore follows that the goddess, being the source of all creation, forms the focal point of both subtle and cosmic bodies. In the physical self, find her in the place of a thousand petals. But lo! May the sadhaka guard well her secret dwelling place upon the earth.'

After a few more pages of this, Savage sighed, closed the book and helped herself to another bowl of muesli. She felt that she'd earned it.

'What, precisely, are you trying to ascertain?'

Detective Constable Farrell, recently returned from Quantico, juggled with his spectacles, a look of polite inquiry upon his strangely unlived-in face. The pomposity of his question almost made Savage laugh out loud, but she managed to check herself. She passed Sarah Blackmore's book over the desk to him.

'Whether there's anything in that book that might account for Major Blackmore's interest in his granddaughter. Plain and simple.'

They were at headquarters. Farrell was sitting at Laverne's desk, something he would never have dared to do had Laverne been in the office. It was ten-thirty. Laverne hadn't turned up for work. Farrell, alone among the officers at York CID, was suspected of possessing an intellect. This suspicion owed much to his gratuitous use of words of more than two syllables and his habit of carrying books of poetry to the lavatory. Despite his pretensions, Farrell possessed an incisive brain. Savage had presented him with *The Black Goddess* in the hope that he might shed light on its contents. She wrote what she wanted to know on a blank sheet of paper that she taped to Laverne's desk.

WHAT EXACTLY DID/DO THE BHAIRAVI CULT BELIEVE? IS THERE ANYTHING IN THOSE BELIEFS THAT COULD ACCOUNT FOR MAJOR BLACKMORE'S INTEREST IN HIS GRANDDAUGHTER?

Farrell glanced at the questions and nodded indifferently. 'Give me an hour,' he said.

'Only an hour? I was going to suggest that you took it home with you.'

'No need. I'll read the introduction, the conclusion, and anything else in between that takes my fancy. And take notes. One hour.'

'I'll hold you to that. I've got to nip out now. Some important business to attend to. See you later.'

Detective Inspector Savage's 'important business' consisted of collecting some clothes from a dry cleaner in town: the suit in which she had rolled about the platform at King's Cross and the skirt that Gudrun Sweet had bled all over. Initially, she'd considered burning these garments, not even offering them to Oxfam, on the grounds that wearing them had brought her bad luck.

On reflection, she had concluded that if clothes could bring bad luck, then she might as well come to work naked.

In the car park, she met Laverne. He was wiping some bird-droppings off the rear bumper of his car. 'Nice to see you working so hard,' she remarked sardonically.

'Bloody pigeons,' he raged. 'I only took it to the car wash yesterday . . . where are you off to?'

When she told him, he offered to act as her chauffeur. 'I really need to talk to you . . .'

Typically, as soon as she was seated beside him in the Rover, his mood altered abruptly. He became cold and darkly laconic. They drove to the city centre without exchanging a word. After they'd collected Savage's dry cleaning, Laverne parked his car outside the minster and they strolled together down Low Petergate. Laverne stopped at a baker's and bought them each a mammoth Danish pastry.

A thin mist hung over the city. Out of the mist fell a steady light dew that moistened the skin and made the pavements glisten. Laverne and Savage joined the city wall at the fourteenth century gatehouse known as Monk Bar and turned left, heading back towards Bootham Bar and the cathedral. On the way, Laverne's mood changed again and he became plaintive and confessional as he told the DI what he'd experienced the night before.

She listened attentively, finally understanding why Laverne was so reluctant to use his extraordinary powers. 'That's appalling. Absolutely dreadful. No wonder you're afraid.'

He faced her accusingly. 'Who said I was afraid?'

She struggled to correct her mistake. 'All I'm saying is, well, when I was attacked at King's Cross, I was scared to death.'

Her honesty defused his blustering pride. 'Yep. OK. You were right the first time. I was afraid. I've been afraid for ... what? Twenty-two years. Since my lad died. It started with him dying, and it's never really stopped. I like to think I'm brave, I like to imagine I'd stand up to anything or anyone to protect those I love ... but you know, Lyn, when it comes down to it, I'd rather sit at home in front of the telly and not have to bother.'

She laughed. For a second he was tempted to laugh with her, but the disquieting image of a half-man floating through the air lingered in his memory. 'Listen, Lyn ... I've got a feeling about Blackmore and this whole situation. That feeling could be summed up as sheer terror. At first, I thought he was just a bit eccentric. I've now reached the conclusion that he could be more dangerous than anyone we've come up against.

'Because of this, I've decided that from now on, Blackmore should be my responsibility. You know I've always respected you. You're a fine detective and a lovely woman. But this isn't your fight. Go back to your family, be good to them, enjoy your life. Leave the Major to me.'

Savage was not, by nature, a litter-bug, but she could not resist rolling up the bag that had contained her pastry and flinging it forcefully at Laverne's head. 'I have never heard such a pile of antiquated, patronizing crap in all my life!'

Laverne was too startled to defend himself.

'I'm a lovely woman, am I?' she demanded, blood rising to her cheeks. 'If I was male, would you be calling me a "lovely man"?'

'Possibly,' he replied lamely.

'Would you hell!' she retorted angrily. 'So you think I should go home and finish the ironing, do you? After all we've been through together?'

The cathedral came into sight, trembling through the mist like a mirage. Laverne seized Savage by the wrist. 'That's not what I meant at all. I'm telling you that I've got a bad feeling about all this.' He paused, struggling to find the right words. 'This feeling ... call it a premonition, if you like. I think I might be about to die. No great tragedy. I'm getting on a bit. Not many years 'til I retire, now. If I go, Dawn'll get a good pension.'

'Oh, don't be so damn morbid!' she exclaimed, and then wished the words away, seeing the sadness in his eyes.

'Not morbid. Just practical. Your kids are still young. They depend on you. I'm not joking, Lyn. If I'm right about this, Blackmore could easily kill us both.'

She slapped him boisterously on the chest. 'You're wrong. It won't come to that. We won't let it.'

Later that afternoon, while Laverne was deliberately filling in the wrong answers to the quick crossword in *The Guardian*, Savage ushered Farrell into his office and closed the door behind them. Laverne shoved the newspaper to one side and raised his eyebrows expectantly.

Savage turned to Farrell. 'Tell the Chief Super what you've just told me.'

Farrell held up a single sheet of foolscap, nudged his spectacles up until they were balanced on the bridge of his nose and recounted his findings. 'Well, sir, to come straight to the point, these Bhairavi people were complete nutters. In the west, we might call them devil-worshippers, although Indian notions of good and evil are slightly more ambivalent than our own. The whole Bhairavi creed was based on the idea that one day, the goddess Kali would come to earth in human form and bring about the end of the world. Bhairavi is the goddess at her most destructive. Her skin is red and she's usually depicted as covered in blood.

'As for why the Bhairavi Cult would be interested in Tess Martin, there's a quote here that may shed light on the matter: "On the darkest night of the New Moon, animals may be used for the sacrifice. But when the moon wears the shadow of the earth like a cloak, only the blood of the truly beloved must be offered to Ma Kali, blood that belongs to saint, a god, a spouse or a dear child."'

Slowly, Laverne rose to his feet. 'Human sacrifice?'

Savage and Farrell nodded sombrely.

'Not just any sacrifice,' added Farrell. 'If it isn't the sacrifice of a loved one, it's no real sacrifice at all. As seen in Genesis. Remember Abraham and Isaac?'

Laverne looked puzzled. Farrell reminded him of a story he'd once learned at Sunday School, and long forgotten. 'If Blackmore loves Miss Martin half as much as Abraham loved Isaac, well . . . I'd say she was in bad trouble.'

'When?' said Savage. 'When's it likely to happen?'

Farrell heaved a sigh, shifting his gaze from Savage to Laverne, then back to Savage. 'I'd have thought that was obvious. Do neither of you watch *The Sky at Night*?'

Impatiently, Laverne snapped, 'Just bloody well tell us!'

'I'm sorry, sir.' Farrell was anything but sorry. His eyes glinted indignantly behind his spectacles. 'I assumed that line about the moon wearing the shadow of the earth was self-explanatory. Tomorrow morning, shortly after midnight, there's going to be a lunar eclipse. If anything's going to happen to that girl, my guess is that it'll happen then.'

14

THE GATES OF PARADISE

'You know what this is called, don't you?'

Savage was speaking with her mouth full as Laverne, his foot pressed down hard on the accelerator, sent his battle-scarred Rover charging down the fast lane of the M5 at full pelt. The Detective Inspector was sucking a boiled sweet, a cherry drop, to be precise.

During Savage's girlhood, her mother had always whiled away long car journeys by passing around bags of boiled sweets, so that by the time they arrived at their destination, the entire family felt as if their teeth were covered with an armour plating of solid sugar. Only old people with no teeth to lose bothered with such confectionary, nowadays. Old people and Laverne, who still possessed his own teeth but had been acting like an old man since he was ten.

'Speeding,' answered Laverne indifferently. 'It's called speeding.'

'I was talking about what we're going to do when we get to Glastonbury . . . a little crime known as kidnapping.'

'Oh, *that* . . .'

'I can't believe what I've got myself involved in here . . .'

'What choice do we have? We can't exactly go to Holebrook and ask for his co-operation. He'd blow the whistle to Geraint John faster than you can say "southern pillock".'

Savage fell silent for a few moments. Laverne swerved into the middle lane to undertake an Audi that was scrupulously obeying the speed limit, then immediately returned to the fast lane without indicating. As they accelerated, the Audi's horn bleated in righteous indignation.

'Nice driving,' commented Savage satirically.

'What do you expect me to do?' he rejoined. 'It's two hundred and seventy miles from York to Glastonbury. We've hardly got time to observe the bloody *Highway Code*.'

They had, indeed, made remarkable progress. As they left the motorway at the twenty-third exit, it was three-fifty in the afternoon. The journey had taken three-and-a-half hours.

At Glastonbury, Laverne parked behind St John's church. Then he and Savage crossed High Street and bought fish and chips, which they ate out of the paper, gazing in shop windows and watching the locals passing by. Laverne estimated that the mystical weirdos outnumbered the ordinary citizens by three-to-one.

At the lower end of High Street, Savage pointed out an edgy young man who was waiting by the Market Cross, circling and flapping his elbows in agitation. 'Look at him. His dealer's late . . .'

'See what we're like?' said Laverne. 'That's what police work does to you. Can't even go for a walk without getting suspicious.' Then he glanced back at the boy, still performing his ritual dance under the cross. A junkie. No doubt about it.

They retired to the snug of the Globe Inn where they each sipped a welcome double brandy. 'OK. Tell me your plan,' said Savage.

'What plan?' said Laverne.

'I presumed you had one.'

'No.'

She tutted and shook her head.

Laverne defended himself. 'A plan wouldn't be much use, Lyn. I might be able to enter the house without being seen. But Tess can't come out without being seen. So my only plan is to leave my body, go in and get her, somehow smuggle her past Blackmore's guards and bring her out to the car. Then I think it might be a good idea to get away from Glastonbury as fast as we bloody well can.'

Savage rotated the brandy glass in her cupped hands, then levelled her eyes at his, her expression sober. 'And go where?'

'Don't know yet. Somewhere that isn't too obvious. Anywhere but York.' He grimaced apologetically. 'I haven't really had time to think about it.'

'Know what?' She was smiling warmly, so that he was unprepared for what followed. 'That's pathetic. That must be the most pathetic scheme I've ever heard in my life, and I've heard a few.'

He stared at her resentfully.

'What about tomorrow?' she persisted. 'What do we do then?'

'Tess won't be in danger tomorrow. All that matters is that we keep her away from Blackmore tonight.'

'She'll still need a home tomorrow. A home and people to look after her and food and clothes and a school to go to.'

'Er, let's just concentrate on keeping her alive, for now.' He swallowed his brandy, then searched her face for evidence of any misgivings. 'That's if you still want to go ahead with this?'

Savage ruminated for a few seconds before answering. A young couple walked into the snug and after choosing a table near the door, gazed into each other's eyes attentively, holding hands across the table. Finally, she said, 'Oh, bugger it. Who needs a career, anyway?'

At seven-thirty, as the sun was sinking, Laverne backed his car into a field and switched off the lights. Then he turned to Savage and smiled. 'Won't be long.'

As she watched, he sat back and closed his eyes. Savage held her breath, mesmerized, while in front of her, her partner divided into two. The physical Laverne remained immobile while his perfect double raised itself from him as casually as someone sitting up in bed. Savage cowered slightly as this second Laverne turned to her, smiled and left the car without opening the door. An instant later, the apparition was standing in front of the car's bonnet, gazing amiably in at her through the windscreen. Although ostensibly solid, and identical in bearing, dress and appearance to its owner, Laverne's spirit seemed to shimmer in the dusk. Savage now understood why mystics sometimes refer to the astral self as the 'body of light'. Laverne's body of light nodded to her once before turning to the east and vanishing. She heard herself grunt in surprise.

Savage turned uncertainly to the man at her side, saw that he was breathing deeply, apparently unconscious. This suited her fine. She was completely exhausted. Gratefully, she closed her eyes and sank into an uneasy doze.

Laverne, floating rather than walking, passed the gatehouse of Paradise House. There was no guard on duty, which struck him as odd. Blackmore was usually so security-conscious. Laverne imagined himself in the lobby, and in an instant was actually there, standing directly in front of the stairs. The hall was silent and dark. A solitary light burned in the gallery above. Superstitiously, Laverne sidestepped the serpents of power on the blood-red lobby floor and floated up the stairs.

At the top, he turned left and skimmed along the gallery to Tess's room, passing through the locked door without stopping. Tess was lying on the bed. She was safe and fully conscious, listening to pop music on a small CD player and flicking through a glossy magazine. Her foot was still manacled. A tray beside the bed contained the remnants of a recent meal.

The force of Laverne's entrance created a gust of wind that swayed the curtains and rustled the pages of her magazine. She glanced in his direction without seeing him, yawned, then turned over another page of the magazine.

Relieved, Laverne left the room and climbed the stairs to the control room. There was no one on duty and the TV screens hissed with white noise. He lifted the bunch of keys off the nail by the door and retraced his steps to the floor below, feeling unhappy and apprehensive. Something was wrong. This was all too easy. Where were the guards?

He slowly re-materialized as he unlocked the door to the girl's room. By the time he'd opened the door and walked inside, he looked solidly, convincingly corporeal. Or, at least Tess seemed to think so. At the sight of him, her face brightened instantly and she sat up. Before she had time to speak, Laverne held a finger to his lips and tapped them. Then, noiselessly, he closed the door behind him.

'You've come to take me away?' she breathed excitedly, while he used the smallest key in the bunch to unfasten her shackle.

'It seems like a good idea, wouldn't you say?' he whispered, rubbing her bruised ankle to restore the circulation. 'What's been going on downstairs?'

'Nothing . . . why? What's happened?'

He shook his head, unwilling to alarm her. 'There's no one about down there. Any idea why?'

'No.' She grinned delightedly. 'I knew you were special. I knew it . . .'

Snorting self-effacingly, he helped her off the bed. She immediately limped over to the dressing table and began to gather together her possessions. Laverne walked up behind her and placed a gentle hand on her shoulder. 'No time for all that. Just take a coat and some comfortable shoes.'

She paused and looked up at him, as if contemplating rebellion, then nodded dutifully. After she had donned a pair of expensive-looking trainers and a pink denim jacket, they walked out on to the landing. Laverne paused and listened. Then a cry from below echoed through the entire house, starting as a furious yell and rising to become a deafening, uncontrolled wail. It was hard to tell whether the voice belonged to a man or a woman.

'What's happening?' Tess whispered.

To Laverne, it sounded more like a cry of terror than pain. He shook his head and steered her towards the stairs. They descended slowly, accompanied by a series of strangled sobs that could have been made by a fretting dog. The cries seemed to be coming from behind the closed drawing room door. At the foot of the stairs, Tess started to panic. 'Kari! What if it's Kari?' Her apparent concern for the wellbeing of her jailer confused Laverne, without surprising him. He had seen so many ungrudging victims in his career that he no longer even attempted to understand the vagaries of the human heart.

There was no time to debate the issue. As Tess broke away from him, he seized her and swung her up into his arms. She tried to cry out, but her voice was drowned by another despairing howl of agony. Laverne opened the front door and carried the tearful girl out into the dusk.

All the way to the gatehouse, Laverne expected to see the cone of fire that had pursued him to Lammas Farm, or hear an invisible sword singing as it swooped to cut him down. He saw and heard nothing. They walked out to the lane without incident.

As they passed through the gates of Paradise House, a car, its headlamps glaring, cruised forward to meet them. Laverne stiffened, knowing that the engine's voice was too polite to belong to the Rover. This car was a Jaguar. Its doors clicked open and two men hurried out to greet them. One of them was small, with a domed hairless skull and a sallow complexion. The other was younger, with high cheekbones and narrow, calculating eyes. Even in the dark, Laverne had no difficulty in recognizing Detective Sergeant Mowart and John Macmillan, the Chief Constable for Avon and Somerset.

'Thank God you're safe,' said Macmillan.

Laverne was lost for words.

'If you'd both get in the car . . .' said Mowart, opening the back door with rather too much haste. But Laverne was reluctant to co-operate, or to let go of the girl.

'Please, Chief Superintendent,' urged Macmillan tightly. Without meaning to, Laverne inhaled the man's noxious aftershave. 'We know all about Blackmore. We know why he's interested in Miss Martin. We're sorry that we ever doubted you.'

Still Laverne hesitated. Chief Constables do not, as a rule, drive around the countryside at night looking for people to rescue. If Macmillan suspected the Major of any serious crime, where were the police cars and vans, the paramedics, the firearms officers surrounding the house?

'How did you know I was here?' challenged Laverne.

Silence. The two men seemed to shrug inwardly.

Laverne felt a sickening lurch in his stomach as he realized that there would be no back-up, no police protection for Tess Martin, that Mowart and Macmillan had other plans for her. By way of confirmation, Mowart reached out and violently snatched Tess from Laverne's arms. Macmillan tried to grab Laverne, who promptly vanished. Macmillan let out a short grunt of surprise, and then staggered back, punched in the chin by an unseen fist. He spun sideways, denting the car with his head as he fell, then lay on the ground, concussed, blood trickling from the corner of his mouth.

Mowart, shouting incoherently, hurriedly shoved the struggling Tess into the back seat, locked her in and ran round to the driver's door. Something pounded across the bonnet, making the car shake. Then an invisible fist clubbed Mowart in the face, cracking his jaw.

Yelling in anger and pain, Mowart reeled backwards and stumbled into the ditch at the side of the road. Looking up, he fancied he saw a small orb of light hovering above him. Was he literally seeing stars? Or was there really something there? The answer to his question was swift and painful. An astral foot encased in an astral brogue collided with his head. Mowart snarled at his phantom attacker and then lay silent.

Tess Martin, biting her knuckles in the back of the Jaguar, suddenly saw the lights of another vehicle reflected in the windscreen. A car pulled up behind, and shortly afterwards, the driver's door of the Jaguar flew open. Laverne, newly returned to his body, thrust his head into the car and, leaning over the front seat, unlocked the back door for her.

'Where did you go?' she complained. 'I was scared to death.'

'Were those two men friends of your grandfather, by any chance?'

'I don't know who they are. I've never seen them before.'

Laverne and the girl got out of the car. Savage was kneeling over the prostrate Chief Constable. 'Have you any idea who you've just clobbered?'

'Yep.'

'He's bleeding.' She was incredulous. 'You've just caused actual bodily harm to Somerset's highest ranking police officer.'

'Serves him right.'

Muttering darkly to herself, Savage helped Tess into the Rover, sharing the back seat with her. Laverne leaned over Mowart, who was groaning as he returned to consciousness. He found the keys to the Jag in Mowart's jacket pocket and slung them into a field. Then he settled into the Rover, reversed without due care and attention, executed a crazy three-point turn and sent the car swerving to the end of the lane.

Savage sighed. 'So now we've got Blackmore *and* the police after us . . .'

'No,' stated Laverne firmly.

'No what?'

'Not the police. Mowart and Macmillan weren't here on police business.'

Savage stared at him fixedly, but was reluctant to question him further in the presence of Tess. Laverne drove through the town cautiously, not wishing to attract any more unwanted attention. But as soon as they reached the Edgarley Road he accelerated aggressively, joining the A371 at East Compton and hurtling south. To their left the full moon, a disc of shimmering ice, climbed the darkening sky.

Savage broke the silence. 'Where are we going?'

'The station,' said Laverne. 'I'm hoping to catch a train.'

They arrived at the village of Castle Cary shortly before eight-fifteen. Laverne, with deep regret, left his faithful Rover in a pub car park, abandoning it to fate and to vandals. Then the three of them, looking for all the world like a real family, walked to the station. The 20.19 for Paddington was gliding into view as they joined the huddle of passengers waiting on the platform.

'This way,' prompted Tess, tugging at Laverne's arm. 'Second class is always at the back.'

'Ah,' said Laverne. 'But we're not travelling second class.'

'You're paying, I take it?' smiled Savage, as they started walking alongside the express.

He nodded. They stopped at a carriage that only contained a handful of passengers. 'First class is quieter. I could do with a bit of peace and quiet.'

He held a door open for Tess and Savage and they boarded the train. As he climbed up after them, he saw a solitary woman slowly limping down the platform towards them, and vaguely considered waiting around to help her, before deciding that chivalry can be carried to extremes. One damsel-in-distress a day ought to be enough for any knight. Decisively, he slammed the heavy door shut and moved into the brightly lit carriage to join his companions.

15

A Garland of Human Heads

They shared a table in the centre of coach G. Tess occupied the forward-facing window seat with Savage at her side. Laverne sat opposite Savage. Travelling with his back to the engine always made him vaguely nauseous, but he was conventional enough to consider women and children before himself, whether he felt sick or not.

'He'll already be looking for me,' said Tess, almost boastfully. 'He won't just give up. You know that, don't you?'

A man two tables away rustled the latest edition of *The Cornishman* irritably, as if resentful of anyone daring to hold a conversation in his proximity. Savage signalled for Tess to keep her voice down. With a slight jerk, the powerful diesel engine tugged the train out of the station. There was a loud 'phut' from the PA system, followed by an elderly West Country voice. 'Ladies and gentlemen, this is your Senior Conductor welcoming you aboard the 20.19 Pullman service from Penzance to London Paddington, calling at Westbury, Reading and due to arrive at Paddington at approximately 22.00 hours. Passengers are reminded that the buffet-bar is open for the sale of hot beverages, beer and spirits and a fine selection of . . .'

'Over-priced inedible filth,' said Laverne, ending the conductor's announcement for him.

'Actually, I'm hungry, actually,' admitted Tess. In the merciless glare of the overhead lights, Laverne was shocked by how pale and ill she looked.

'Actually you're hungry actually, are you?' he joked. She kicked his shin under the table. He winked at Savage. 'Actually, are you hungry actually, too, Detective Inspector Savage?'

Savage had already risen to her feet. She checked that her purse was in her bag and asked them both what they wanted. Tess insisted on accompanying her to the buffet. Laverne requested coffee and a hot bacon roll, or anything hot, or failing that, anything. While the women were absent, the conductor wobbled down the aisle, a small man with fish-eyes behind pebble glasses who reminded Laverne of Arthur Askey. 'I thank you . . . tickets from Castle Cary, please . . .'

Laverne stopped the guard, noting how the old man's mouth turned down at the corners on learning that Laverne and his 'family' had no tickets. Laverne asked for three first class singles to Paddington; the conductor opened a flimsy ticket book and took an infernally long time filling in the travel details. Then he asked for one hundred and thirty-five pounds, and it was time for Laverne's mouth to turn down at the corners.

Savage and Tess returned with bags containing coffee, Laverne's hot bacon and tomato roll, some crisps and Danish pastries. Tess was sinking her teeth into something that she cheerfully referred to as a dog-burger.

'It's crowded in second class,' said Tess. 'Absolutely packed.'

'Hmm?' said Laverne, feigning interest through a mouthful of rubbery microwaved bacon.

'Dad never let us travel first class. He said we couldn't afford it, but even if we could, he said that British Rail are so crap it'd be a crime to pay them more money.'

'Your dad said that, did he?' grinned Savage. 'Sounds like a sensible fella, your dad.'

'He was.' The girl made the words sound like a challenge. 'He was great.'

There was a clatter from the wheels as the train crossed over a set of points. Tess chewed her burger in silence and the two police officers felt the terrible black weight of her loneliness, like a fourth presence at the table.

Laverne made his way towards the rear of the carriage, on the pretext of visiting the WC. Once outside in the passage, however, he rolled down a window and lit a guilty cigarette with the stars and stripes lighter that he had accidentally acquired from Agent Roth at Lammas Farm. He noticed how his hand trembled as he raised the cigarette to his lips. He could have been at home now, on his second malt of the evening, relaxing in front of the telly with his feet up on the sofa. What the bloody hell had he got himself into?

The train gathered speed, rolling and swaying eastwards through the dark meadows towards Wiltshire. From the open window, Laverne smelt searingly clean country air, saw the scattered lights of cottages and homesteads. When he lifted his hand to peer at his watch, he experienced an odd feeling of unreality. In the heavens, the moon slid through a white dagger of cloud. And in that cloud, Laverne thought he could discern the hollow eyes and the fleshless leer of a death's head.

Something prodded his elbow. It was the girl, eating crisps and staring up at him in cold disapproval. 'What?' he said. 'What is it?'

'I thought you were supposed to be protecting me.'

'Why? What's happened?'

'She's asleep. Your fancy-woman's nodded off.'

'Do you mean Detective Inspector Savage?' He suddenly realized what the girl had said. 'And she's not my "fancy-woman". She's my colleague.'

'Well, she's supposed to be protecting me, so why's she bloody asleep?'

'Oi!' warned Laverne. 'You're too young to use words like that.'

'Shut up and give me a cig,' she said.

'Actually, I don't smoke,' said Laverne, flicking his half-finished cigarette out of the window. This made her laugh.

'Actually, neither do I, actually,' she said, in between giggles.

The sound of her laughter lit a small fire in Laverne's guts, for he knew that if she was relaxed enough to laugh, then she obviously felt secure in his company.

'What are we going to do now, eh?' he said calmly. 'Because I'm buggered if I know. I don't know what to do when we get to London. I've made no plans, you know. No plans at all.'

'You've got me away from Granddad,' she said. 'I asked you to take me away from him, and that's what you've done. I can't ask any more of you.'

Laverne needed to know how much the girl knew, without alarming her unnecessarily. 'Have you any idea why he did it? Kept you locked up like that?'

'Oh, he thinks I'm the Bhairavi,' she answered, with a bitter half-laugh. 'An incarnation of the goddess Kali. He's round the twist, but mental illness runs in the family. My great-grandma was an even bigger looney than Granddad. She dedicated her life to all this Indian stuff, just so Kali could one day come to earth in human form. That's who Granddad thinks I am. Not much of a compliment. Ever seen pictures of her? She's a right old bag.'

She offered him a crisp. Laverne waved the bag away. 'He's told you this himself, has he?'

'Sure.'

'Did your parents know that he believed this?'

'Did they hell. He only told me when they were dead and buried. When he'd got me all to himself.'

'Do you hate your granddad?'

'No.' There was no hesitation. 'No. He's just not a fit person to look after me.' She saw Laverne's mind creaking into detective-mode. 'And I don't mean in that way. He never touched me or anything. I just mean he's mad. He thinks I'm a bloody goddess, for God's sake!'

'If he thinks you're a goddess, why did he keep you chained up?'

'Because he said that evil people were out to get me. People like you, I suppose.' She laughed mirthlessly as she folded her empty crisp bag into a neat little square. 'Oh, he's going to absolutely love you.'

A woman brushed past them on the way to the lavatory. They stayed silent until the door had closed behind her.

'You don't think your grandfather might be evil, then?'

She laughed. 'Nah. Just a bit whacko.'

'You're certain?' He wondered how to phrase his next question, then opted for traditional Yorkshire tact. 'No chance that he might have killed anyone, for instance?'

'Who? Granddad? Get real.' Tess, reading the stern look on his face, laughed incredulously. 'What? You think he killed Mum and Dad? His own grandchildren? You're mad.'

'Am I?' Laverne suffered a nauseating spasm of self-doubt.

'He loved us! He loved all of us.'

'That doesn't mean he isn't a murderer, Tess. Or that he wasn't planning to murder you.'

She tutted at the gross inadequacy of Laverne's mental powers. 'You don't get it, do you? He worships me. Granddad thinks I'm holy.' She grinned. 'A holy cow! Of course, I told him he was round the bend, but he never listened to me. Even though I was the goddess, he wouldn't listen. I'd call that a bit blasphemous.'

Laverne studied her face for signs of artifice and found none. If she was telling the truth, they were all in serious trouble. 'And you're satisfied that your granddad's made a mistake, are you?'

'Well, do I look like a goddess?'

He smiled. 'I wouldn't know. I don't exactly move in divine circles.'

'Well, listen. I'm not religious. I've never had any visions, or funny dreams, or worked miracles, and I haven't got the slightest bit of interest in India. My mum liked all that stuff, but I take after my dad. Logical, you see. I'm a scientist. I've lived with myself for thirteen-and-a-half years ... if there was anything that unusual about me, don't you think I'd have noticed?'

Laverne nodded, persuaded by her reasoning. The train was slowing to a crawl, despite being nowhere near a station. He peered through the window and saw only open country. Glancing back at the girl, he caught her watching him dolefully. He said, 'What is it?'

'You remind me of someone.'

'Yes, I know,' he answered flippantly. 'Sean Connery.'

'No.'

He could see that his attempt at humour had fallen flat. 'OK. Who do I remind you of?'

She shook her head, unable to speak. The automatic doors whisked open for no particular reason. Taking this as his cue, Laverne said, 'Come on. Let's go and see how my fancy-woman is getting on ...'

Savage was waking as they returned to their table. The slow-moving express suddenly stopped dead. Then the engine was turned off. Tess groaned with dismay. The man who had been reading *The Cornishman* sighed self-consciously and tapped out a number on his cellphone.

Laverne stared into space, deep in thought. A delay to the journey was the last thing they needed. By now, Blackmore and his minions might easily have found his car parked at Castle Cary. It wouldn't require a considerable intellect to guess their destination. Now they were stuck in a broken-down train, somewhere on the Great Western line. Macmillan, Mowart and God knows who else might already be speeding towards Westbury to intercept them. Savage gazed across at him, no doubt sharing his anxiety. He tried to give her a smile of reassurance.

'If you'd given me more time, I could have brought my Walkman,' Tess complained.

'But we didn't have more time,' said Savage reasonably.

Ominously, the Senior Conductor passed by on his way towards the driver's cabin. He wore a yellow safety jacket and carried an old-fashioned lantern.

'What's the hold-up?' snapped the businessman.

The conductor doffed his cap. 'Obstruction on the line. We're working as fast as we can.'

'Why don't I go back to the buffet?' suggested Savage. 'Might as well have more coffee while we wait.'

'I'll go,' offered Tess.

'You haven't got any money,' mocked Savage. 'Come on. We'll go together.'

The two women walked off through the restaurant car. Sensing danger, Laverne got to his feet and followed the conductor. As he did so, he studied the faces of the carriage's other occupants. There was an elderly woman reading a magazine, a middle-aged couple who were merrily drinking their way through every spirit from the buffet, and a Greta Garbo type swaddled in a head scarf and sunglasses who was asleep with her mouth open. By the exit sat a young man with wild, gravity-defying hair, typing frantically into a personal computer. Coach D was more crowded, partly because it was the only coach for smokers who wished to travel first class.

At the end of the coach, the conductor unlocked a door. Laverne tapped him on the shoulder, explained that he was a police officer and asked what the trouble seemed to be. Not listening, the odd little man said, 'No passengers beyond this point, sir. Strictly not, train staff only.'

Laverne held his ID in front of the man's face. After reading it in confusion, the conductor's expression altered. 'Oh, well that's different. Right this way, sir.'

Laverne followed him through into the driver's van. The conduc-

202

tor led him to the exit, which was open to the night and the silent track. 'See what you make of this, sir. We've all had a look and we can't make head nor tail of it . . .'

With stumbling difficulty, the conductor edged through the door and descended a set of metal steps. Laverne followed him. They joined two other men, both of whom were aiming bulky engineer's flashlights up the line. 'This gentleman's a police officer, lads. Maybe he should take a look.'

One of the men, a fatherly type with Brylcreemed hair, was so relieved to see Laverne that he shook him by the hand. Laverne guessed that this man was the engine driver. Beside him stood a man in his early twenties, perhaps some kind of trainee. The younger man nodded to Laverne.

'What's it doing now?' inquired the conductor.

'Nothing,' said the driver. 'It just stays there, 'til we move towards it. Then it moves off, just like before . . .'

Laverne stared past the three men. One hundred and fifty yards up the line, suspended above the glimmering moonlit rails like a ghostly sentinel, burned the cone of living fire that he had seen at Lammas Farm. It looked larger now, larger and brighter, as if the coming eclipse had concentrated its sense of purpose.

'It's them bloody vandals. They built a bonfire on the line, that's all,' opined the conductor.

The driver stopped listening to his radio for a moment in order to annihilate this theory. 'Don't be bloody silly. Bonfires don't bloody walk away when you chase 'em, Walt.' He pulled a face for Laverne's benefit to indicate that the conductor was a buffoon.

To illustrate his point, the driver advanced a few paces. The distant blaze moved backwards and away from the line, drifting over the embankment and remaining there until the driver retreated, when it returned to occupy its previous position. 'See?' The driver spat vigorously at the rails. 'Show me a bonfire that knows how to play hide-and-seek.'

'I reckon it might be a UFO,' said the younger man. When no one responded to his utterance, he muttered under his breath, 'That's what I reckon, anyhow.'

Laverne said, 'I'd like you all to get back on board the train and stay there.'

This utterance was greeted with a long silence, as if all three members of the train crew thought that Laverne was overstepping the mark by giving them orders. 'Why?' demanded the driver. 'Do you know what it is, then?'

The pillar of flame seemed to be edging forward. With greater urgency, Laverne said, 'Yes, I do. Now get back on the bloody train.'

Something about his manner and the tone of his voice infected them all with fear. They required no further admonition. As they boarded the express, Laverne, his mouth dry, walked up the lonely track towards his shining enemy.

The cone of fire remained where it was as Laverne advanced. It had no reason to avoid him. Laverne was its reason for being there. The fire, or the fiend within the fire, was actually waiting for him. When he was about fifty yards away, the blaze briefly flared up, as if in recognition.

Drawing closer, Laverne expected to see Blackmore enshrined within the light. Instead, he saw a woman, a woman that he recognized. Grinning lewdly at him through the cold flames, she bowed once in greeting. Then, with a ferocious roar of combustion, the vision shrank and compressed, becoming a spitting, sizzling white globe with a woman's face inside it.

Laverne was too bewildered to speak. While he looked on, the face in the flames became Blackmore, then Savage, then Laverne himself, before resuming, with laughter in its eyes, its true likeness.

The luminescent orb of pure hatred now hung above the Chief Superintendent's head, as if passing judgement. Then it shot downwards, hitting his brow with the force of a falling rock. And the last thing Laverne saw before losing consciousness was the face of Angela Roth, the Butcher of Glastonbury.

Savage and Tess, returning from the buffet, found themselves waylaid outside the crowded restaurant car by an unwelcome admirer. A short young man, can of lager in hand, barred their way through the automatic door. He was stocky, impudent and rather drunk. Addressing Savage, he said, 'Has anyone ever told you that you are a very sexy lady?'

Gently, she tried to shoulder him out of the way. He wobbled slightly, but stood his ground. 'I mean it. A helluvan attractive piece.'

'Get out of the way, idiot,' growled Tess.

The young man switched his attention to the girl. 'And you're not bad yourself, darlin'.'

Savage was about to resort to the old 'I'm a police officer' threat, when a shout from the next coach attracted her attention. Peering over the drunk's broad shoulder, she saw something extraordinary. At the far end of the carriage, a cloud of red liquid exploded into the air. Then someone without a head fell sideways in their seat and dangled in the aisle while their own blood rained down upon them.

In the time that it took Savage to gasp, there was a second eruption. The occupants of the next two tables seemed to burst apart, launching a fresh geyser of blood and minced meat at the walls and windows of the carriage. Seconds later, a fresh harvest of dismembered heads and limbs rolled into the passage, as if the oncoming carnage was synchronized to the rhythm of some demonic heart that breathed in life and spewed out death.

The drunk was blocking Tess's view, and he himself was too far gone to interpret the dread in Savage's face as anything more than the overblown distaste of a woman who was playing hard to get. Savage grabbed Tess's arm and tried the handle of the nearest door. It was locked, centrally locked. There was no escape, not for anyone.

'What?' yelled Tess, not understanding why Savage was dragging her down the train with such urgency and haste. 'You're hurting. What is it?'

'Follow me! Hurry!'

Before they had cleared the coach, Tess understood the policewoman's haste. She heard a chorus of snuffling grunts, like the noise of pigs at the trough. The girl glanced back. The people who had been queueing for the buffet were now scrambling over each other in terror. Then a tidal wave of blood burst into the carriage.

When he returned to his senses, Vernon Laverne was already stumbling through the train, and like any sleepwalker who awakes in mid-stroll, his first sensation was one of acute disorientation. He thought he had returned to the abbatoir where he'd worked thirty-five years ago, before getting the sack for being kind to the animals.

The abbatoir had reeked of sweet, fresh blood and excrement. It was an odour that Laverne had re-encountered many times in the course of his career, and he could smell it now. Similarly, at slaughter-time, showers of blood had run down the stinking walls. Those walls surrounded him again.

When he remembered that he was on an Intercity train that had stopped a few miles out of Westbury, Laverne's sense of *déjà-vu* was complete. He was a boy again, shaken by pity and disgust in equal measures, walking among the dumb animals as they bled upon their hooks.

There must have been at least six hundred passengers on the train. They were all dead. The aisles of the coaches were swimming with blood. Yet Laverne was unscathed, without the slightest stain or scratch upon his person. He took no pleasure in this fact, slipping and staggering as he made his faltering way through an avenue of soft limbs and spliced carcasses. He had never seen so many dead people in one place before.

At first, he failed to recognize Lyn Savage. He walked the length of the train and back again before he identified her. She was lying across one of the tables, the only person in sight with a full complement of limbs. A single red hole under her shoulder blades showed where the sword had entered her body. The exit wound was slightly to one side of her left breast, exactly over the heart.

Her right fist was curled around a small metal hammer. It was the hammer that British Rail supply to their passengers for breaking the train windows in an emergency. In the window above Savage's head was a small jagged hole. Fresh air blew through this hole, into the carriage, cooling Laverne's shocked white face.

Showing exceptional self-control, Laverne left his friend's side and walked up and down the train, searching for Tess Martin. Only when he was satisfied that neither the girl nor her remains were on board did he return to Savage's body. The Detective Inspector's eyes were closed. Her mouth appeared to be smiling serenely, as if she was privy to some marvellous secret. Perhaps, after all, death was nothing to fear. Lovingly, Laverne reached out and placed a protective hand over her head.

16

THE BLACK GODDESS REBORN

Laverne had no idea how long he'd been walking before he reached the road to Shepton Mallet. His watch had stopped at eight fifty-one, when he had found Lyn Savage dead. The moon above remained clear, inviolate. The eclipse was not yet underway.

During his trek across the fields, he had caught the odd fleeting glimpse of his own astral body, walking alongside him. He was beside himself with grief. Literally. He had failed on a truly cosmic scale. Failed to protect Savage and the girl, and along the way, just for good measure, provoked a demon into slaughtering six hundred people. But if he could at least get the girl back, alive and unharmed, he might begin to atone for his atrocious mistakes.

Already, he was trying to deny the identity of the spirit he had seen. It had already assumed the form of Blackmore, Roth, and Kali. Perhaps it was capable of impersonating anyone, alive or dead, a non-human assassin with no identity of its own.

But Laverne knew in his heart that this was not the case. He had been deceived and manipulated by a powerful human being, a woman he had respected. A woman who was also a powerful sorceress, the Jadugar of Dakshineswar.

Even this knowledge, hopelessly bleak as it made his prospects, was not the greatest cause of his distress. What perplexed him most was his own continued survival. For the third time, someone that he knew to be capable of his total extermination had spared his life.

Why? What crime had he committed to earn the mercy of a monster?

Whatever its cause, his privileged status was surely Tess Martin's only hope. For all he knew, he was the only person on earth who could climb Glastonbury Tor, snatch her from his enemies and walk away unchallenged. He was certain that Tor Hill was where he'd find her, having already deduced that Roth and the lunatics who followed her believed the Tor to be Mount Meru, the legendary centre of the universe.

Somewhere behind him, he heard the deep drone of a powerful engine. He turned to see the double gleam of approaching head-lights. The vehicle, a Range Rover, roared past him, then braked two hundred metres further on, its tyres squealing.

There it waited, lights blazing, the big engine ticking over comfortably. Laverne walked to the car window and peered in. The driver was leaning sideways, holding the passenger door open for him. In the glow of the interior light, Laverne recognized the pale, commanding face of Major Aden Blackmore.

Instinctively, Laverne took a step backwards.

'All right, you bloody fool!' bellowed Blackmore. 'What've you done with her?'

Blackmore got out of the truck. He was holding a bulky assault rifle. 'I've just passed a fleet of bloody ambulances,' barked Blackmore, whisky on his breath. 'No one at Westbury would tell me a thing.' Blackmore stood next to Laverne at the roadside and waved the rifle in his face. 'Those bastards have got Tess, I take it?'

Laverne staggered slightly and walked on. Blackmore, who had seen battle-fatigued men before, relented and helped the Chief Superintendent into the Range Rover. 'What's happened, man?'

By way of response, Laverne gave a single, terrible sob. But the tears he wanted and needed to shed would not come. Blackmore took a left turn off the highway into a narrow lane and parked outside a dark church.

Then the Major lifted a half-empty bottle of The Old White Stag from the back of the truck, unscrewed the cap and passed it to Laverne. 'Here. Get a belly-full of this. And when you're ready to tell me, I'd like to know what happened on that train . . .'

Slowly, in halting, inadequate words, Laverne recounted the events of that night. Blackmore listened in silence, then let out a sigh of immense weariness. 'Dear God. No wonder you're shaken up.' After a long pause, he said, 'And you saw Roth's face clearly?'

Laverne nodded.

'So you realize that it was Roth and not me who murdered all those people?' Laverne nodded again, with less certainty than before. 'She's the Jadugar, you see. Her spirit can take any form. She can make herself look like me or you, anyone, alive or dead. When she kills, she assumes the shape of Kali Ma, the Black Goddess. Roth has the power to expel souls from their own bodies – exactly what she did to that poor Snape fella. She's the devil, Laverne, and you delivered my granddaughter straight into her hands.'

The Chief Superintendent accepted Blackmore's analysis of the situation calmly. After all, it was the truth. Laverne downed more whisky, feeling his courage gradually returning. And, by God, it was a wonderful malt. In the midst of death, we are in life.

Blackmore, his keen bright eyes undimmed by his inner desolation, watched Laverne closely. This is a good man, he thought. He's not too proud to admit to his mistakes. In spite of everything he's been through, he still has plenty of fight left in him. Mildly, Blackmore said, 'And don't think I haven't seen your astral body blundering around my house. What did you think you were playing at?'

'I was confused,' conceded Laverne. 'I admit that I've made an absolute balls-up of everything. But can you blame me for jumping to the wrong conclusions? Roth was impersonating you, and doing a bloody good job of it. And you were keeping a thirteen-year-old girl prisoner. You even chained her to the floor, for Christ's sake. What was I supposed to think?'

Blackmore sniffed. 'I wasn't keeping her prisoner. I was protecting her, you chump. While she was in my house, Roth couldn't get at her.' He paused to observe Laverne's reaction. 'You realize that Roth is my mother returned to earth?'

Laverne, who had never been quite certain of Blackmore's sanity, was careful not to react.

'I always knew that my mother would be reincarnated, and I knew she'd return as a woman,' continued Blackmore. 'I even knew that the goddess would descend to earth on this night, of this year, and that Sarah, in an unfamiliar body, would return to act as tutor and guardian to the holy child. Getting the Avatar of Kali ready to destroy the world, you see. That was why I wouldn't let women in my house.

'The day you brought Roth to my door, I swear I saw my dead mother staring at me out of Roth's eyes. Shook me up quite a bit, I can tell you.' Disturbed by the memory, Blackmore snatched the whisky bottle and took a long swig. 'But I knew that as long as I didn't let the bitch over the threshold, her spirit couldn't come back for Tessy.'

'I don't understand,' said Laverne.

The Major gave Laverne a tired smile. 'Don't understand much, do you? Your spirit walks through walls, yet you haven't the faintest idea why or how. What's the matter with you, man? Did you never think to read a book about it?'

Reminded of Savage, Laverne shook his head violently.

Seeing suppressed emotion in the policeman's face, the old man softened. 'All right. Then you won't know the age-old rule of astral travel, or indeed any kind of haunting. Which is that to enter a house, any spirit, good or bad, alive or dead, must either *know the way or be invited over the threshold.*

'Think about it. Has your astral body ever gone anywhere that you haven't been invited to, or haven't visited in the flesh beforehand?'

'I'm not sure,' answered Laverne truthfully. Then he recalled the night when the cone of fire had pursued him back to his cottage in Huntington, without harming his family. Roth had not visited his home. Nor, on the basis of her recent activities, was she likely to receive an invitation.

Blackmore thumped the dashboard. 'It's true, Laverne. Even the most powerful spirits can only enter a house at the bidding of its inhabitants. Unless, of course, those spirits have lived and died in that house, in which case they already inhabit it. But my mother, Sarah, never set foot in Paradise House. Spent all her married life out in India, you see. My paternal grandparents, showing remarkably good taste, disapproved of her.'

Laverne was not convinced. 'But Roth'd never been to Tess Martin's house, either. And no one invited her. Yet she still found a way in.'

'You're wrong, Laverne. Tess's mother invited her. After my marriage broke up, my wife took our daughter, Pat, out to stay with the old woman in India. For a holiday, y'know. The old girl seems to have made a fuss of her. It's an odd fact that very few people are entirely evil. Anyway, Pat remembered her granny with fondness. It was my daughter's love for Sarah that brought her into the house that night. Invitation, you see. No finer invitation than love . . .'

Laverne pondered this. 'OK. So Roth's *spirit* couldn't get at Tess. But in the real world, she was pretty well-connected. She had a Chief Constable on her side. What was to stop Roth and the police from walking in and taking her?'

'Me. My sheer bloody-mindedness,' replied Blackmore. 'The buggers knew that if push came to shove, I'd kill them, then shoot Tess and myself. These people don't expose themselves to any kind

212

of risk, you see. By the same token, I knew that if I stepped outside my door, the spirit of the Jadugar would be waiting to cut me apart. Stalemate.

'Roth's been prowling around my house, waiting for my defences to drop. Today, one of my guards actually saw her peering in through the window. You might have heard him screaming? God knows what form she took. Anyway, the guards took fright and scarpered. Not many real men left in the world, Laverne.'

'Except us.'

Blackmore gave his sharp bark of a laugh. 'Yes! We'll do, all right.'

Laverne peered through the windscreen. A shadow was crawling across the southern edge of the moon. The eclipse was underway. 'Better get a move on,' he said.

Blackmore put his foot down hard on the accelerator and they sped westward, avoiding the main roads, keeping to the winding, narrow country lanes. While the dark farms, woods and fields hurtled by, Blackmore stiffly apologized for his earlier rudeness. 'You must have felt like strangling me. But at least I understand why Mother let me walk out of the house unmolested. The murdering bitch was otherwise engaged.'

Laverne had never really seen the point of reincarnation, believing that one visit to this miserable world ought to be more than enough for anyone. 'You're sure that Roth is your mother, then?'

Blackmore laughed drily. 'Indeed I am. A friend at the Pentagon checked Agent Roth's records for me. She was born on 12 August 1960 in New Haven, Connecticut. My mother died earlier that same year, on the tenth of February.'

'Well, that doesn't add up, surely,' objected Laverne. 'By my reckoning, Roth was already a three-month-old foetus when your mother died.'

'My dear chap, you really are an ignoramus, aren't you?'

Laverne resisted the impulse to refute this charge.

'The soul doesn't enter the foetus at conception. It waits until the child is three months old. Thought everybody knew that.'

Once again, Laverne found himself wondering whether the Major was deranged. 'Explain something to me,' he said. 'If Tess is, er, well, holy . . .'

'She's the Bhairavi,' insisted Blackmore. 'No question.'

'All right . . . well, in that case, why do they want to kill her?'

'They don't.'

'No?'

'Of course not. They want her to become the goddess.'

'I thought she was already the goddess.'

'Not exactly. She has no awareness of her divinity, you see. Her godhead has not been awakened. Take Jesus, for example. He was undoubtedly divine, but if he hadn't met John the Baptist, his powers would have remained dormant. Same goes for Tess. Tonight, when the earth's shadow covers the moon above Mount Meru, the Black Goddess will descend to her, just as the Holy Spirit came down to Christ in the form of a dove when he went to the River Jordan. If that happens . . . well, she'll destroy the world.

'But if we can get her away from Tor Hill, Roth and her cronies will have missed their chance. Tess will just grow up to be an ordinary young woman. Just as Jesus, without his baptism, would have remained a carpenter. So no, old son. They don't want to kill her. They want her alive. It's the rest of humanity they want to see dead.'

Laverne sank into an unhappy silence. Blackmore, reading his mind, said, 'And you're wondering why you're still alive, are you?'

Laverne nodded once, with slow emphasis.

'That I can't answer,' said Blackmore. 'Is Roth partial to you, would you say?'

'I don't know. She tried to kiss me once.'

'That's strange,' mused Blackmore quietly.

'Why? I'm not *that* ugly, am I?'

'No. I've just never known my mother to kiss anyone.'

They were entering Glastonbury. The town appeared to be in the grip of a major power failure. The streets and buildings were in utter darkness.

'Where is everyone?' breathed Laverne.

The Range Rover's lights illuminated what looked like a bundle of dirty washing, strewn across the middle of the road. Blackmore slowed down. Laverne lowered the window at his side to get a closer look. It was as he had suspected: the clothes contained people, or parts of people. Another massacre had taken place here.

Blackmore turned off the lights and cruised forward to the corner of Wellhouse Lane, drawing level with a Volkswagon saloon that had spilled its headless driver on to the road. There were bodies and smashed cars everywhere. Blackmore turned to Laverne. 'You see how powerful she's become? There's every likelihood that she'll kill the pair of us.'

Laverne sighed. 'If she gets her way tonight, we'll both die anyway. Why prolong the agony?'

Blackmore clasped Laverne's hand warmly. 'You're a decent sort.' It was the kind of stiff-upper-lip understatement that Laverne associated with old Jack Hawkins movies. He found the tribute strangely touching. Not knowing whether to cry or laugh out loud, he did neither.

The Major pushed the gear lever into first and sent the vehicle growling up the steep, narrow lane with its headlamps doused. At the top of Stone Down, a macabre vision came into view. St Michael's church was on fire. The tower had become a glowing chimney, dribbling black smoke into the sky.

'The maniacs,' breathed Blackmore, almost admiringly.

They stepped out of the Range Rover. Blackmore removed his assault rifle from the back of the vehicle and held it up for

215

inspection. 'This is an M16. Classic weapon. Range: four hundred metres. Fires an average of eight hundred rounds a minute. I'll leave the safety catch off. If I go down, pick it up and just keep firing.'

Reasoning that there was no way that they could approach undetected, they crossed the field to the foot of the hill and started to climb. Intermittently, shrieks of agony drifted down to them on the wind. The moon at their backs was now almost completely obscured by a cowl of darkness.

A cluster of lights bobbed down to meet them. Four men in black robes, bearing burning torches, had descended to block their way. Laverne recognized one of the men as Underwood, the constable that had gone missing from Lammas Farm. The party was led by Macmillan, his face bearing the bruise of Laverne's recent attack.

'Only the Lord Nilakantha may pass this point,' said the Chief Constable in a sonorous voice.

'What?' said Blackmore, incredulous.

Fixing his cadaverous eyes on Blackmore, John Macmillan spoke again. 'The Lord Nilakantha is welcome. You are not welcome.'

Rashly, Macmillan attempted to underline his point by shoving Blackmore out of the way. The barrel of the M16 caught light and the harsh clatter of automatic fire resounded through the hills. Macmillan's face opened like a ripe watermelon. He slumped to his knees and rolled down the slope. The other three men started to back away. Before Laverne had time to protest, Blackmore fired again, cutting them down like vermin.

Then Blackmore turned to Laverne and yelled in his face. 'Run, man! It's you they want! Run!'

Instantly, there came a thin whistling sound, and Major Aden Blackmore came apart before Laverne's eyes, belching blood as he divided at the waist and both halves of his sundered body began to slither downhill. Then his head parted from his shoulders, and his arms came away from his torso, so that he fell, fell away to nothing, his body scattered over the steps of the Tor.

Laverne screamed in anger and distress, and reached for the fallen rifle. But an inner lurch of disgust stayed his hand. No. Guns were not his style. There had to be a better way. He left the weapon on the cold earth and continued to climb.

As he approached, the smell of burning meat filled his lungs. The Bhairavi faithful, about fifty men and women of all ages and nationalities, parted to let him through, smiling in rapture, casting white lotus flowers before his feet. There was no resistance. His presence was clearly welcomed.

A bonfire raged in the belly of St Michael's church. The screams he had heard emanated from this fire. Two disciples were feeding a constant stream of goats and lambs, their legs trussed, through the doorway into the flames. And the plaintive screeches of the animals being burned alive mingled with the bleating fear of those awaiting incineration, filling the night with the music of the pit.

The compass rose at the end of the eastern path had been covered by a gilded throne. The throne faced the tower and contained Tess Martin, her auburn hair highlighted by the flames. She was clad in a crimson robe, her shoulders extravagantly garlanded with red and white lotus blossoms. Two young handmaidens, also garbed in crimson, held her steady in the chair. Tess was barely conscious, swaying and drooping, either drugged or shocked beyond endurance by the horrors of the day.

Then a familiar voice shouted, 'Jai Shiva! Jai Nilakantha!'

From the north side of the blazing ruin came a figure swaddled entirely in black, veiled and hooded, but whose proud bearing revealed her to be Angela Roth, high priestess of the Bhairavi Cult. Roth gestured to the men tending the bonfire. The slaughter stopped, and the surviving animals were herded away.

'Jai Nilakantha!' she shouted.

This cry was echoed by Roth's disciples, who threw themselves to the ground and hid their faces. Apart from the crackle of the fire, there was deep silence as Roth walked over to Laverne. She was barefoot, unadorned by jewels or bracelets, carrying a nosegay of white lotus blossoms which she laid before his feet. Then she stood and lifted her black veil.

Laverne half expected to see a face made hideous and corrupt by the crimes of its owner. But Roth looked exactly like the woman he remembered: strong-jawed and defiant, handsome rather than beautiful, but hardly a devil. When she spoke, however, her voice carried no trace of the truculent stage-American who had hounded him with her notebook. That Angela Roth had gone for ever. In her place stood the icy, remorseless assassin he had glimpsed at Lammas Farm. In a low voice she said, 'My Lord Nilakantha.'

'What are you talking about, woman?' spluttered Laverne. He was shaking so much that his teeth chattered. 'You know damn well who I am.'

'Yes,' she said humbly. 'You are Shiva, who drank a sea of poison to save the world. This sacrifice left you with a blue mark upon your throat.' She touched the bruise on his neck. 'Thus giving you the name "Nilakantha" or "Blue throat".'

Laverne laughed at the blatant absurdity of it all. 'I'm a god too, am I?'

She nodded eagerly. 'When I heard about you in America, I knew that you were an avatar of Shiva. You are brave and selfless. You would drink a million seas of poison to save the lives of others. And when you die, the Bhairavi will ride upon your corpse and absolute power shall be hers.'

Laverne tried to push the priestess aside. She stood firm and smiled. 'I hoped you might kill Blackmore for me. I even stabbed my own body, so that I'd be the last person you suspected.' She seized Laverne's right hand and tried to guide it to the wound on her back. Angrily, he yanked himself free. 'But you saw through me, briefly, that night at Lammas Farm. And now, together at last, we need pretend no longer. My lord!'

With this, Roth joined her disciples on the ground before him. Laverne rushed over to Tess. Gently, he tried to lift her. She resisted, her eyes tightly closed, clawing at his face in confused anguish. At her feet, the two handmaidens, eyes upturned, wailed and threshed on the ground, white froth bubbling from their mouths.

On an impulse, Laverne turned to look behind him. Above him, with the black moon behind her, loomed the figure of a nine-foot woman. She stank of putrefaction, and she danced in a tower of cold fire. Her naked body was shining black. She had the face of a satanic ape. Blood coursed from the corners of her crimson mouth. Her eyes – wild, vibrant, gleefully murderous – belonged to a soul in hell.

She was Ma Kali, Time the Destroyer, the goddess who brings mourning in her wake. Laverne, paralysed with fear, stared up at her. And the Black Goddess gazed down at him, not with anger or loathing, but with love.

Each of her four arms wielded a weapon. Both of the right hands held a bloody two-edged sword. In her left hands, she gripped a dagger and an axe. Around her neck, between her dead, withered breasts, hung a garland of shrunken human heads which rattled as she moved. The belt at her waist was laden with the amputated hands of children.

Roth's physical body remained where he had left it. But her soul danced before him in its favourite guise, imitating the Black Goddess as skilfully as it had imitated Blackmore. Roth had assumed the form of the goddess when she murdered, making each killing an act of homage as well as a personal indulgence.

And Laverne, whose spirit could assume no form other than that of a middle-aged man in a brown suit, knew that he could never be a match for this woman. Yet he was the only real hope that Tess

219

Martin had. The frantic apparition was dancing steadily closer. In seconds, her blades and axe would descend to slice him apart.

Laverne knew he had to act now, or not at all.

With a last, immense effort of will, he leapt out of himself and hurled his spirit into the prone and vacant body of the high priestess. He had never possessed anyone in his life, and it was an extraordinary sensation to suddenly find himself in the body of a woman, breathing with her lungs, seeing with her eyes, even tasting her tongue in his mouth. But there was no time to savour the novelty of the experience.

Roth's dancing spirit, realizing what had happened, let out a harrowing wail. Laverne, running in Roth's body, dashed past her astral self and dived head-first into the bonfire, feeling Roth's pain and screaming with her voice as the white heat blistered and branded her flesh. It took less than a second for her hair and robe to kindle. Then Laverne's spirit could stand the agony no more, and he fled to the safety of his own flesh and bones, leaving Roth to burn.

The murderous apparition had vanished. Perhaps she no longer had much to dance about. But nor had Laverne. Back in his body, he found that he could no longer breathe. He looked down at himself and saw why. The priestess had been too quick for him. His chest had been riven by a single axe-wound. Laverne fell, his blood pumping into the earth, knowing that his life was coming to an end.

Whining, charred blacker than the goddess she revered, Roth crawled out of the fire and her followers put out the flames that clung to her head and back.

The darkness became absolute. The moon was totally eclipsed, a dense black hole, ringed by pale fire. Mowart, taking charge, pointed to heaven and shouted, 'Jai Kali! Jai Ma Kali!'

The assembly took up his chant. A shower of liquid fell down from heaven, spattering the upturned faces of the faithful. Mowart

220

held out his hands to catch the dark droplets that tumbled from the cloudless sky. Blood. It was raining blood. The goddess Bhairavi had come to earth.

In ecstasy, the believers turned to their saviour, the Bhairavi. Slowly, Tess opened her eyes and arose from her golden throne. With a sigh of awe, her worshippers bowed low before her. Tess, indifferent to their devotion, looked down at the weathered, grey-haired man lying at her feet. Tess knew this man, remembered his smile and the simple, easy warmth that reminded her so much of her father. Thinking to help, she stooped to touch his open wound. But Laverne died before she could reach him.

She surveyed the grovelling acolytes, and the oily, smouldering thing that crawled across the ground towards her, moaning, its heat-fused fingers groping for her feet. The girl knew what this thing was called, and what it had done in her name.

So she opened her mouth and roared. And the universe turned black.

17

THE KILLER OF ALL TIME

There is a bridge in Glastonbury; an old timbered bridge that spans a quiet brook. On the northern side of the bridge, a rough dirt track curves away into a dense pocket of woodland. In the opposite direction lies a house where nothing tragic will ever occur.

A young girl stands on the bridge, watching the cold stars, listening to the water running over the rocks. From the nearby house comes the sound of a piano, played with a reassuring lack of feeling. Tess smiles with recognition.

She now knows that Blackmore and Roth were right. She is truly the Avatar of Kali, the goddess who embodies the destructive power of time. But if Kali turns men into spirits, and the spirit exists outside time, then Kali is also the destroyer of time itself. And this is what Tess has done. She has returned the world to that chill night in early spring, before the killing began in Glastonbury.

Her followers murdered in her name, but they were misguided, for only the ignorant equate the terrible goddess with cruelty. Her true nature is pure joy, and at this moment, that is precisely what Tess Martin feels.

At his home in Evercreech, Sergeant Mowart sits by the phone with his superior, John Macmillan. They were anxiously awaiting an international call, but now, turning blue in their chairs, they wait only for the coroner, the priest and the undertaker. Both men have suffered massive, inexplicable heart attacks.

Across the ocean, in the state of Virginia, a promising and respected federal agent has expired during an afternoon nap. She has been dead for less than a minute, yet her body is already stiff and cold. When her flat-mate discovers her that evening, Angela Roth's body will have decomposed beyond recognition.

Back in England, Detective Inspector Lyn Savage laughs as she reads a story to her children. It's well past their bedtime, but tonight, for some reason, Savage has been unwilling to let the girls out of her sight. She's feeling clingy and protective. She knows that Jane and Michaela won't be young for ever.

Savage is right to feel that time robs us of those we love. But tonight, time and destiny have been reversed. Trevor Snape, returned to his small flat, thanks his God for another day free from temptation. Major Aden Blackmore, getting sentimentally drunk in his study, decides that tomorrow, just for the hell of it, he might leave the safety of Paradise House and visit his family on the other side of the Tor.

Those that were slain now live again, while their future killers breathe no more. And a goddess in human form now walks upon the Earth.

At his home in Huntington, Chief Superintendent Vernon Laverne glances up at the stars as he opens the back door to put out the cat. The animal attempts to outwit him by doubling back into the house, but Laverne deftly fields his advance with a gentle swipe of the foot. As the cat accepts defeat and ambles away, something bright falls off the step. Laverne stoops to retrieve a posy of lotus blossoms, fragrant and white. He frowns. These flowers are the only real mystery he's encountered in months. Recently, his life has been slow and uneventful, and that's the way he likes it.

From the draining board, Laverne takes a glass tumbler and half-fills it with water. Then he stands the white blooms in the tumbler, making a half-hearted attempt to arrange them. Humming to himself, he places two large mugs of tea and the flowers on a stainless steel tray. Then he carries the tray into the living room where Dawn, his wife, is waiting.